Run. Run. Run.

All around me, they could taste it. They could feel it. Furred bodies pushed at each other to get closer to me, to touch me, to sniff me, to be with me, and the roar from their minds was overwhelming.

Alpha. Alpha. Alpha.

I forgot about Chase, about Devon, about each and every one of them as anything other than my brothers, my sisters, my people, my pack.

Mine.

This was what I'd been born for. This was all that I wanted and all that I was, and as one overwhelming, unstoppable, incredible force, we ran.

Trial by Fire

A RAISED BY WOLVES NOVEL

Jennifer Lynn Barnes

EGMONT
USA
NEW YORK

EGMONT

We bring stories to life

First published by Egmont USA, 2011
This paperback edition published by Egmont USA, 2012
443 Park Avenue South, Suite 806
New York, NY 10016

1 3 5 7 9 8 6 4 2

www.egmontusa.com
www.jenniferlynnbarnes.com

THE LIBRARY OF CONGRESS HAS CATALOGED THE HARDCOVER EDITION AS FOLLOWS:

Barnes, Jennifer (Jennifer Lynn)
Trial by fire / Jennifer Lynn Barnes.
p.   cm.
Summary: Bryn, the new alpha of her werewolf pack, must deal with an opposing pack
led by her friend when a runaway begs her for help and protection from abuse.
ISBN 978-1-60684-168-6 (hardcover) — ISBN 978-1-60684-202-7 (electronic book)
[1. Werewolves—Fiction. 2. Runaways—Fiction. 3. High schools—Fiction. 4. Schools—
Fiction.] I. Title.
PZ7.B26225Tr 2011
[Fic]—dc22
2011002853

Paperback ISBN 978-1-60684-333-8

Printed in the United States of America

For Daddy, from his not-quite-human girl.

CHAPTER ONE

―◦―

"NO MORE SCHOOL, NO MORE BOOKS, NO MORE teachers' dirty looks..."

For a two-hundred-twenty-pound werewolf, Devon Macalister had a wicked falsetto. Leaning back in his chair with casual grace, he shot a mischievous look around our lunch table. "Everyone sing along!"

As the leader of our little group—not to mention the alpha of Devon's pack and his best friend since kindergarten—the responsibility for shutting down his boy-band tendencies fell to me. "It's Thanksgiving break, Dev, not summer vacation, and technically, it hasn't even started yet."

My words fell on deaf ears. The smile on Devon's face widened, making him look—to my eyes, at least—more puppy than wolf. To my left, Lake, whose history with Devon's flare for the dramatic stretched back almost as far as mine did, rolled her eyes, but her lips parted in a grin every bit as irrepressible and lupine as Devon's.

A wave of energy—pure, undiluted, and animalistic—

vibrated through my own body, and I closed my eyes for one second ... two.

Three.

In control of the impulse to leap out of my chair and run for the woods, I glanced across the table at the last member of our little quartet. Maddy was sitting perfectly still, blinking her gray eyes owlishly, a soft smile on her lips. Images—of the night sky, of running—leapt from her mind to mine through our pack-bond, as natural as words falling off lips.

The impending full moon might have been giving the rest of our table werewolf ADD, but Maddy was perfectly Zen— much more relaxed than she normally would have been when all eyes were on the four of us.

Despite our continued efforts to blend in, the buzz of power in the air and the unspoken promise that within hours, my friends would shed their human skin were palpable. I recognized the feeling for what it was, but our very human—and easily fascinated—classmates had no idea. To them, the four of us were mysterious and magnetic and just a bit unreal— even me.

In the past nine months, my life had changed in more ways than I could count, but one of the most striking was the fact that at my new high school, I wasn't an outsider, ignored and avoided by humans who had no idea why people like Devon and Lake—and to a lesser extent me—felt *off*. Instead, the other students at Weston High had developed a strange fascination with us. They didn't approach. They didn't try to penetrate our tight-knit group, but they watched and they whispered, and whenever Devon—*Devon!*—met their eyes, the girls sighed and fluttered their eyelashes in some kind of human mating ritual that I probably wouldn't have completely understood even if I'd grown up like a normal girl.

Given that I'd been raised as the only human child in the largest werewolf pack in North America, the batting of eyelashes was every bit as foreign to me as running through the woods, surrounded by bodies and warmth and the feeling of *home*, would have been to anyone else. Some days, I felt like I knew more about being a werewolf than I would ever know about being a teenage girl.

It was getting easier and easier to forget that I was human.

Soon. Soon. Soon.

The bond that tied me to the rest of the pack vibrated with the inevitability of the coming moon, and even though I knew better than to encourage Devon, I couldn't help the way my own lips tilted up at the corners. The only things that stood between the four of us and Thanksgiving break were a couple of hours and a quiz on Shakespeare.

The only thing standing between us and delicious, feral freedom was the setting of the sun.

And the only thing that stood between me and Chase—*my* Chase—was a distance I could feel the boy in question closing mile by mile, heartbeat by heartbeat, second by second.

"Bronwyn, please, you're making me blush." Dev—who could read me like a book, with or without whatever I was projecting through the pack-bond—adopted a scandalized tone and brought a hand to his chest, like he was seconds away from demanding smelling salts and going faint. But I sensed his wolf stirring beneath the surface and knew that it was hard for Devon on a day like today to be reminded that I wasn't his to protect in the same way anymore.

That I was alpha.

That Chase and I were . . . whatever Chase and I were.

"Fine," I said, flicking a French fry in Devon's general direction. "Have it your way. No more school, no more books . . ."

Dev made an attempt at harmonizing with me, but given my complete lack of vocal chops, it did not go well, and a horrified silence descended over our entire table.

After several seconds, Devon regarded the rest of us with mock solemnity. "We shall never speak of this moment again."

"In your dreams, Broadway boy." Shaking out her long blonde hair—a motion laden with excess adrenaline—Lake stood and stretched her mile-long legs. If the girls in school were all secretly pining for Devon, the boys were absolutely smitten with Lake. Clearly, they'd never met the business end of her shotgun or had their butts whipped at pool.

Soon. Soon. Soon.

Across the table, Maddy sighed, and Devon bumped her shoulder with his, a comforting gesture meant to communicate that he understood. Soon, our entire pack would be gathered in the woods. Soon, the Weres would Shift and I would let their power flow through me, until I forgot I was human and the difference between four legs and two virtually disappeared.

Soon—but not soon enough.

"So," I said, my voice low and soothing, intent on keeping my pack-mates focused, however briefly, on the here and now. "*Hamlet.* What do I need to know?"

"New girl."

I balked at Lake's answer. "I was thinking more along the lines of Guildencrantz and Frankenstein."

"Rosencrantz and Guildenstern," Devon corrected absent-mindedly as he followed Lake's gaze to the double archway at the front of the cafeteria. I turned to look, too, and the rest of the student body took their cue from us, until everyone was eyeballing the girl who stood there.

She was small—the word *tiny* wouldn't have been a misnomer—and her eyes seemed to take up a disproportionate amount of her face. Her skin was very pale, and she was dressed almost entirely in black, save for a pair of white leather gloves that covered her arms from the elbows down.

She looked like a porcelain doll, and she felt like a threat. Given that I could tell, even from a distance, that she wasn't a Were, I had no idea why something inside me insisted I track her every move.

"The natives are getting kind of restless," Devon commented

offhand. Weston wasn't a big school, and mid-semester trans-fers were practically unheard of, so White Leather Gloves was garnering more than her fair share of murmurs and stares.

Including mine.

"Mayhaps I should go play the white knight, divert the spotlight a little?"

Devon's suggestion was enough to make me switch my gaze from the new girl to him.

"No."

I wasn't sure who was more shocked by the sharpness with which that word exited my mouth—Devon or me. Our pack didn't *do* orders. Given the way I felt about people get-ting dictatorial with me, I wasn't prone to pulling rank on anyone else. Besides, Devon and I had spent so much time together growing up that even if he hadn't been my second-in-command, I still wouldn't have been able to force my will on him. The closest I could come to ordering him to do anything was threatening to decapitate him if he didn't stop singing *The Best of ABBA* at the top of his lungs, and even that was mostly futile.

With a lightly inquisitive noise, Devon caught my gaze and held it. "Something you'd like to share with the class there, Bryn?" he asked, arching one eyebrow to ridiculous heights while keeping the other perfectly in place.

I debated answering, but it was probably nothing—just that time of the month, with emotions running high and my heart beating with the power of the impending full moon. Still, I hadn't spent my entire life growing up around people capable of snapping my neck like a Popsicle stick without learning to pay attention when my instincts put me on high alert.

If my gut said someone was a threat, I had to at least consider the possibility that it was true—even if the *someone* in question was five foot nothing and human down to the tips of her leather-clad fingers.

Instead of mentioning any of this to Devon and opening that can of worms, I threw another French fry in his general direction, and the tension between us melted away as he reached for his plate and armed himself. "You know, of course," he said, pitching his voice low, "that this means war."

I couldn't help glancing back toward the archway and the new girl who'd been standing there a moment before, but she was already gone.

Pack. Pack. Pack.

Protect. Protect. Protect.

I let the feeling wash over me, absorbed it, and then relegated it to the back of my head, with the promise of *soon, soon, soon* and the desire to *run*. At the moment, I had more immediate concerns—like my retention of *Hamlet* definitely leaving something to be desired and the incoming French fry flying directly at my face.

That night, I was the first one to arrive at the clearing. We hadn't had a fresh snowfall since the second week in November, but this time of year, the layer of white on the ground never fully melted away, and I breathed in the smell of cedar and snow. I was wearing wool mittens and my second-heaviest winter coat, and for a moment, I closed my eyes and imagined, as I always did just before the Shift, what it would be like to shed my clothes, my skin, and my ability to think as a human.

There had been a time in my life when the last thing I wanted was the collective werewolf psyche taking up even a tiny corner of my brain, but a lot had changed since then.

Different pack.

Different forest.

Different me.

Without opening my eyes, my hands found their way to the bottom of my puffy jacket, and I pulled it upward, exposing the T-shirt I wore underneath. My fingers tugged at the end of the shirt, and my bare skin stung under the onslaught of winter-cold air.

Opening my eyes, I traced the pattern rising over the band of my jeans: three parallel marks, scars I would carry for the rest of my life. For most of my childhood, the Mark had been a visible symbol to the pack that had raised me that I was one of their own, that anyone who messed with me messed with the werewolf who'd dug his fingers into my flesh hard enough to leave scars.

Callum.

He was the alpha of alphas, the Were who'd saved my life when I was four years old and spent the next decade plus grooming me for a future I'd never even imagined. No matter how many months passed, every time my pack assembled, every time I lost myself and ran as one of them, I thought of the first time, of Callum and his wolves and knowing that for once in my life, I belonged.

Every time I heard the word *alpha* beckoning to me from my pack's minds, I thought of the man who'd once been mine—and then I thought of the other alphas, none of whom would have been particularly distraught if I went to sleep one night and never woke up.

Ah, werewolf politics. My favorite.

Bryn.

The moment I heard Chase's voice, soft and unassuming, in my mind, every other thought vanished. It was always this way with the two of us, and the anticipation of seeing him, touching him, taking in his scent was almost as powerful as the feeling that washed over my body the moment he emerged from the forest, clothed in shorts and a T-shirt that didn't quite fit.

Chase had been a werewolf for less than a year. Ironically, that made him seem far less human than Weres who'd been born that way or the members of our pack who'd been Changed as kids. The difference was visible in the way he moved, the tilt of his head. For as long as I'd known him, he'd been in flux, defined by the wolf inside as much as the boy he'd been before the attack.

Now, slowly, things I'd felt in his memories and dreams, quirks he'd shown only in flashes seemed to be fighting their way back to the surface. Each time he came home from patrolling our territory as my eyes and ears, I saw a little bit more of his human side.

Each time, he was a little more *Chase*.

"Hey, you." Chase smiled, more with one side of his mouth than the other.

"Hey," I echoed, a smile tugging at my own lips. "How's tricks?"

I took those words leaving my mouth as a sign that I'd been hanging around Devon for way, way too long, but Chase didn't so much as blink.

"Same old, same old." He was quiet, this boy I was getting to know piece by piece—thoughtful, observant, and restrained, even as the power in his stride betrayed the wolf inside. "How's school going?"

"Same old, same old."

"There's no such thing as 'same old, same old' with you," Chase said wryly. "You're *Bryn*."

Given my track record, he kind of had a point there, but I wasn't about to admit it out loud.

With that same half smile, he leaned toward me, hesitant, but inhumanly graceful. I answered the question in his eyes, reached for the back of his head, brought his lips down to mine.

Soon. Soon. Soon.

I could feel his heart beating, feel his mind and thoughts blending with my own as the two of us stood there, bathed in moonlight and feeling its effects like a drug.

Whoever Chase was, he was mine.

"Ahem."

I'd known before I kissed Chase that we'd be interrupted. There was no such thing as a secret in a wolf pack—let alone privacy. But I'd been foolishly optimistic and hoped that the interrupter would be Lake or Maddy or one of the younger kids.

Instead, as Chase and I pulled away from each other, we were confronted with the oldest member of our pack, a gruff, weatherworn man who didn't look a day over thirty-five. Based on the way his lips were twitching, I concluded that the man in question was torn between smiling and scowling.

"Hey, Mr. Mitchell," I said, hoping to push him toward the smiling end of the spectrum. A guarded look settled over Chase's eyes, but he echoed my greeting, and Lake's dad gave us a long, measuring stare in return.

"I suspect the earth would keep rotating round the sun even if the two of you called me Mitch."

In the time I'd been living on the Mitchells' land, Mitch and I had had this conversation more than once, but I wasn't really the type to give in once I dug my heels in about something.

"So noted, Mr. Mitchell."

The smile finally won out over his scowl, but it lasted only a second or two before Mitch eyed the space (or lack thereof) between my body and Chase's. "Last I heard, Ali was on her way here with the twins," he said, which I took as a not-so-subtle hint that Chase and I should give each other some breathing room. Chase must have interpreted it the same way, because he stepped back—away from me and away from Mitch, who delivered the rest of his update with a nod. "Lake and Maddy are rounding up the troops, and I believe Devon said something about making an entrance."

I was fairly certain that I was the only alpha in the history of the world to have a second-in-command who appreciated the impact of arriving fashionably late. Then again, I was also the only alpha with as many females in her pack as males and more toddlers and tweens than grown men.

Besides, it wasn't like the whole *human* thing was status quo.

"Bryn!" The unmistakable sound of a very small person bellowing ripped me from my thoughts, and I smiled. There was nothing quite like hearing my name yelled at the top of a three-year-old's lungs—unless it was having the aforementioned three-year-old barrel into me full blast and throw her arms around my legs like she was afraid that if she let go, I'd disappear off the face of the earth forever.

"Hello, Lily," I said wryly. The kid acted like she hadn't

seen me in a lifetime or two, even though it had only been an hour, if that.

Moon! Happy! Fun!

With the older wolves, I had to go looking for thoughts, unless someone was using the pack-bond to actively send them my way, but with Lily, everything was right there on the surface, bubbling up the way only the strongest emotions did in adults.

Alpha-alpha-alpha! Bryn-Bryn-Bryn!

The two words—*alpha* and *Bryn*—blended together in her mind. As the youngest of the kids I'd saved from the werewolf equivalent of a psychopath, Lily was one of the only ones who couldn't remember the time before our pack, or the things that the Rabid had done to her, to all of them.

In Lily's mind, *Bryn* meant *alpha*, and *alpha* meant *Bryn*. It was as simple as that.

"Can we Change yet?" Lily asked. "Can we, can we, can we?"

Not yet, Lily, I answered silently, and she stilled, mesmerized by a power I'd never asked to hold over anyone.

"Lily, I told you to wait." The voice that issued that statement was aggrieved, and the look on its owner's face was one I recognized all too well from my own childhood.

Come to think of it, it was a look I recognized all too well from about a week ago, two tops.

"Hey, Ali," I said, glad that Chase and I had heeded Mitch's warning and put a little space between my body and his.

"Hey, baby," Ali replied, a twin on each hip. "Everyone's been fed, but I make no guarantees about their state of mind."

For most of my life, it had been just Ali and me, but she'd taken to managing an entire brood with the same efficiency with which she'd once transformed herself from a twenty-year-old college student into my protector within Callum's pack. Ali was human, but the words *force of nature* still applied, and I would infinitely rather have tangled with an irritated werewolf than Ali in mama bear mode.

"Now?" Lily asked, right on cue with Ali's disclaimer about the younger werewolves' state of mind. "Now-now-now?"

"Shhhh," I said, and Lily closed her mouth and laid her head against my knee.

"You know, Bryn," Ali said thoughtfully, "if Lily minded me half as well as she minds you, I wouldn't be considering renaming her Bryn Two."

"Ha-ha," I retorted. "Very funny."

Ali smiled. "I try." She looked toward Mitch, and without saying a word, he walked over and took Katie and Alex from her arms. Not even a year old, Ali's babies already looked more like toddlers, and in identical motions, their hands found their way almost immediately to Mitch's beard.

He smiled. "I've got them," he told Ali, and she nodded before kissing the twins and turning to walk back out of the woods. Ali never stayed to run with the pack.

As far as I knew, she never had.

Now, Bryn? Now?

Lily refrained from asking the question out loud, but I heard it through the pack-bond all the same, and this time, the answer—*soon, soon, soon*—seemed to come from outside my body, from instincts I couldn't have explained to the human world. Lily seemed to feel it, too, and a keening, whimpering sound built in the back of her throat. I ran a hand gently over her bright red hair and she began rocking back and forth on her feet. Within moments, the others had arrived, filling the clearing, and the effect was magnified a hundred times.

Our pack was small—twenty-two total, only eighteen there that night—but the air was electric, and as their thoughts swirled with my own, the connection between us became a living, breathing thing. I felt them, all of them: Lake and Maddy, Lily and the twins, Chase. From the youngest to the oldest, from those who thirsted for a hunt to those who wanted nothing more in life than to run...

They were *mine*.

Devon slid in beside me, and the moment I felt the brush of his arm against mine, I knew.

It was time.

In other packs, this was formal. There were petitions and ceremonies and marks carved into flesh, but here and now, I didn't have words, and they didn't need them.

Now. Now. Now.

I couldn't deny the Change any more than they could. The

treetops scattered moonlight across our faces, and I inclined my head. That was all it took.

At any other time of the month, the sound of tearing fabric and crunching bones wasn't a pleasant one, but under the full moon, the effect was like the beating of a drum.

Run. Run. Run.

All around me, they could taste it. They could feel it. Furred bodies pushed at each other to get closer to me, to touch me, to sniff me, to be with me, and the roar from their minds was overwhelming.

Alpha. Alpha. Alpha.

I forgot about Chase, about Devon, about each and every one of them as anything other than my brothers, my sisters, my people, my pack.

Mine.

This was what I'd been born for. This was all that I wanted and all that I was, and as one overwhelming, unstoppable, incredible force, we ran.

CHAPTER TWO

SATED AND SOOTHED, THE PACK SLEPT. MY ALL-TOO-human body was worn past all endurance, but for the first time in days, my pack-sense was calm, and the others' minds were quiet in my own. Their presences ebbed and flowed at the edge of my consciousness, and as I finally collapsed onto my bed, the protests of my aching body dissolved into infinity, into nothing.

I dreamed of wet grass and fallen leaves that crunched under my bare feet as I walked. I couldn't see my body, couldn't make out the outline of a single rock or tree, but I shrugged off the blindness as a mild inconvenience. My body knew what it was doing better than I did, and the scents I took in with each step were rich and familiar: damp soil and dew, cedar and cinnamon.

A sound. To my left.

My nose twitched and I whirled, my hair fanning out around me, my knees bent, ready to pounce.

Ready, if necessary, to run.

For a moment, there was silence. A twig snapped. Leaves rustled, and then I made out the faint sound of paws on wet ground.

A wolf.

I knew that much with certainty, but who the wolf was and why it had come here, I had no idea. The list of people who wanted to see me dead wasn't short enough that I could ignore the possibility of a threat. Still, no matter how hard I tried, I couldn't coerce my feet into moving, couldn't keep my body from crouching down or my arm from moving to hold out a beckoning hand, palm up.

What was I doing?

The wolf moved closer, until I could feel the heat of its body, the warmth of its breath against my palm. I wanted to see, willed myself to see, and then there was light.

The wolf in question was female, larger than some but, based on the size of her paws, not quite full grown. She was thin—and, I knew instinctively, *fast*—built along lean, muscular lines that were almost masked by thick honey-brown fur that gave way to darker markings around her face and a bit of white near each of her paws.

She brought her eyes to mine, and there was something regal about the motion. I held my breath. I waited. She showed her teeth. She ducked her head. Finally, slowly, she stepped forward, that much closer to my outstretched hand.

And then the world froze and we were caught like that,

inches apart, neither one of us able to close the gap. I fought the paralysis, but it didn't break until the scene around me had shifted and I found myself back in the clearing, the ground covered in snow, my body wrapped up in layers and layers of clothing and the wind whipping my hair at my face. It took me a moment to remember that after our run, I'd gone back to the cabin and fallen asleep in my own bed.

I'm still asleep, I thought. *I'm at home in my bed, asleep. This is just a dream.*

Despite the realization, I looked for the rest of my pack. I searched for them, with my eyes and with the part of me that knew each and every one of them like they were extensions of my own body.

I looked for the strange wolf who'd almost brought her nose to touch my hand.

But all I saw was a human, a stranger. A man. The part of my brain that thought like a girl recognized the cockiness in his expression and put his age at five or six years older than me.

The part of me that thought like Pack felt his presence like white noise, high-pitched and deafening.

Threat. Threat. Threat.

My instincts returned full throttle, and I braced myself for a fight, but the man never blinked, his light eyes focused on mine, his head tilted slightly to one side. Slowly, he raised his right hand, the same way I'd beckoned forward the wolf.

I felt the fight drain out of me, like a tire going flat.

Mesmerized, I walked toward the stranger with the diamond-hard eyes, and a serpentine smile spread over his face. Flames leapt to life at the ends of his fingertips, and I froze.

Eyes glittering, he lifted one flaming hand and waved.

Just a dream, I told myself. *It's just a dream.*

With the smell of smoke thick in my nostrils, I woke up.

"Have to say, Bryn, you look like the kind of happy that's *not*." Keely softened those words by setting a root beer float down in front of me on the bar and dangling a straw just out of my grasp. "What gives, kid?"

By profession, Keely was a bartender. By nature, she was supernaturally good at getting secrets out of people, and in the past six months, she'd become the third in the trio of adults in all of our lives, the cool aunt to Mitch's and Ali's more parental presences.

Long story short: no matter how much I didn't want to talk about the way I'd woken up that morning, covered in sweat and ready to swear that the house was on fire, I didn't stand a chance of keeping my mouth shut.

Knowing my own limitations, I leaned forward and grabbed the straw out of her hand. "Nothing gives. I just didn't sleep very well."

Because werewolves had a habit of sniffing out lies—

literally—I'd spent years training myself to tiptoe around the truth. Rather than fight the compulsion to tell Keely everything she wanted to know, I made an effort at telling her the most abbreviated version of the truth I could manage.

"Bad dreams."

Keely tilted her head to the side. "What kind of bad dreams?"

I thought on the question for a couple of seconds before the bartender's uncanny ability for getting answers—which we called a *knack*—had my lips moving completely of their own volition.

"One second, I was dreaming, and the next, it was like I was being watched." I shuddered, remembering the way the cocky stranger had observed me, like I was some kind of specimen under a microscope.

"Do you think it was anything?" Keely's question was deceptively simple, and she masked its significance by turning her back on me and going to get refills for the handful of other patrons who'd found themselves at the Wayfarer on Thanksgiving Day.

Grateful for the temporary respite, I considered her question: did I think there was something to this dream?

Yes.

Whether the answer was mine as a human or the result of the pack-sense that had long since woven itself into the pattern of my thoughts, I couldn't say. In either case, I wasn't keen to share it with Keely, who would relay my answer to Mitch, who told everything to Ali, no questions asked.

Sometimes Keely's knack really sucked.

Taking a final slurp of my root beer float, I slipped off the bar stool and headed for the exit. "Bye, Keely."

Behind me, Keely snorted. "Leaving so soon?"

Once I was safely out of range, I paused to give Keely a disgruntled look and caught sight of Lake plunking her elbows down on a nearby pool table. I could tell by Lake's posture that she was preparing to lecture a couple of our twelve-year-old pack-mates on the art of the hustle.

"If you go in looking like you could tear them to pieces, they'll hedge their bets. The trick is to look completely defenseless."

I found myself nodding in agreement with Lake's lesson, because those were words to live by—in pool and in life.

The way Keely looked and the fact that she was human kept most Weres from realizing that she had a way of making people admit things they had no desire to say out loud, and it wasn't like *I* looked like much of a threat. Our entire pack was a testament to the power of being underestimated. We were younger and smaller and newer to the werewolf game than any of the other packs, but like Keely—like me—my charges were more than they appeared to be.

Most werewolves had at least one werewolf parent, but my pack—aside from Devon and Lake and a few others—was different. I was human, and the others had been at one point, too. The only difference was that they'd been bitten, and I hadn't.

Most humans didn't have what it took to survive a major werewolf attack, but those of us who did had one thing in common—a knack for survival.

We called it Resilience.

I'd spent most of my life as the underdog (no pun intended), so supernaturally good survival instincts had come in handy more than once—and I was fairly certain they would again. Or at least, I hoped they would.

Soon.

Images from my dream—eyes watching me, flaming finger-tips, waving hello—flashed like lightning through my brain, leaving an impression in their wake that I couldn't quite shake, but I did my best to keep them from bleeding out to the rest of the pack. Leaving Lake to her lecturing, I pushed the front door open and was greeted by a chilly breeze and a feeling of wrongness that I recognized all too well: the sound of finger-nails on a chalkboard, the smell of black pepper and rotting leaves.

My back arched, and the only thing that saved me from growling was that I wasn't actually a Were.

Wolf. Foreign wolf.

My pack-sense went into overdrive, as it always did when a strange werewolf stepped foot onto Cedar Ridge land.

Territory was everything to people like us, and though we allowed peripheral males from other packs to cross through our slice of Montana on a semi-regular basis, my reaction to their presence was always, for the first few seconds at least, completely visceral. Instinctively, my eyes scanned the grass lot, looking for the intruder in question, and the moment they landed on a familiar form, my pack-sense relaxed, and my stomach tightened with nausea and guilt.

"Casey." I greeted him with a nod, giving no visible indication of weakness. I'd been taught to hide my emotions by the master, and even though my temper had a tendency to get away from me, I could have written the book on pretending to be okay when a major part of you wasn't.

"Bryn." Casey returned my nod but didn't quite meet my gaze. Within my own pack, everything seemed so natural, but interacting with people from other packs—older male people in particular—was a jarring reminder of my alpha status. I was sixteen, female, and human and had at one point been this man's subordinate.

The only thing that made his deference now *more* awkward was the fact that a lifetime ago, he'd been married to Ali.

If it hadn't been for me, he still would be.

"Ali's back in the kitchen," I said, trying not to let my mind go back to the night less than a year ago when Casey had stood by and watched me being ceremonially beaten for breaking faith with Callum's pack. That Ali's then-husband had done nothing to stop it was something my foster mother would never, even for a moment, forget. "She and Mitch are working on getting dinner rolling. The twins are around here somewhere—you know how it is."

Babies were prized in any pack, and Katie and Alex had no end of teen and preteen admirers anxious to pull babysitting duty whenever Ali needed a break.

"I know how it is, Bryn."

Before Ali had left Casey, the twins had been the darlings of Callum's pack. Now even their father was relegated to the occasional holiday visit, which reminded me . . .

"Ali didn't say you were coming." I met Casey's eyes, and he glanced away.

"It's Thanksgiving," he said with a shrug that looked—to my eyes—almost like a challenge. "My family is here."

Werewolf law dictated that Casey's ability to visit Cedar Ridge lands depended on my consent, but given that I was a large part of the reason he'd lost Ali—and the twins—I wasn't about to bring Pack politics into this.

"Kitchen's right through the back. You can go surprise Ali and Mitch yourself."

Casey's jaw clenched when I said Mitch's name, and I kicked myself for inadvertently baiting him. Werewolves tended to be possessive of their females, and one very human divorce hadn't managed to convince Casey's inner wolf that Ali wasn't his anymore.

Luckily, however, I had no illusions whatsoever about Ali being incapable of taking care of herself. She had even less tolerance for dominance maneuvers than I did, and if there was something going on between her and Mitch, I doubted she'd think it was Casey's business any more than she thought it was mine.

"Good luck."

My words caught Casey off guard, and for a moment, he looked like he might actually smile. Instead, he held out a small package wrapped in brown paper.

"From Callum," he said. "For you."

I took the package and pushed down the urge to tear immediately through the paper, the way I'd opened Callum's gifts when I was little. Things were different now, and this was a token from one alpha to another. The situation called for a little dignity.

The second Casey stepped inside the Wayfarer and the door shut behind him, I ripped through the paper, shredding it to reveal a small green box underneath. Since I seriously doubted Callum had sent me a box, I dropped the paper and began gently tugging the lid off the top of the package to reveal...

A teeny, tiny stallion?

Carved from dark cherry wood, it bore the mark of Callum's craftsmanship: smooth, even strokes of a carving knife he'd carried in his pocket for as long as I could remember. As an artist, I favored materials lifted from the recycling bin or stolen off bulletin boards around town. Callum carved wood, and apparently, he'd carved this piece for me.

I turned the box upside down, and the horse, no bigger across than the width of my hand, fell out into my palm. There was no note, no explanation—just a little wooden horse that, for whatever reason, Callum had sent to me.

A year earlier, I might have rolled my eyes at the gesture and been secretly pleased that he'd thought to give me anything at all.

Now I was suspicious. Highly suspicious.

What are you playing at, Callum?

There was a part of me that expected a response to my silent question, even though my pack-sense no longer extended to Callum or any of the other members of the Stone River Pack. They were Stone River, I was Cedar Ridge, and we might as well all have been human when it came to feeling each other's thoughts.

Seriously, Callum. A miniature horse?

I knew this wasn't just a gift, the same way I knew that Casey was here as much for Ali as for the twins. Werewolves were creatures of habit, and if there was one thing I'd learned about Callum in a lifetime of growing up in his pack, it was that he never did anything without purpose.

Easy there, Bryn-girl. Everything I've done, I've done for you.

It was easy to imagine Callum saying those words, just like it was easy to imagine him whittling, the knife moving in a blur of motion, wood dust gathering on the backs of his fingers as they moved.

"So," I said out loud, turning the horse over in my hands, "the only question is why."

The horse was not very forthcoming with answers, so I tucked it into the front pocket of my jeans, annoyingly sure that someday this little gift of Callum's would make perfect, crystalline sense and that I'd probably kick myself for not seeing the *why* sooner. Until then, I'd just have to be patient.

I hated being patient.

In search of a distraction, I went to look for Chase and found him sitting at the edge of the woods, almost out of sight from the restaurant and small cabins that dotted the rest of the Mitchells' land.

"You out here alone?" I asked Chase. "Don't tell me Lake and Devon have scared you off already."

I was only half joking. Lake had a fondness for weaponry and a habit of treating firearms like they were pets. If you weren't used to it, it could be downright disturbing.

"I haven't seen Lake," Chase replied. "And Devon's fine."

Of all the words I'd heard used to describe Devon Macalister, *fine* wasn't a particularly common one. People either loved Dev or hated him; there wasn't much in between.

"Was it the kids, then? Ali swears Lily's worse at three than she was at two."

Chase smiled and shook his head. "I just needed a minute," he said. "Quiet."

It took me a moment to realize that Chase wasn't talking about the kind of quiet you heard with your ears. The rest of the pack couldn't sense one another as strongly as I could sense them, being alpha—but I remembered what it was like to have the whisper of a pack constantly pulling at the edges of your mind. For Chase, who spent so much of his time at the edges of our territory, the noise level here was probably deafening.

"Quiet, huh?" I said, trying to remember what that was like.

Chase reached up to take my hand and nodded, rubbing his thumb back and forth over the surface of my palm. Without meaning to, I saw a flash of his thoughts, saw that he could have shielded his mind against the others but had chosen not to, because that would have meant closing me out, too.

I settled down on the ground next to him, matching his silence with my own. With Devon and Lake and even Maddy, I was always talking, joking, arguing, laughing, but with Chase, I didn't have to say anything, didn't even have to think it.

Given everything I had to think about—Callum's cryptic gift, Casey's arrival, the feeling that my dream the night before hadn't been just a dream—there was something calming about sitting there, just the two of us.

Right up until it wasn't.

For someone with the size and build of an NFL linebacker,

Devon was impressively light-footed, and he appeared above us without any forewarning, oblivious to—or possibly ignoring—the implication that if he'd arrived a few minutes later, he might have interrupted something else.

"Who's ready for some food?" he asked, all smiles. "Dare I hope Ali is making her scrumptious cranberry sauce of awesomeness?"

I was on the verge of answering, but Chase beat me to it. "I could eat," he said simply.

I rolled my eyes. Chase was a werewolf, and he was a boy. He could *always* eat.

"It's Thanksgiving," Chase said in his own defense. "I've heard that food is kind of a tradition."

A flash of something passed between us, and I knew that Thanksgiving really was something Chase had heard about but never experienced—at least not in a way he cared to remember.

I added that to the list of things I knew about the boy independent of the wolf. From what I'd already gathered about Chase's human life, being attacked by a rabid werewolf and waking up in a cage in Callum's basement was pretty much the best thing ever to happen to him. My own childhood hadn't exactly been sunshine and rainbows, but I didn't push the issue—not with Devon standing right there, looking at the two of us and processing just how close my body was to Chase's.

The two of them were remarkably chill for werewolves. They didn't play mind games with each other, and they never made me feel like property—but there was still only one of me and two of them, one of whom had been my best friend forever, and the other of whom made my heart beat faster, just by touching my hand.

Awk-ward.

"So," I said, climbing to my feet and changing the subject ASAP, "I had a dream last night that someone tried to burn me alive, and I'm not entirely sure it was just a dream."

Devon stiffened. Chase's pupils pulsed.

Subject successfully changed.

"Now, who's ready to eat?"

CHAPTER THREE

AFTER—BUT ONLY PARTIALLY BECAUSE OF—THE bombshell I'd dropped on the boys, Thanksgiving dinner proved to be a tense state of affairs. Casey had to leave the table twice: once when Mitch's hand brushed Ali's as he reached for the salt, and once when Katie started bawling and Mitch was the one to reach out and distract the temperamental little miss from the indignity of being stuck in a high chair. As for Devon and Chase, they were acting even more high-strung than Ali's ex.

Apparently, my distraction had worked a little too well, leaving the two of them closing rank around me, like the Thanksgiving steak—a vaunted Were tradition—might leap off the table at any moment and attempt an assassination.

It was just a dream, guys.

I sent the words to the two of them through the bond, thankful that I'd mastered this part of being an alpha and didn't have to worry about other members of our pack over-hearing.

I'm fine. I'm going to be fine, and if either of you move your chairs even a centimeter closer to me, you're going to be picking stuffing out of your hair while trying to pry my foot out of your you-know-what.

The humorless expression on my face sold that threat. I wasn't some weak little human girl anymore. For that matter, I'd never been some weak little human girl. I was a survivor, I was their *alpha*, and I could take care of myself.

"Ouch!" The cry escaped my mouth before I could stop it, and on either side of me, Chase and Devon leapt to their feet.

"Problem?" Ali asked mildly, amusement dancing in the corners of her eyes. Given the whole Casey thing, I didn't think she had call to be in such a good mood, but what did I know?

"No problem," I said darkly, rubbing my shin. "Somebody just accidentally kicked me under the table." I narrowed my eyes at Lake, and she helped herself to another T-bone and smothered it in steak sauce.

"Wasn't an accident," she said cheerfully.

"Lake." Mitch didn't say more than his daughter's name, and she rolled her eyes.

"It's not like I *shot* her."

There was a retort on the tip of my tongue, but I was pretty sure Lake had kicked me because she'd picked up on my saying things she couldn't hear, and I really didn't want to open up that topic of conversation to the table at large. The boys' over-protective act was conspicuous enough as it was.

Note to self: in the future, I need to be more careful about how I change the subject.

I'll tell you later, Lake, I said silently. *Promise.*

Lake met my eyes and nodded, all thoughts of further under-the-table violence (hopefully) forgotten.

I reached out to dish up seconds, and the door to the restaurant opened. Casey crossed the room and slid back into his seat, composure regained. Even though I'd gotten used to his presence, something shifted inside my body. I took a long drink of water and gave my pack-sense a chance to acclimate again, only this time, it didn't.

Foreign. Wolf.

Through the heavy scent of homemade gravy and pies baking in the oven, I couldn't even pick Casey's scent out of the crowd's, but what I was feeling now had nothing to do with the five senses and everything to do with my psychic bond to the Pack. The niggling sensation persisted, and the longer I waited for it to pass, the larger it got.

Foreign. Wolf.

That was when I realized that I wasn't sensing Casey. It was something else. Someone else.

Across the table, Mitch glanced toward the door, and then he looked at me.

"Get the kids to the back," he said.

I turned immediately to Maddy, and with the quiet efficiency that had always made her a leader among the Rabid's pint-sized victims, she ushered the others away from the table, even Lily, who let loose a comically high-pitched growl at the thought of being separated from her food.

"Now, Lily." I added my voice to Maddy's, but my thoughts were on Mitch, who'd already started reaching for the gun he and Keely kept behind the counter.

Ali didn't ask what was happening. She didn't have to. Within seconds, she had Katie in one arm and Alex in the other, and she met Casey's eyes.

"Are you staying or coming?" she asked him calmly.

I could see the temptation of going with Ali warring with Casey's lupine desire to prove himself—to Ali and to the rest of her pack.

"This is Cedar Ridge business," I told Casey quietly. "We've got it covered."

The dagger eyes Casey shot me in that moment made me realize that he hadn't forgiven me for being the straw that broke his marriage's back.

He wouldn't ever forgive me.

Foreign. Wolf.

Right now, I had bigger issues than Casey.

"If I asked you to come with us, would you come?" It took me a second to figure out that Ali was addressing that question to me, not Casey.

I didn't answer.

Ali started again. "If I told you to come, would you— You

know what? Never mind, but if there's a hair out of place on your head when I get back, be forewarned, I will kill you, alpha or not."

With those words, Ali followed Maddy and the rest of the younger kids back into the kitchen, out of sight and, hopefully, out of harm's way. After a long moment, and another glare in my direction, Casey retreated, leaving only five of us to meet the coming threat.

Devon, Lake, Mitch, Chase, and me.

Foreign. Wolf.

This time, the feeling was so strong that it brought me onto the balls of my feet. There was a foreign wolf on our territory. *My* territory. He'd come without permission, on an evening when the bar was closed. Teeth gnashed in the recesses of my brain, painting the walls of my mind red with blood as I realized the potential for this to end badly.

Very badly.

The werewolf Senate hadn't been happy with the idea of a human alpha, and there wasn't a day that went by that I didn't think about the fact that I had something most male Weres wanted very, very badly.

Maddy. Lake. Lily, Katie, Sloane, Ava, Sophie . . .

Their names blended together in my mind, and the adrenaline pumping through my veins turned angry and cool. Most werewolves were male. Natural-born females, like Katie and Lake, survived to birth only because they'd been half of a set of twins, and most packs didn't have more than a handful of females, period.

Ours had nine, all of them young, none of them mated. As long-lived as werewolves were, most wouldn't have batted an eye at the idea of taking possession of a female and waiting a decade or two for her to grow up.

If I had to, I'd tear this intruder to shreds with my bare hands to keep our girls safe.

"You even think of telling me to turn tail and hide, and I'll laugh you out of Montana proper." Lake's words left no room for argument, but we both knew that if I wanted her to leave, I could make her leave. That was what it meant to be alpha.

I met Lake's eyes. "Wouldn't dream of it," I said. Alpha or not, forcing my will on someone else wasn't what it meant to be me.

An alien smell—snake oil and vinegar, feces and blood—permeated the thick wooden door, strong enough that even my human nose could make it out, and though none of the five of us moved, the shift in the room was unmistakable. My pack was ready to fight, and I was ready to let them—and to do what I could to back them up—but whoever the intruder was, he never crossed the threshold of the door.

There was a loud thump outside, like a duffel bag being dropped onto cement, and then a high-pitched gargle—half choke, half whine—filled the air.

Blood.

The smell—and the meaning behind it—finally registered, and I pushed my way through my werewolf bodyguards until the only thing standing between me and the door was Mitch.

"Someone's hurt." I said those two words like they were all that mattered. For a moment, I didn't think Mitch was going to get out of the way or even open the door. He'd spent a long time living on the periphery of Callum's pack, with Callum his alpha in name only. Mitch wasn't used to taking orders, and even though he'd joined our pack shortly after Lake had, I wasn't used to giving them to him.

Please, Mitch. I met his eyes.

With a slight nod and his gun at the ready, Mitch opened the door. I didn't push him, didn't rush it, but when Mitch knelt down next to a heap of bones and fur, I couldn't hold back any longer. I was beside him in an instant—not within biting range, but close enough that I could make out every inch of this ravaged Were's body.

He looked like he'd been taken apart piece by piece and sewn back together—badly. He was stuck halfway between his human form and his animal one, and the patches of skin that weren't covered with fur were angry and red, welts layered over bruises layered over burns.

Why didn't he finish Shifting?

Bile rose in my throat with the question. Weres healed extremely quickly, but you couldn't Shift and heal at the same time; it was like trying to eat while throwing up. That explained why the body in front of us was still battered to a pulp, but not why its owner had let himself be caught in the throes of Shifting for any extended period of time.

Without meaning to, I moved my gaze to Chase. The expression on his face was completely impassive. Even I couldn't read it, but I didn't need to, because the last time I'd seen a Were caught between one form and another, Shifting back and forth with excruciating results, it was Chase. We'd been hunting the Rabid who'd Changed him into a Were, and the monster had turned the hunt back on us, infiltrating Chase's head.

"Is somebody doing this to him?" I kept my voice low, and it was almost drowned out by the heavy, tortured breaths coming from the porch. "Should I try to break off the connection?"

That was what I'd done to free Chase from the Rabid. I'd gone into Chase's head, taken the connection the Rabid had formed when he'd Changed him, and snapped it in two.

If I had to, I could do it again.

"No." Mitch's voice was sharper than I'd ever heard it. "This wolf isn't yours, Bryn. Unless you're wanting war, you'll keep your little alpha nose out of his pack-bonds. Not all alphas are as forgiving as Callum when it comes to other people stealing their wolves."

I felt like Mitch had slapped me, like I was stupid and young and completely incompetent as an alpha and a person.

"Whose is he?" I asked quietly, trying to place the wolf's scent but thrown off by the smell of blood and the mewling sound now making its way out of the creature's monstrous hybrid mouth.

Mitch didn't reply; instead, he pointed to the creature's neck. "There's what's keeping him from Shifting."

My eyes adjusted to the darkness on the porch, and I saw the object Mitch had referenced: a long, thin metal shaft that glowed in the light of the nearly full moon.

Silver.

"Dev?" I could have removed it myself, but impulsive or not, even I wasn't stupid enough to think that my going that close to an injured Were was a good idea. Whoever he was, the mass of flesh and bones on our porch was out of his mind with pain, and pain had a habit of making Weres unpredictable.

If Devon got bitten, he'd heal in a matter of moments. If I got bitten, I might never heal, and if I got bitten badly enough, I'd end up either dead or Changed—and neither one of those was a future I would particularly relish.

Devon walked forward, and without waiting a beat, he knelt, closed a hand around the shaft, and pulled. Most werewolves were allergic to silver, but as in many areas of life, Devon was an exception. As he jerked the hated object out of the wound, the injured Were reared back, and I heard teeth snapping and the sound of flesh—though whose, I wasn't sure—giving way.

Chase came to my side, and I thought of that moment of quiet in the woods—how fragile it had been, how fleeting.

Dev tossed the silver rod to one side. "We'll want to pick that up," he said, almost absentmindedly. "Wouldn't want one of the kiddos to get ahold of it."

Our visitor's body registered the silver's removal. It shuddered and finally gave way to one form.

Human form.

If I'd been horrified before, I was sickened now. There wasn't a piece of flesh that had been left untouched, and for a moment, I thought I might throw up or cry or both.

The injured Were was a boy. Not a man, not a threat. A boy—maybe a year or so younger than me. All business, Mitch bent and hefted the boy into his arms, eliciting a high-pitched whine more lupine than not.

"Tell Ali I'll need medical supplies," he said. "Lake knows where they are." With those words, Mitch turned to carry the boy away, leaving the rest of us standing there, slack-jawed and tense.

Lake was the first to snap out of it, and she hurried back to the kitchen to relay the message to Ali. Chase's eyes followed Mitch's progression, and I could see the gears in his head turning as he analyzed the situation. He ran a hand through my hair, assuring himself with every light touch that I was all right, convincing the wolf inside him to still.

Devon didn't move, and this time, I said his name silently.

Dev?

After a long moment, Devon managed to drag his eyes away

from the blood seeping into the wooden planks of the porch. His fists clenched, and he turned toward me. "Bryn."

There was a wealth of information in that one word, and I knew that whatever Devon said next was going to send a tremor through our pack, like static feedback or a punch to the gut.

"I caught his scent, and it wasn't pretty."

I waited for Devon to make a comment about Calvin Klein cologne or something equally flippant, but he didn't. Instead, he cut right to the chase.

"This kid is from the Snake Bend Pack, Bryn. His alpha is Shay."

CHAPTER FOUR

❧

I ONLY KNEW THREE THINGS ABOUT SHAY MACALISTER.

One: he was a purebred werewolf, one of a relatively small number in the country who'd been born to two werewolf parents instead of just one. Purebreds were larger, stronger, and faster and had fewer weaknesses than werewolves with human blood flowing in their veins.

Two: Shay wanted me dead. It wasn't personal. I had something he wanted. More females in a pack meant more live births and stronger, purebred children, and the only thing standing between the other alphas and doubling their numbers—and their power base—was me.

And, okay, maybe it was a little personal for Shay, since I'd been responsible for destroying a Rabid who knew the secret to changing human girls into Weres. It was also possible that once I'd done so, I'd derived great satisfaction from putting the screws to the other alphas—and Shay in particular—flaunting the laws that forbid one alpha from taking wolves who belonged to another, even if that other alpha was a teenage, human female.

43

At the moment, however, it was Shay's third distinguishing characteristic that turned my stomach to lead and blew a cold chill down the length of my spine.

Shay was Devon's—*my* Devon's—brother. He was everything Dev didn't want to be, everything he'd spent his entire life rebelling against, and already the presence of one of Shay's wolves on my land had sapped the mirth from Devon's features and left something stone hard and formidable in its place.

"Hey." I reached out for Devon's arm. "You okay?"

Devon stood there, every muscle in his body tensed. He didn't answer my question. Callum would have forced Dev's eyes to his and repeated the query, but I nudged Devon's shoulder with my head, a gesture of comfort far less human than I was and not particularly alpha in the least.

On instinct, Dev nudged me back, his muscles relaxing— but not by much. "Only you," he said crisply, "would be worried about me at a time like this."

Like Shay, Devon was purebred. Boy-band tendencies aside, he could take care of himself—physically.

"Seriously, Dev. You want to tell me this isn't messing with your head at all?" I didn't have to put even an ounce of my power as alpha behind the words. Best-friend privilege said it all.

"Well, of course it is," Devon replied. "One of Brother Dearest's wolves showed up on our land, beaten within an inch of his life and caught between Shifts. If you'd been the one to open that door instead of Mitch, the smell of human blood probably would have sent him rabid, and you'd be significantly less charming as a decimated pile of meat."

Dev—do you think Shay sent him? I couldn't make myself ask the question out loud, and Devon responded in key.

I don't think anything is below Shay. He's not like other people, Bryn. You know he's not.

"If your brother wanted Bryn dead, is this how he'd do it?" Chase's words took me off guard—not because I had forgotten that he was in the room (though I had), but because his tone, understated and detached, contrasted so sharply with the animal set to his features. His wolf wanted to *touch* me, to *protect* me, to tear Shay to pieces, but Chase's human side wanted answers—whether asking the question was like driving an elbow into Devon's gut or not.

"I don't know," Devon said shortly, his jaw turning to granite, his gaze averted from mine. "I'm not exactly an expert on the inner workings of Shay's dark and twisted mind."

By the time Devon had come along, his much older brother was already the alpha of the Snake Bend Pack. They weren't exactly what one would call *close*.

"Okay. I had to ask. If you think of anything, let us know." With that, Chase turned his attention from Dev to me. "What do you need?"

The look in Chase's pale blue eyes was still feral, the desire to protect me simmering just under the surface—but he'd grown up in a world very different from the one I'd known as part of Callum's pack, a world where females weren't shuffled off into a back room or given bodyguards at the first sign of trouble. Chase was asking, not telling; thinking instead of acting on instinct.

I'd never been so glad that Chase was *Chase* and that neither one of us had been born a Were.

"I need to talk to Mitch," I said, following his example and trying to think this through, even though I wasn't exactly known for an overdeveloped tendency to look before I leapt. "Whatever happens, our first priority is making sure that whoever this visitor is, he doesn't die."

I hadn't been an alpha for long, but even I knew that having a Snake Bend wolf die on my territory wouldn't look good. Until I knew exactly what was going on, and how to proceed, I couldn't afford to give Shay any reason to come here, looking like the injured party and demanding something—or worse, some*one*—in return.

It was two days before they let me anywhere near the injured boy—two days for his injuries to heal enough that he was in control of his wolf, two days that I spent gnashing my teeth and trying to unravel the tangled web of political possibilities surrounding his entry to our territory.

Had Shay sent him here, on the verge of death, with the

hope that he'd attack me? Would the other alphas blame Shay for the action of a wolf who was clearly Rabid? Had someone attacked one of Shay's wolves on our land—and if so, who? A member of one of the other packs, crossing into our territory to make trouble? A Rabid, gone rogue or mad and hunting anyone and anything in his way? Or, God forbid, one of my own peripherals?

By Senate law, our peripherals could attack trespassers, but what had been done to this boy wasn't animal retribution.

It was torture.

I had to talk to him, and after two days of letting Mitch— and more importantly, Ali—tell me no, I was done listening to the word. In a happy coincidence, they also appeared to be done saying it, so I didn't have to go through the awkward and unquestionably ill-fated process of trying to pull rank on the woman who'd been my mother since I was four.

"I want to go with you." Devon's voice was perfectly pleasant, but I recognized the look in his eye, because the exact same expression had been staring out at me from the mirror for days.

"Can you behave yourself?" I asked mildly.

Devon did a good impression of someone who was offended. *"Moi?"* He ruined the effect somewhat by brushing invisible dust off the tips of his fingers, a motion as close to popping his knuckles as someone with Devon's sensibilities could come.

I reached out to him with my mind but hit a smooth, blank wall. Of all the wolves in my pack, Dev was the one most clearly poised to become alpha himself someday. The promise of his future dominance made him an ideal second-in-command, but there was power there, too, and that power meant that if he wanted to, Dev could guard his mind from me absolutely, in a way that no one else in our pack could.

"Dev."

"What do you expect me to say, Bronwyn?" he asked, adopting Callum's habit of calling me by my full first name when he was irked. "This boy—who belongs to *Shay*—came here, to our territory, half mad and out of control of his Shift, and plopped himself down more or less on your front porch. He could have killed you, and accident or not, that's not the kind of thing you can expect me to shrug off like a hideous hair day."

Challenge.

There was a whisper of it in the bond between us, and I brought my eyes to Devon's in a staring contest that neither one of us wanted to be engaging in. For several seconds, we stood there, locked in something we didn't completely understand, and then Devon blinked.

Literally.

He didn't avert his gaze. He didn't round his shoulders, but he blinked, and that was enough.

I'd won.

"I'm still coming with you, you impossibly irritating little wench."

From Dev, that was a term of endearment, and I took the degree to which he sounded on the verge of slipping into an exaggerated British accent as an indication that he was in control of himself—and that unless my life was in immediate danger, he'd behave when cross-examining Shay's wolf.

"Yeah," I said, punching him lightly in the stomach, "I love you, too."

Taking a deep breath, I knocked on the door of Cabin 13, where Mitch had been tending to the injured wolf.

Lake answered the door and pulled me inside. "'Bout time you got here," she said. "Now would you please tell him I can stay and to stop picking at me to take to the hills?"

Based on the mutinous expression on her father's face, I inferred that the "him" Lake was referring to was Mitch.

"Well, go on. Tell him." Lake folded her arms over her chest, the expression on her face an exact mirror of the scowl on Mitch's.

Are you crazy? I asked, sending the words from my mind to hers. In response, Lake shrugged, which I took to mean something along the lines of "Yes, in fact, I am."

"It's okay by me if she stays," I said, but that was as far as I was willing to go; I hadn't thrown down with Ali on my own behalf, so I wasn't about to press the issue with Mitch for Lake. Besides, why she would want to be anywhere near a male Were from a pack that was, in all likelihood, less female-friendly than ours was a mystery to me.

"Please," Lake snorted in response to the expression on my face. "Have you seen this kid? I reckon I could take him with three paws tied behind my back, no shotguns, no knives."

"If you had paws," Devon volunteered helpfully, "you wouldn't be able to use a shotgun."

In her human form, Lake fought dirty, which for a Were meant using weapons other than claws and teeth. In wolf form, she was faster than just about anyone I'd ever seen, but she wasn't as big as most males and couldn't match them in brute strength—so she improvised.

"You three gonna squabble like children, or do you want to talk to the boy?"

I took Mitch's question as implicit permission for Lake to stay. I could almost pretend this was just another adventure, with Devon and Lake and me alternating between keeping one another out of trouble and getting into it.

Almost.

"I'll do the talking." I said the words quietly, more to psych myself up for the coming interrogation than anything else. Mitch nodded his approval, and then he stepped aside to allow the three of us entry to a small hallway.

Wolf. Foreign.

The feeling washed over me as I walked forward, but it receded more quickly than it had before, like my instincts knew as well as I did that even if the boy was a threat, they were no longer needed to sound the alarm. That thought in mind, I breathed through the unmistakable smell of Snake Bend in the air, noting that it was tinged with antiseptic and something that smelled like coffee or chocolate: the boy's scent, separate from the smell of his pack.

Lucas, Bryn. Mitch's voice was rough in my mind, and my brain itched just listening to it. *The boy's name is Lucas.*

Mitch was Pack, but even living at the center of our territory, he seemed more like a peripheral, less connected to me and the others than we were to one another. It was a testament to Mitch's experience and age—a few hundred years, at least—that he was able to keep his mental distance *and* still make his words heard in my mind at will.

"Lucas," I repeated out loud. I stepped into the room and was greeted with a face so blank that I had to wonder if he'd heard me say his name or registered my presence here at all.

The boy in question was olive-skinned, but pallor had settled over his cheeks, and he didn't twitch or move at all as I approached. The stillness was unnatural on a Were, and watching him felt as odd as seeing a lion lying faint on the floor. He looked like someone had drained the blood from his body and then leeched his will to live straight from his soul.

I crossed the room to stand at the foot of his bed, keeping myself just out of his reach. "I'm Bryn," I said, for lack of a better opening, "and you're on Cedar Ridge land."

"I know." His voice wasn't quiet or raspy or anything else I'd expected of it. Instead, it had an almost musical quality to it, like he would have been more at home singing along to an acoustic guitar than forcing his mouth to speak regularly. "I came here for you."

Devon was beside me in an instant. To his credit, he didn't stand straight, and his lip didn't curl back to reveal canines, but his size and presence spoke for themselves. "Did your alpha send you?" Devon asked, refusing to refer to Shay by name.

The boy on the bed shuddered and then his body fell almost immediately back into stillness, like even shivering was too much for his fractured mind to bear.

"When you say you came here for Bryn," Lake added, her eyes glittering and utterly lethal, "what exactly would you be meaning by that?"

So much for my doing the talking.

"I can't . . . I can't live like that. Not anymore. It's—" The boy blinked and even that seemed to take gargantuan effort. "I just can't do it." Ignoring Lake and Devon, Lucas looked at me—not at my eyes, but close enough that I felt the weight of each word out of his mouth. "They say you help people. That you save them. Callum's Bryn. That's you, right?"

"You didn't come here to kill Bryn." Devon's voice matched the tone in Lucas's almost exactly, and I wondered if Dev even realized he was doing it. "And your alpha didn't send you?"

Lucas moved, and I braced myself. At first, I thought he was leaping to his feet, but when he stopped moving, he was still on the bed, kneeling and no longer covered by the threadbare sheet.

Angry white scars crisscrossed his torso and arms like tiny *X*s and *O*s. He'd been cut, long and deep, over and over again. "You want to know if Shay sent me?" he asked Devon. "If *your brother* sent me?" Lucas breathed in raggedly and lowered his voice. "You look just like him."

Devon didn't even blink, but inside, I winced for him, knowing that Lucas's words would undoubtedly have left a mark.

"I suppose whether or not Shay sent me depends on your definition of the word *sent*. He beat me. He hounded me. And when it got to the point that I couldn't think of fighting back, couldn't even muster up the strength to keep wishing he was dead, when I thought that things couldn't get any worse for me in Snake Bend"—Lucas settled back, his eyes blank, his voice soft—"they did."

"Why?" The word burst out of Lake's mouth a second before I could give voice to the question myself. "Why would your own alpha do something like that?"

Now Lucas didn't look at Lake, or at me. He looked at Devon, and I wondered if he was really seeing Dev or if he was still caught up in memory, seeing Shay in the features the brothers shared.

"Why?" Lucas repeated. "My alpha is the type who needs a punching bag when things are going badly." He shifted his gaze from Devon to me. "And lately, things haven't exactly been going well."

Lucas's words hit me hard, the image of his bloodied body interwoven in my mind with that of the scars that still marred his flesh. Shay had done that to Lucas. He'd done it because he was a bully and because he couldn't touch the person he most wanted to hurt, the *reason* things had not been going according to his master plan.

Me.

Six months earlier, Shay had gone to Alpine Creek, Wyoming, expecting to return with fresh blood and females for the Snake Bend Pack, and because of me, he'd gone home empty-handed and watched as a human girl walked away with everything he'd wanted for himself.

I'd seen the bloodlust in Shay's eyes. I knew how badly he'd wanted to slam me into a wall, to rip out my insides and watch my body crumble to the ground. But thanks to the power Callum held over the rest of the werewolf Senate, thanks to the Senate's own laws, Shay couldn't touch me.

In the wild, when an animal is forced to pull back from attacking an adversary and turned its wrath on an easier target instead, they called it redirected aggression.

There was a chance—a good one—that what Shay had done to Lucas he'd done because of me.

"What do you want from us?" I asked Lucas, unable to keep myself from taking a step closer to the dead eyes that looked up at me from the bed. "Why did you come here?"

I didn't bother telling myself that the only one to blame for Shay's actions was Shay. It didn't even matter if I believed it. I wasn't the kind of person who could look at someone like Lucas and walk away with something as pat as an "it's not my fault."

In response to my question, Lucas tilted his head to the side, a gesture more animal than not. "I want you to claim me," he said, like it was the simplest, most obvious thing in the world. "I don't want to be Snake Bend anymore. I want to be Cedar Ridge."

CHAPTER FIVE

⁓

"HE WANTS TO TRANSFER PACKS?"

No matter how many times I said those words, I still couldn't quite believe that was why Lucas had come all the way to the Wayfarer, a place that must have felt like enemy territory to his wolf, the same way he felt foreign to me. Bleeding and bloody, beaten within an inch of his life and unable to Shift, he'd limped and stumbled his way over mountains and through the forest and around God knew how many towns where he might have been spotted and shot—and he'd done all of that in the single-minded pursuit of one thing.

Me.

They say you help people. Callum's Bryn.

I struggled to keep my head up under the memory of Lucas's words and the hope I'd seen in his otherwise dead eyes. I didn't want to be anyone's last hope any more than I wanted to be some kind of werewolf legend: the Little Human That Could.

"What this kid is asking," Chase said slowly, mulling over the words, "is it even possible?"

After meeting with Lucas, I'd retreated to the forest to process his request. Chase had been waiting for me when I got there, and everything that had happened passed between us with a single touch. Devon and Lake had followed on my heels, and now, there we were, the four of us. I breathed in deeply through my nose, banishing Lucas's scent with theirs and reminding myself that, alpha or not, I wasn't in this alone.

"People do transfer packs," Devon said slowly. "It's a coming-of-age thing."

I snorted. "Coming-of-age? Please, Dev. This isn't *Catcher in the Rye*. Pack transfers happen when a wolf gets exiled from one pack and picked up by another, or after someone's been peripheral for years. That's how it happened when Mitch left Callum's pack. That's how it happened a hundred years ago when Shay transferred to Snake Bend. That's how it works. It's nature's way of shaking up the gene pool—and it doesn't happen like this."

I wasn't telling Devon anything he didn't know, but in a show of grace, he didn't call me on it. I took that as a sign that he knew how uncomfortable I was with Lucas's coming here, looking at me like I was different from the others, like I could be his savior. Being alpha was one thing with my own pack—we were young, and we were family, and I would have died for any of them, no questions asked. I *needed* to protect them, more than I needed water or air or any kind of human connection.

But this?

Lucas wasn't a member of our pack. I didn't know him, didn't love him, couldn't see inside his mind or feel his emotions as my own. I knew from experience—first with Callum's pack and later with the Rabid—that I had the ability to rewire pack-bonds, breaking another alpha's hold over a wolf and psychically instating my own, but I also knew that doing so wasn't something the powers that be in our world would let me get away with a second time. Mitch had said it himself—not all alphas were as forgiving as Callum had been when I'd claimed Devon, Lake, and Chase.

The same law that kept the other alphas from coming here and raiding our ranks for child brides forbade me from interfering with Lucas's ties to Shay's pack. I couldn't just welcome him with open arms and say, "Hey, sorry your alpha has been torturing you on my account. Make yourself at home."

"Shay has to agree," I said slowly, realizing even as I did that I might as well be saying something about hell freezing over or pigs taking flight. "For Lucas to transfer from Snake Bend to Cedar Ridge, Shay would have to agree."

Anything less could start a war—or worse, give the other alphas, Shay included, the justification they needed to take what was mine.

I wanted to help Lucas. I did. The idea of sending him back to Shay, knowing what Shay would do to him for running away, made me want to vomit.

But I couldn't risk my pack's safety for his.

—*Maddy*—

The part of me that was alpha felt her approaching, and I wondered how long she'd debated before joining the four of us in the woods. She was the newest recruit to our inner circle, and even though we were Pack, even though that made us family, I knew she was still getting used to trusting other people, to believing that they could care about her the way we did.

Being raised by a psychopath will do that to you.

"Hey, Mads." Devon greeted her with a smile, and I knew he felt the same tug I did: to protect Maddy, to make her feel safe, to make sure she knew that on four legs or two, she belonged. Only this time, those mandates were in conflict with each other. Protecting Maddy meant telling her that everything was fine, that we would take care of this, that she didn't need to worry about Snake Bend or Shay or the battered boy in Cabin 13. But doing that would put up a wall between her and the rest of us. It would be saying that Maddy was weak or broken, that because she'd been a victim, she'd never get to be anything else.

I couldn't do that any more than I could have stripped Lake of her weapons or demanded that Chase open up at the next run and tell the entire pack his human life story.

"The boy is part of the Snake Bend Pack. His alpha has been abusing him, and he came here hoping we could help." *Hoping I could help*, I corrected myself silently. "He wants to transfer packs, but Senate law says I need his alpha's permission first."

Maddy absorbed this information in an instant, and something dark and animal settled over her gray eyes. When she spoke, her voice was absolutely calm, but there was something almost regal about it.

Something deadly.

"His alpha won't give permission," she said softly. "He'll be furious that the boy got away, that he came here. He won't like being outsmarted. Monsters like that don't like knowing there's a part of people that you can't touch unless they let you." Maddy shrugged, like her words weren't important, like she wasn't talking about herself every bit as much as she was talking about Lucas. "If you send this boy back, his alpha will kill him."

I wanted to tell Maddy that she was wrong, that Shay wouldn't kill Lucas, that Pack Law wouldn't allow it.

Unfortunately, it did, and Shay would, and I knew, just looking at Maddy, that she wouldn't understand how I could ever let that happen.

I couldn't.

If things had gone differently, I might have grown up in Maddy's place, attacked and raised by a killer who stripped away everything that made me a person, everything that made me *me*. The others knew me better and had known me longer, but Maddy and I were the most alike, the two of us separated only by winds of chance that had blown her one way and me the other.

I couldn't let Shay kill Lucas.

If I didn't do something to save this battered foreign boy, Maddy would never forgive me, and I would never, ever forgive myself.

Alpha. Alpha. Alpha.

The thrum of the bond at the gateway of my mind was a constant, incessant reminder that being alpha meant making tough decisions. It meant protecting my pack to the detriment of anything and everything else. I knew that. I accepted it, but I was human, too, and I hadn't grown up under Callum's tutelage for nothing.

There was always a way around orders, a way to be the exception instead of the rule. I just needed to find it. I was going to find it.

Even if it killed me.

Chase arched one eyebrow at me, and Devon narrowed his eyes slightly. "Let the record show that I don't trust the expression on your face right now. I know that expression, Bronwyn."

Lake smiled beatifically, ready and willing to misbehave. "So do I."

When it came to the ins and outs of werewolf politics, my resources were severely limited. Of the members of our pack, fourteen had been the taught the ways of the world by a Rabid, two were infants, two had spent their lives as peripherals, one had been a werewolf for less than a year, and the remaining three were Devon, Ali, and me.

Long story short: it wasn't like I had a werewolf Yoda to show me the ropes. My best bet in our pack was probably Mitch, and if he had information he wanted to share, he would have already given it to me. Ali probably knew more about werewolves than any human on the planet, but somehow, I didn't think approaching my legal guardian and saying, "Hey, I need to find a loophole so I can steal another alpha's werewolf and give him even more reason to want me dead," would go over terribly well.

That left me with exactly two options: Google and Callum. Since I didn't think a random internet search was going to reveal even a fraction of what I needed to know, I went back to the cabin I shared with Ali and the twins, and sequestered myself in my bedroom to make a call.

Convincing myself to dial the number was harder than it should have been. The part of me that was alpha objected to the idea of bringing another pack into this, and the part of me that had once considered Callum like family balked at the idea of hearing his voice.

There were things—more of them than I wanted to admit—that were easier to forget when Callum stayed in his territory and I stayed in mine.

Flopping down on my bed, I reached for my nightstand and picked up the carving he'd sent me. I still had no idea what it was supposed to mean, but I was positive that it did mean something, and that if and when I called Callum, nothing I had to say would surprise him in the least.

I'd spent my entire life growing up under Callum's watch without realizing that he had a psychic knack. Sometimes it felt like everyone but me had known that Callum saw flashes of the future and made a routine practice of nudging it in one direction or another. He was fallible. He wasn't omniscient— but he'd probably known that I was going to call him before the option had even occurred to me, and if I chickened out, he'd probably know that, too.

Screw that.

My fingers were dialing before my mind had processed the decision to do so, and my breath caught in my throat with the first ring. I pictured Callum's house and saw the landline ringing over and over again.

Maybe I should have called his cell.

The moment that thought crossed my mind, someone picked up the phone, and a smooth, even voice said hello.

Not Callum's.

The voice was female, and even if I hadn't recognized it, the process of elimination would have told me that it was Sora— the only female Were in Callum's pack now that Katie and Lake were in mine. Unfortunately, Sora was also Devon's mother, which meant that she was Shay's mother. I was going to go out on a limb and guess she probably wasn't the best person to ask about how to legally steal a wolf out from under the monstrous product of her loins.

Ew. I so did not want to be thinking about Devon's mother's loins.

"Hello?" Sora repeated for what was probably the third or fourth time.

"It's me." I'd spent as much time at Devon's house as my own growing up, so I took it for granted that Sora would know who the *me* in question was.

"Bryn." There was a faint trace of a smile in Sora's voice, and I pulled my knees tight to my chest, surprised at how short a mental hop it was from hearing her say my name to thinking about the last time I'd seen her.

I could almost hear my ribs popping, feel my mouth bleeding as she came at me again and again.

I tried to force myself out of the memory. When I'd broken faith with Callum's pack and he'd ordered me beaten, Sora was the one who had carried out the sentence. I knew now that the entire ordeal had been part of a larger plan, one that had led me to the founding of the Cedar Ridge Pack, but that didn't make me hate Sora for it any less.

"Did you want something, Bryn?" Sora's voice was unbothered and calm, and I wondered if she'd thought, even for a second, about asking me about Devon.

"I need to talk to Callum," I replied tersely. "Is he around?"

"He's otherwise occupied at the moment."

I recognized the half-truth for what it was. For all I knew, Callum was "otherwise occupied" with watching Sora talk to me.

"You might as well just say he doesn't want to talk to me," I said dryly. "It's not going to hurt my tender feelings. This is business."

Sora snorted. "Some of us have manners."

"Yeah," I replied, "and some of us are alphas, so if the Stone River big guy can't spare the time to talk to the head of Cedar Ridge, just say so."

The silence on the other end of the line was deafening. I counted to ten in my head and wondered if Sora was doing the same.

"The Stone River alpha can't officially advise the Cedar Ridge alpha on matters of inter-pack relations," she said finally, her words clipped and precise. "Were the Stone River alpha to do so, the remainder of the Senate might interpret that as evidence of a political alliance and might therefore feel compelled to make alliances of their own. The Stone River alpha would prefer to avoid such complications."

I huffed and blew a strand of hair out of my face. "In other words, Callum can't help me."

"Officially."

I translated Sora's reply to mean that Callum could and

would help me unofficially. The trick would be figuring out how exactly a thing like that might work.

"You're not an alpha," I said slowly, and this time, I wasn't throwing the words in Sora's face. "So technically, if you were to give me advice, it would be . . ."

"Unofficial?" Sora suggested.

"Exactly."

Now the reason that Sora was answering the phone at Callum's house was perfectly clear. Callum couldn't tell me what to do, but he could send me cryptic homemade gifts and arrange for another knowledgeable source to answer his phone when I happened to call.

It was unfortunate that the knowledgeable source in question was related to the alpha I had in my sights.

"What has Callum told you about why I'm calling?" I asked, wondering how much Sora knew—and, for that matter, how much of what was happening now Callum had foreseen.

"Callum said you might have some questions, and that since my son is now in your pack, if I wanted to answer them for Devon's sake, that decision was up to me."

To the best of my knowledge, Devon hadn't spoken a word to Sora since she'd carried out Callum's sentence against me. He'd left their pack and hadn't been home since. Maybe Sora figured this was the least she could do for Dev, and if not mentioning Shay prevented her loyalties from being split . . .

Well, I wasn't above telling half-truths myself.

"I need to know if there's a way for a Were to transfer into another pack against his alpha's will."

"Both alphas have to sign off on all transfers." Sora's answer was immediate—and not at all what I wanted to hear. "The first alpha relinquishes his hold over the wolf, who then becomes a lone wolf, and the lone wolf can then be claimed by another alpha, with or against his will."

"What if the first alpha is abusive?" I asked, knowing even as I did that it was a wasted question. Sora had broken my ribs at Callum's request, and she was my best friend's mother. Words like *abuse* didn't have the same kind of meaning to people with animal instincts. "What if he's doing horrible things to his pack for no reason other than that he can?"

That question was a little more precise, but still, it didn't get me the answer I wanted.

"What one alpha does with his pack is not another alpha's business," Sora said. "However . . ." She trailed off after a moment. "Callum has been known, on occasion, to make it in another alpha's best interest to cut ties with a particular wolf."

"Well, that's nice and vague."

Sora didn't respond, but I could picture the expression on her angular features almost exactly. It was an expression that said, *It's a miracle nobody has strangled you yet, you obnoxious human child.* Since Sora was trying to help me, I attempted to dial the attitude back a notch.

"So you're saying that if I want another alpha to sign off on letting one of his wolves go, I should ..."

"Give him something he wants more than he wants to keep the wolf." Sora paused, and I sensed her debating whether she should continue talking. "Before you were born, Callum's territory used to include the northern part of Oklahoma. He gave it up in exchange for Marcus."

"Marcus?" I couldn't help the incredulous tone in my voice. Marcus was a greasy, antisocial, horrific a-hole who'd hated me for as long as I could remember. I was pretty sure he hated everyone except for Callum, to whom he was unfailingly loyal.

And now I knew why.

"That's all I'm willing to tell you, Bryn. Just tread carefully here."

"Is that the nice way of telling me not to do anything stupid?"

Sora let out a sharp bark of laughter. "That's the nice way of saying that if you misstep and put yourself in danger, I know Devon will follow you, right to the brink of hell. He may hate me now, but we've got the next thousand years to get past that, and I'd prefer you not get him killed before he has a chance to become what he's meant to be."

I was going to reply, but before I could, I heard a click, and then the other side of the line went dead. Sora had hung up on me, and I was no closer to finding a loophole than I'd been before I called.

Great. Just great.

To save Lucas, I'd have to give Shay something he wanted more than a punching bag, and without even asking, I knew what he'd want in return.

A female Were.

CHAPTER SIX

THE NEXT MORNING, I WOKE UP WITH A FEELING of dread in my stomach and an unnatural heat playing across the surface of my skin. The smell of smoke was a ghost in my memory, and though I didn't remember the details of the dream I'd just had, a sense of déjà vu, hazy and ominous, seemed to cloud the rest of my thoughts.

A night plagued by nightmares I couldn't quite remember had done little to shed light on my current predicament. In an ideal world, I would have woken up knowing exactly what to do and how to read between the lines of what Sora had told me to derive a solution that didn't involve either turning Lucas back over to Shay or brokering some kind of deal with him and trading one wolf for another.

This, however, wasn't an ideal world, and no matter how hard I tried to think of an answer, I had nothing.

At this point, the best I could do was stall. Until Shay contacted me, asking if Lucas was staying at the Wayfarer, I was under no obligation to tell him, and Shay couldn't come here to get Lucas unless I gave him permission. With any luck, distance would have strained Lucas's bond with the Snake Bend Pack enough that his alpha wouldn't be able to pinpoint his exact location, and by the time Shay figured out where Lucas had gotten off to—assuming Lucas had been straight with us about how he'd gotten here in the first place—I'd have managed to think of a way to play the Snake Bend Alpha, the same way Callum had been expertly playing all of us for years.

Unfortunately, unlike Callum, *I* didn't catch even minor glimpses of the future, so I had no way of knowing that my "wait and see" plan would be effective for less than three hours.

Shay contacted all the alphas, including me, via email, which just felt wrong. Our world was brutal, the kind of place where issues of dominance were settled with a fight to the death. The idea of Shay sitting down and typing out a polite query about whether any of the other alphas had seen his "missing runt" was completely bizarre.

It also didn't leave me any wiggle room regarding how or when to reply. Once the other alphas started sending in their statements, I had no choice but to send mine and CC it for the rest of the Senate alphas to view.

Treading lightly, I channeled Callum and wrote a polite but pointed reply—one that said that Shay's wolf had trespassed on my territory, that he'd been out of control of his Shift, and that I'd gladly send the trespasser back Shay's way as soon as

I determined whether he'd been acting on his own agenda or someone else's, and assured myself that he wouldn't be a future threat.

Shay didn't have to agree to give up his claim on Lucas, but by Senate Law, I had the right to deal with trespassers as I saw fit. And if the other alphas wanted to read between the lines and infer that perhaps Shay had sent Lucas here to kill me . . .

Well, I figured that couldn't hurt.

After I hit send, I spent the next three hours refreshing my inbox, but the internet was silent, and I was left wondering if I'd done the right thing, or if I'd somehow crossed a line in the sand already.

With only a few hours left in my Thanksgiving break, I tried to distract myself with homework, and when that didn't work, I played with the twins. Unfortunately, even Katie's puppy antics couldn't take my mind off the threat hovering above me and mine, so I went for a walk and ended up at Cabin 13.

The others wouldn't be happy that I'd gone to see Lucas alone, but I figured they could deal. I wasn't happy about having to choose between sending an abused kid back to his abuser and risking the safety of people I'd sworn to spend the rest of my life protecting.

I opened the door to the cabin, half expecting Mitch to be standing guard, but he was nowhere in sight, and my pack-sense sent an unpleasant chill down my spine, a way of reminding me that taking your eyes off the enemy was always a mistake.

Even if the enemy in question was a person I was desperately trying to save.

As I came to the doorway of Lucas's bedroom, I wondered if I would get over feeling this way around him, or if as long as Lucas was Snake Bend, a part of me would always want to bare my teeth at his presence on our land. He wasn't a threat, but he also wasn't mine, and I wasn't sure I could convince my gut that there was a distinction to be made there.

Lucas, however much he didn't want to be, was an extension of Shay. He smelled like Shay, and Shay would be a presence—no matter how faint—in his mind, the same way I was connected to Maddy, to Lake, to Dev.

"Is your alpha trying to talk to you through your pack-bond?" I asked, not bothering to say hello as I entered the room. "Is he telling you to come home?"

Except in the most extreme circumstances, werewolves couldn't disobey their alphas. The stronger ones—purebreds, like Dev, or Resilients, like Chase and the rest of the Changed Weres in our pack—could fight it, but even for them, holding out against a direct order was like trying to keep from blinking when a sharp object was flying straight for your eye.

"He's trying," Lucas murmured, face downcast, body stiff, "but I'm too far away."

That smacked of the truth to me, even though I didn't have

a Were's ability to smell lies. A wolf's tie to his pack depended on how close he was to its other members—especially the alpha. The same principle that made the Wayfarer unbearably loud for Chase would have shielded Lucas more and more from Shay's influence the farther away from Snake Bend territory he got.

"Your alpha emailed looking for you." I wanted to soften my words but instead found myself saying them in a completely neutral tone and observing Lucas's reaction. I'd spent too many years watching Callum do the same thing, and the experience had left its mark. "Shay wants you returned. I stalled, but unless we figure out a way around it, I'm going to have to send you back."

"No."

Lucas had opened his mouth to say the word, but the sound came from behind me. I turned.

Standing in the doorway, Maddy didn't elaborate on her *no*. She didn't challenge me. She just came to sit on a chair next to Lucas's bed, her legs tucked under her body, her head tilted slightly toward his. She didn't say another word. She didn't introduce herself. She just sat there, watching over him, and his body curled toward hers, like they were pups in the same litter.

Like he could feel her presence the way I'd always felt Chase's.

"Maddy." It was on the tip of my tongue to tell her to be

careful, but then I realized the irony of the situation: of the two of us, she was the one more capable of fighting back if Lucas made a move. Still, I didn't like it. Didn't like the idea that someone—anyone—might hurt her, after everything she'd been through already.

I'll be careful, Bryn, Maddy promised silently, *but someone has to keep an eye on him. It might as well be me.*

I brought my gaze to meet Lucas's. "I'm going to try to find a way to help you, but you need to know up front that I won't trade my pack's safety for yours. If I have to send you back to Shay to keep them safe, I'll do it."

I hated myself for saying those words and hated Callum for raising me to be the kind of person who could say them—but they just kept coming.

"If you lay a hand on Maddy, if you hurt her or any of mine in any way, I'll kill you myself."

As an alpha, I was bound by those words, and in that moment, I didn't have a single doubt about my ability to follow through on the threat. Maddy could probably take care of herself, but if Lucas wasn't what he appeared to be, if he attacked her or tried to force his will on hers in any way, Shay would be taking home a body instead of a live wolf.

On the bed, Lucas lowered his head in a sign of submission, and even from a distance, I could see an angry red scar on the back of his neck. Its edges were jagged, like it had been carved into his flesh with a knife, and the shape—a four-pointed star laid over a half circle—looked too deliberate to have been the product of anything but a steady hand.

How could Shay have done something like that? How could anyone?

Seeing Lucas sitting so close to Maddy made me imagine her in his shoes, and I knew without probing the edges of her mind that she was thinking the same thing, seeing herself— and the things she'd survived at the hands of the Rabid—in this boy.

"Unless you force me to act, I won't turn you over until I have to." I addressed Lucas, though he seemed to know that I was saying the words for Maddy's benefit as much as his. "But right now, I don't really have a plan, Lucas, so if you've got any ideas here, I'm all ears."

Lucas retreated, pressing himself back and down into the mattress, and I cringed at the motion and the knowledge that I'd just established dominance over a person who had experience with only one kind of alpha.

"He doesn't know anything." Maddy lifted her chin and looked just over my left shoulder, a guarded, faraway gaze in her eyes. "They don't want you to think. They don't want you to believe it could be different." She turned her face away from mine, but she didn't look directly at Lucas, either. "It takes a while."

I know, Maddy, I told her silently. *I know.*

Out loud, I directed my words to the boy on the bed. "I'll

give you as much time as I can, Lucas, but you need to know that I'm not magic. I'm not fearless. I can't just pull a miracle out of my hat."

"You're Bryn." Lucas lifted his head slightly. "That's going to be enough."

After a long moment's consideration, I left Lucas under Maddy's watchful eye, confident that, if nothing else, she wouldn't let him slip off into the night unnoticed, leaving the rest of us to explain to the Senate exactly how I'd gone about losing a wolf that I'd already admitted to having, one who another alpha was within his rights to want back, once I'd dealt with the matter of trespassing in the first place.

Call me if you need me, Maddy, I told her silently, not even realizing until after I gave the order that to her ears, my mind-voice vibrated with the kind of power most werewolves couldn't deny.

I'll call you if I need you, Bryn, Maddy replied. *I always do.*

She trusted me, relied on me the way I'd once counted on Callum, before he'd taught me that sometimes things—and people—got caught in the crossfire of the greater good.

"Hey, you." Chase had been expecting me, which was ironic, because even after I'd left Cabin 13 and started walking toward the woods, I hadn't realized I was looking for him.

"Hey," I replied, all too aware of the difference between the last time we'd had this conversation and now. There were times when it felt like Chase and I were the only two people in the world, when I was a girl and he was a boy and everything else just faded away.

This was not one of those times.

"I'm not sure there's a way out of this." I wouldn't have been able to admit that to anyone but Chase, the same way he wouldn't have wanted Devon to know that this year had been his first real Thanksgiving. "I can stall Shay, but eventually, unless I think of something else..."

The rest of that sentence, the very idea of sending Lucas back to Shay, was unthinkable.

What kind of person could do something like that?

What kind of alpha would I be if I refused and my pack got hurt as a result?

"You do what you have to do," Chase said in a way that told me he'd crossed lines and seen the point of no return firsthand himself. "You can't save everyone, Bryn. You do what you can, when you can. You try. But sometimes, at the end of the day, you just have to take care of yourself."

I couldn't help giving Chase an incredulous look. "Who said anything about taking care of myself?"

I was worried about Maddy, about Lucas, about the precedent I might set if I stepped on the wrong side of certain political lines. I was worried about the pack, about being the kind of alpha that Callum was, and about *not* being that kind of alpha. The last thing on my mind was *me*.

Chase reached up and brushed a stray hair out of my face, his thumb tracing a gentle line from my cheekbone to my jaw. "I know," he said, "but you can't blame a guy for trying."

The rest of his words flowed straight from his mind into mine. *Your job is watching out for the pack, Bryn. Let my job be watching out for you.*

He held up his palm, waiting for me to accept his offer. After a long moment, I mimicked the motion, pressing my hand against his. A jolt of energy ran up the length of my arm.

"If you want to watch out for me," I said, as single-minded as a dog with a bone, "then help me find a way out of this that doesn't involve sending Lucas back to Shay."

Chase didn't reply. He stared at me for several seconds, and then he gave in to the wolf inside. He leaned forward, rubbed his cheek against my neck—and turned to walk away.

"Where are you going?" I called after him, wanting to hear the answer from his lips, even though I could have pulled it from his mind.

Chase turned, his features caught in the light of the moon. He didn't say anything, but suddenly, I knew.

Chase, who rarely spoke to the people in our own pack, was going to talk to Lucas.

To try to come up with a plan, find a way out of this.

For me.

Just before I went to bed that night, I got an email from Shay. He hadn't CC'ed the other alphas this time, and reading over his message, I could hear the condescension dripping from his honeyed words. Underneath the condescension, I could sense something a thousand times worse.

Satisfaction.

Shay didn't demand that I return Lucas immediately. He didn't contradict my claim that I had the right to deal with a trespasser as I saw fit. Instead, he said, very politely, that he would be more than happy to retrieve Lucas as soon as I'd handled the situation to Cedar Ridge's satisfaction, and then he signed off with a final line.

> *I feel it only fair to warn you—I'm not the only one with a vested interest in his whereabouts, and the others might not be quite so understanding.*

Others? I thought, my heart dropping to my stomach. *What others?*

CHAPTER SEVEN

THAT NIGHT, I DIDN'T SLEEP. I READ SHAY'S EMAIL A half dozen times, paced the full length of my room, and read it a half dozen more. No matter how many ways I looked at it, I could only think of two possible interpretations.

Either Shay was lying to me, or Lucas was.

If Shay was lying, he was probably doing it just to get under my skin. Psychological warfare was the closest he could come to an assault, and if his objective had been to keep me up at night, turning the possibilities over and over again in my head, he'd succeeded.

I'm not the only one with a vested interest in his whereabouts . . .

Who else could possibly care where Shay's whipping boy was? Since I hadn't heard from any of the other alphas, all of whom had received my email admitting that Lucas was here, I doubted that any of them were the "others" Shay was referring to, and that left, what? One of the few lone wolves who weren't associated with any pack? Lucas's family, who—depending on whether he'd been born Snake Bend or transferred in—might or might not be a part of Shay's pack?

A Rabid?

None of the possibilities were good ones, and they all seemed far-fetched. If Lucas had family outside of Shay's pack, he would have gone to them, not me, looking for salvation, and I couldn't imagine that he'd done anything to attract the attention of someone who lived in No-Man's-Land, between one alpha's territory and the next.

Shay was probably just messing with me. There was nothing to keep a Were from lying in an email. For Lucas to mislead me, in person, with Maddy, Lake, Devon, Chase, or some combination thereof in the room, would have been significantly harder, given the werewolf ability to smell lies.

Then again, I knew the power of telling half-truths better than just about anyone. Lucas hadn't said that anyone besides Shay was after him, but I hadn't asked.

At three in the morning, unable to sleep or lie down or even sit still, I decided it was time to remedy that.

Ali was a light sleeper, but her hearing was completely human, and I used my hold over the twins to keep them in a nice, quiet, undisturbed sleep as I snuck out my window. After I'd made my escape, I ran to Cabin 13, eased open the door, and slipped inside before shutting it behind me and moving quickly through the front hall.

"Watching you try to be stealthy is just plain sad."

Lake didn't bother whispering, and the sudden sound of her voice took me off guard just enough that I felt a flash of irritation—at her for sneaking up on me and at myself for being so focused on my Lucas mission that I hadn't heard or felt her coming at all.

"What are you doing here?" I snapped, keeping my voice low.

"Bryn, just about everyone in these parts has hearing like mine. Whispering isn't going to do you a lick of good." One second, Lake was sitting, and the next, she was on her feet beside me. I never even saw her stand up. "Luckily for you, my dad sleeps like the dead, and nobody else within range would bat an eye at you taking a midnight stroll that just happens to bring you up close and personal with the only werewolf in the state of Montana who wouldn't die to keep you safe."

"Did you follow me here?" I asked.

Lake shrugged. "The word *follow* seems to suggest you got here first."

I rolled my eyes. "This isn't a race, Lake."

"If it was, I would've given you a head start. Now, you want to tell me why the alpha of the Cedar Ridge Pack is sneaking out windows and putting herself in a potentially dangerous situation without backup?"

It was on the tip of my tongue to remind Lake that she'd scoffed at the idea of Lucas being a threat, but I bit the retort back. Just because Lake thought *she* could take someone with three paws tied behind her back didn't mean that I'd stand a chance against him in a fair fight. The best I could hope for in a fight against a Were—any Were—was catching him off guard enough that I could take to higher ground and wait out the assault. With weapons, I might stand a chance at inflicting some damage, but I hadn't exactly come here armed.

Rather than acknowledge that Lake might actually have a point, I met her eyes. "You breathe a word of this to Devon or Chase, and I *will* kill you."

Lake smiled. "I'll take that under advisement. Now, you care to clue me in to what we're doing here, or should I start making educated guesses?"

I glanced at the door to Lucas's room. If he was awake, he was hearing every word we said, and I didn't want to give up the element of surprise.

I got an email from Shay, I told Lake silently. *He said that I'm welcome to deal with Lucas's trespassing as I see fit, but that he thought it fair to warn me that he wasn't the only one with an interest in Lucas's whereabouts.*

Lake's lips twitched, and though a normal person might have mistaken her for someone holding back laughter, I knew instinctively that she was holding back a growl.

Shay Macalister is a piece of work, Lake said. *And if we can help it, neither one of us is breathing a word of this to Dev.*

On that, Lake and I were in absolute agreement. The last— and only—time Shay and I had come face-to-face, Devon had come dangerously close to fighting him on my behalf. In size and brute power, the two were evenly matched, but Shay had at least a hundred years of experience on Devon, and I didn't want to add any fuel whatsoever to that fire.

You ready to see what our visitor has to say? I asked Lake.

I was born ready, Bronwyn. Lake punctuated that statement by releasing the safety on a shotgun I hadn't even realized she was holding.

Is that really necessary? I said, giving her a look. *It's not like you're actually going to shoot him.*

He doesn't know that. Lake waggled her eyebrows. *And for the record, I'm packing silver, just in case.*

My gut twisted at the idea of using fear as leverage with someone who'd come here looking for protection, but as Lake had made abundantly clear, injured or not, Lucas was a Were, and he was healing. In a fight, Lake could take him, but she might not be able to get to him before he got to me. I didn't think Lucas would attack either one of us, but in life-or-death situations, thinking wasn't enough.

You needed to *know.*

The door to Lucas's temporary room creaked as I opened it. It took my eyes a moment to find him, because Maddy was asleep on the bed. The covers were bunched up around her, and I knew that in her sleep, she'd burrowed into them, turning Lucas's bed into her den.

The fact that he'd let her—and that he was sleeping on the

floor so she could have the bed—did not go unnoticed. That Maddy had fallen asleep in his presence was even more staggering. She wasn't the type to trust blindly, and whatever else Lucas was, he wasn't Pack. She shouldn't have felt that comfortable around him; he shouldn't have been willing to sleep on the floor for her.

I felt a stab of possession spike through me—Maddy was *ours*; she trusted *us*—but that didn't stop me from sending a silent message to Lake, asking her to put the shotgun down.

With a glance at Maddy and a sharp intake of breath, Lake complied. I heard the click of the safety, and she set the gun near the door, her eyes on Lucas's as she crossed the room and put her body between his and mine.

"He's coming for me, isn't he?" Lucas was awake. His voice was dull, and on the bed, Maddy made a noise halfway between a whimper and a whine.

"No." I wanted to kneel down next to Lucas, to put myself on his level, but I didn't move, allowing Lake—long-limbed and lethal—to stay between us at all times. "Shay isn't coming, at least not yet, but he said something, and I need to know if it's true."

Lucas pushed himself farther into the corner. Through the pack-bond, I caught a flash of an image from Maddy's dream: the back of a hand connecting with a toddler's chubby cheeks. I didn't know when and I didn't know who, but the fractured memory was enough for me to feel, just for a second, the intensity with which Maddy looked at Lucas and saw the life she and the others had lived with the Rabid. I glanced at Lake, and since I couldn't kneel next to Lucas, she did.

"We're not looking to hurt you," she said. "Not unless you're looking to hurt us."

"I've never hurt anyone." Lucas's words rang with the kind of truth that I didn't need a werewolf's sense of smell to recognize as honest and bare. "I'm the one who gets hurt."

His words twisted like a knife in my gut, but I soldiered on, softening my voice but delivering the message all the same.

"Shay says he's not the only one after you." I paused and measured Lucas's reaction, but his eyes were as dull as his voice, and I couldn't see anything in them but what I already knew. "Is he lying?"

For several seconds, Lucas didn't reply. Then he looked up, right at my eyes, for a single beat of my heart. "I don't know."

"You don't know as in you're not certain, or you don't know as in you have no clue why Shay might say such a thing?"

Lucas retreated even further into himself, and when he replied, his voice was barely audible to my human ears.

"The first one."

"So when Shay says there might be someone else after you, that's not crazy talk, is it?" Lake kept her voice soft, and she didn't make a single move toward him, but there was no way for him not to answer.

Lake Mitchell wasn't the kind of person you just shrugged off.

"No. It's not crazy talk."

The air whooshed out of my lungs as I processed our visitor's answer. Lucas didn't know for sure if Shay was lying, but he knew that it was possible that his alpha was telling the truth.

That someone else was after him.

And he'd come here, to my land, and asked for my help, without so much as a word of warning.

"Assume that whoever might be coming after you is coming," I told him sharply. "Who is it?"

Lucas didn't answer. I took a step forward, pitching my voice low and staring directly into his eyes with an intensity none of my wolves could have denied. "Is it one of the other alphas?"

"No."

"Is it a Rabid werewolf?"

"No."

"Is it your family?"

"I don't have a family."

"Lucas, we can't help you if we don't know what we're up against. Keeping this information to yourself is the same as lying, and if you lie to me, I *will* send you back."

I felt, rather than saw, Maddy stirring, but she didn't object to my words. If Lucas was a threat—if the people after him were a threat—we needed to know. She knew that. She trusted me.

Lucas turned to look at her and took a ragged breath, and then he answered my question, his words coming out in a rushed whisper. "They're human, okay? The Snake Bend Pack has dealings with humans, and Shay . . . loaned me out."

"He *what*?" Lake and I spoke at the same time. Maddy didn't even blink.

"Shay gave me to some humans, okay? Not forever, just for a little while, to punish me for *whatever he was punishing me for*." Lucas brought one hand to the scar on the back of his neck, and in that moment, I knew that Shay wasn't the only one who'd left a mark on his body.

Whoever these humans were, whatever they wanted with a Were, they'd left their mark, too.

"Humans aren't even supposed to know about us," Lake said. "The Senate kills people when they find out."

It was an ugly truth of our world that sometimes the secret of a pack's existence took precedence over a single human life—even now. In all the time I'd known Callum, he had never lifted a lethal hand to a human, but I wasn't naïve enough to think that the other alphas batted an eye at safeguarding our secret with that kind of force.

Most Weres hadn't been thrilled with the idea of Callum allowing Ali and me into his pack. Human females were for breeding, and most Weres accepted that only because there were so few females of their own kind to go around. The idea of an alpha handing one of his wolves over to *humans* was unfathomable.

Lucas tore his eyes away from Maddy and spoke directly to me. "I don't know why Shay does what he does. Most of the time, it's not exactly advisable to ask, but when he got tired of beating me, he gave me to some humans and let them do the same. They were strong, and they had weapons, and I was restrained."

As strong as werewolves were, they could still be out-numbered, and Lucas wasn't really on the more formidable end of the werewolf spectrum to begin with.

"So, yes, Shay might be telling the truth when he says that he's not the only one looking for me. They had me, and they hurt me, and when I finally got loose, I ran away. I turned tail, and I ran, and they might come looking for their pet werewolf, okay?" Lucas's voice grew louder as he spoke, but the neutral expression on his face never wavered. "It's not like the alpha is going to give them anyone else."

The alpha.

The words echoed in my head, and I wanted to drive my fist through a wall—or better yet, through Shay's small intestine.

Alphas were supposed to *protect* their packs. Sometimes that meant fighting an outside threat. Sometimes that meant being the bad guy to keep order within the pack, sacrificing the needs of the few to ensure the best outcome for the pack as a whole. But being alpha never meant throwing someone out like he was garbage.

It never meant letting a bunch of humans cut into one of your Weres like he was some kind of science experiment or a slice of meat.

"Are you sending me back?" Lucas's voice was devoid of any emotion, quiet and clear.

"We'll see," I said, which was the best I could give him. Still, for the first time since I'd read Shay's email, the muscles in my neck and back began to relax. A known threat was preferable to an unknown one.

Besides, we had an entire werewolf pack at our disposal. A small one, granted, and young, but still—how much of a threat could a bunch of humans possibly be?

CHAPTER EIGHT

I MADE THE EXECUTIVE DECISION NOT TO TELL Devon or Chase about my correspondence with Shay—Chase because I wanted him to form his own impressions of Lucas, and Devon because Lake and I had agreed that the less Devon knew about Shay's machinations, the better. I did, however, tell Mitch everything. If someone was after Lucas—human or not—I couldn't just leave the Wayfarer and the youngest, most vulnerable members of our pack without cluing someone in to what was going on, and there was no way to skip school without raising a pack-wide alarm.

The fact that I was one of nine werewolf alphas in North America *and* had to suffer through the tenth grade was wrong on so, so many levels, but try telling that to Ali "Education Is Your Future" Clare.

I had, multiple times, and it wasn't an experience I was looking to repeat.

So instead, I let Lake drive me to school and watched Maddy stare out the window as we drove, knowing without probing her thoughts that her mind was on Lucas—and unable to think of a single thing to say to distract her. Devon spent the entire drive looking at me with a familiar expression—suspicion, exasperation, and steely calm—on his face, and I dug my heels in and refused to allow my mouth to form as much as a single syllable of what he wanted to know.

I could handle this, and besides, it wasn't like I told Devon *everything*.

Somehow, I made it through first period without giving my human classmates any visible indication that something was wrong. The last thing I needed was to fan the rumor mill flames, but for once, fate was on my side. With Thanksgiving break over, the entire high school was living on borrowed time. Finals were looming and winter vacation was less than three weeks away. My eyes were bloodshot, and with each passing lecture, I became more and more aware of the sleep I hadn't gotten the night before, but that did little to nothing to separate me from my classmates.

If anything, it made me blend in.

At the front of my third-period classroom, my history teacher droned on about Oliver Cromwell, and the pages of my three-ring binder began to look increasingly inviting. My head drooped. Each blink lasted just a little bit longer than the one before. Every time I closed my eyes, I let the bond that tied me to the pack flare, assuring myself that everyone was still there, that everyone was in one piece, that they were okay.

I breathed in and out.

They breathed in and out.

Somewhere, one of the younger ones Shifted, and with her transition, my entire body relaxed.

I blinked.

She blinked.

And then I fell asleep.

Smells! Smells! I wanted to inhale them, to eat them, to make them mine. My back arched, and I pressed my paws into the thick carpet. Oh, that felt good! The world was bronzed, the colors dulled, and the sounds—the *words*—all around me meant nothing.

I rolled over onto my back and threw my head from one side to the other, going after carpet fuzz like it was some kind of worthier prey: a butterfly or a cricket or something soft and warm with a heart that went *thump thump thump*.

Out! I wanted out, but something kept me here, inside, near to . . . something.

Near to *them*.

A flash of motion in the corner of my eye sent my body rolling over, and I bounded to my feet. Others! I could feel the pack! I could feel Lily!

I flattened my ears and bent my legs. Opposite me, my pack-sister bobbed her head.

Ready.

Ready.

Ready.

Pounce!

One second, I was inside my little sister's head, and the next, I was watching Katie and Lily, both in puppy form, rolling around on the carpet. For a moment, I felt a pang of loss—for the excitement, the knowing, the smells—but then I was elsewhere, the pack silent in my head, and my ears ringing with the high-pitched whistle of a biting winter wind.

Though it was dark, I could see perfectly. The world was awash in purples and black and deep, velvety gray. Like shadows, the trees melded into one another, and one foot after the other, I walked toward them.

There, in the clearing, was a female wolf—*the* female wolf—her head held high, her coat snow-kissed and damp. I wanted to go to her, but by the time I got to the place where she'd stood a moment before, she was gone, and I was alone.

"Too bad," a light but resonating voice said. "So sad. Guess it's just you and me."

I whirled to see the man from my earlier dream leaning back against a tree, his eyes locked onto my body, his face twisted with an expression halfway between intrigue and revulsion.

"Hello, mutt-lover." His tone was deceptively pleasant—

rat poison dipped in chocolate. My temples pounded, and I could feel him inside my head, feel him turning me inside out, *touching* me—

I took a step backward, but there was nowhere to go.

Nowhere to run.

I thought of the pack, tried to conjure up an image of them, a memory, the pack-bond—anything that might free my limbs enough that I could move, fight back, at least *respond*.

"Isn't that sweet? You think there's a way out." The man's voice wove its way around my limbs, like a snake climbing up one leg, around my torso, and down the opposite arm. "You're awfully young, aren't you, wolf girl?"

A flash of unadulterated loathing passed across his face, but I couldn't tell if it was aimed at himself or at me. "Poor little girl, lost in her own mind. Poor little girl, lost in the woods."

He took one step toward me, then another, his dilated pupils turning indigo eyes nearly entirely black.

Sweat rose on the surface of my skin.

A circle of flame burst to life at my feet.

I wheezed. I bit back a scream, and just before my body caught on fire, the roar of the pack broke through to my mind, and I felt a phantom hand latch on to my shoulder and pull.

With a gasp, I woke up. My entire body jerked in my seat, and my history teacher stopped her lecture just long enough to ask, very pointedly, if I was okay. I nodded, but with the smell of smoke thick in my nostrils and sweat running down the back of my neck, even that tiny gesture was a lie.

Hello, mutt-lover.

I couldn't shake the memory of the voice, and even as the rest of the pack flooded my senses with reassurances, gentle nudges and nips at the edge of my mind, I shuddered.

The bell rang, and after a moment, I gathered my notebook and stood, my limbs stiff, the movement painful and awkward.

And that was when I realized that my skin was angry, pink, and warm to the touch. To all appearances, I was sunburned.

In the middle of winter. Inside my high school.

I brought my right hand to my left and pressed my index finger down on my left wrist. I winced slightly at the subtle burn and then let go. My fingerprint appeared as a white mark on my reddish skin, but after a few seconds, the mark faded.

My memory of the dream—and the expression on the face of the man who'd attacked me—did not. I could feel his stare, see the fire leaping to life at my feet, and even though he hadn't actually said it, looking back, I could hear a promise passing from his lips to my ears.

You're going to burn.

I barely made it to lunch, and I knew before Devon said a word that the others had picked up on at least some portion of what had happened to me—not the details, but enough to know that I was on edge, that the part of me that was Pack was calling for blood.

An animal backed into a corner either cowers or snaps. Most werewolves weren't any different, and human or not, I wasn't the type to cower.

"Dare I guess we're eating outside today?" Devon asked, the set of his jaw belying the casual tone with which he'd issued the question. His hair might have been gelled; his shirt might have been fitted, but beneath the surface of his skin, the wolf was restless.

He'd sensed the threat—they all had.

"We're eating outside," I confirmed, taking a step away from Devon and trying not to listen to the quiet rumble of the wolf beneath his skin. I had enough going on in my own mind right now; I didn't need to deal with Devon's animal desire to protect me at all costs.

I also didn't need to deal with below-freezing temperatures and a wind chill disturbingly close to zero, but beggars couldn't be choosers, and the conversation I was about to have with Devon, Maddy, and Lake wasn't the kind you could have in the middle of the high school cafeteria.

Despite the intense chill, sitting on the ledge outside the cafeteria loosened the knot in my chest and stomach. I could smell the wind, the trees, cedar and cinnamon, pine needles and morning dew.

"Chase." Devon said his name before I could process the scents or let the warmth of his presence wash over me, and I followed my friend's gaze out past the parking lot, to the line of trees that marked the spot where forest gave way to the town.

There, standing guard, was a wolf as dark as midnight, smaller than some, but bigger than any natural wolf.

Chase, I called out to him. *Someone might see you.*

In wolf form, Chase didn't speak back to me in words. Instead, I got pictures—mostly of me—and the distinct sense that if the wolf had had its way, he and Chase would never have let me out of their sight in the first place. I was what mattered to them, and my urge to find this threat and tear it to pieces was nothing compared to how much Chase and his wolf wanted to see me, smell me, *protect me.*

Fine, Chase, I said silently, giving in because if he had been the one under attack, I probably would have done something a lot rasher than standing guard at the edge of the woods. *Just stay hidden.*

This time, I caught a hint of Chase's human side in his reply, something that told me that he was good at blending in to the background, that he'd spent most of his human life trying not to be noticed.

"Hey, sleeping beauty." Lake tried for nonchalance in her tone but couldn't quite sell it, and her voice quivered as she pressed on. "Want to tell us what's going on, and why exactly you look like you've seen the wrong side of a barbeque?" She plopped down next to me and stretched out her legs.

You guys remember that thing we weren't going to tell Devon? I asked Lake and Maddy silently. They both shifted slightly in response. Devon narrowed his eyes, and Lake batted her eyelashes in a show of innocence that was just this side of terrifying.

I think we're going to have to tell him, I continued. *Any volunteers?*

"Not it," Lake said out loud.

"Not it," Maddy chimed in quickly.

I sighed. "Hey, Dev, funny story..."

Shockingly, Devon didn't find the story of the previous night's events very funny, and none of them—not Lake, not Devon, not Maddy, not Chase in wolf form, lurking in the distance—was overly amused by the morning's development.

"You had a dream that someone was trying to set you on fire, and when you woke up, your skin was burned," Lake repeated humorlessly.

I leaned back on my wrists and blew out a breath, watching it take shape in the winter air. "That about covers it."

"Except, of course, for the part where my brother sent you veiled threats about someone else coming after Lucas, and the part where our gentleman visitor looked you straight in the eye and told you the threat was human."

When Devon got irked, he had a tendency to over-enunciate, and by the end of that sentence, his pronunciation was sharp enough to draw blood.

"Lucas wasn't lying." Maddy was the only one willing to speak up and voluntarily step into Devon's line of fire. "I was there. Lake was there. We would have smelled it."

"There's lying and there's not-lying," Lake replied, mulling over each word. "If you ask me, Lucas was not-lying. His words weren't exactly false, but for someone who wants our help, the boy isn't really what you would call forthcoming."

Lucas hadn't ever explicitly said that the people after him weren't a threat. He'd never said that they weren't dangerous. He'd said that they were human, and I'd filled in the blanks on my own. The irony of the situation—that I of all people had assumed that by virtue of being human, a person couldn't possibly be a threat—did not escape me.

Devon leaned over and pressed two fingers deliberately against my cheek, watching the skin go pale and then pink again. After a moment, he repeated the action.

"Are you done yet?" I asked, shoving him, to absolutely no avail.

"Depends. Is my bestie done lying to me and pretending things are okay when they aren't? Hmmmmm?"

Devon poked me again. I was on the verge of giving in and promising him that whatever happened next, I would tell him, whether I thought hearing it would be good for him or not, but before I could say the words, our conversation was interrupted.

At first, the interrupter didn't say anything. She just walked up to us—right up to us—so close that the tips of her black leather boots almost touched my jean-clad legs. She didn't kneel to our level to speak. She didn't even look down. Instead, she stared off into the distance.

Into the forest.

At Chase.

"Hello there," Devon said, shifting position to move a fraction of an inch closer to the intruder. "Is there something I can help you with? Directions to the gymnasium? Personal tutoring on *Hamlet*? Predictions on this year's Oscar favorites?"

Personally, I thought he was laying the drama geek vibe on a little thick, but the girl—the same one I'd seen in the cafeteria the week before—didn't so much as bat an eye. In fact, I would have gone as far as to say that she paid less attention to Dev than any female had in a very long time.

When she did shift her gaze from the forest, the girl had eyes only for me.

"I'm Caroline," she said, "and you're the wolf girl."

I'd certainly been called worse, but my breath caught in my throat the moment she said the word *wolf*.

I stood up and looked down at her. Humans didn't know about the existence of werewolves, and they especially didn't know about the existence of my pack here, in my territory, at my high school.

"Who are you?" I took a step forward. If we'd been anywhere near the same height, my face would have been right in hers, but she was so small that the top of her head didn't even reach my chin.

"I'm Caroline," she repeated. "Keep up."

Caroline. Looked like a porcelain doll, felt like a threat.

My brain absorbed the information and fed it automatically to the rest of the pack, a transfer as simple and reflexive as taking a breath and then breathing out.

"I believe you have something that belongs to us."

Us?

I glanced over Caroline's shoulder, half expecting to see an army of pint-sized leather-clad divas, but as best I could tell, she was alone.

"Define *something*," I said, pushing down the urge to place a hand on each of her shoulders and force her, belly up, to the ground.

Not here, I told myself. *Not now.*

"I believe its name is Lucas." Caroline scuffed the heel of her boot into the ground, and it took me a minute to realize that she was etching a symbol into the snow. "On the off chance that you've had multiple Lucases show up at the home front in the past couple of days, ours should have been fairly clearly marked."

For a split second, it was like I was staring right at the back of Lucas's neck again, and the scar I'd seen there, ugly and puckered, was an exact reflection of the shape in the snow: a four-pointed star laid over a half circle.

"You recognize it," Caroline said. "Very good. You get a sticker. Sadly, you won't be able to really enjoy that sticker if we're forced to put you down like a rabid dog."

The second the threat left her mouth, Devon, Lake, and Maddy were on their feet, and I could feel the hackles rising on Chase's back in the distance.

For the first time, Caroline flicked her eyes around the rest of our little group, and she held one gloved hand out to Devon. "Down, boy," she said, not even bothering to reply to Maddy or Lake. "That wasn't a threat. It was a conditional statement. If we get back what's ours, everyone lives to howl at the moon another day. If we don't..."

Caroline shrugged delicately. A low growl ripped its way out of Maddy's throat. I glanced at her, and she swallowed the inhuman noise, but not without taking a step closer to the little blonde girl with the great big mouth.

"Who's *we*?" My voice gave no hint of the deafening barrage of thoughts in my mind. I was cool, calm, collected.

So was she.

"My family." Caroline dragged her eyes up and down my body, and they settled on my sunburned cheeks. "I see you've already met Archer. He has an uncanny way of getting under your skin, wouldn't you say?"

She gave me time to reply, then smiled when I didn't say a

word. "You'll have to excuse his manners, though. Archer's all about the hunt."

Hello, mutt-lover. The voice echoed through my memory, and my temples throbbed just thinking about it.

"My mother told him to wait, but Archer was anxious to meet you in person. If she tells him to pull back, though, he'll listen. My mother can be a very persuasive woman, and she has no desire for bloodshed, especially not yours, Bryn."

They knew my name.

"I think you'll find us reasonable. We won't attack. We won't rush you. My family can be very patient—some of us, anyway." Caroline folded her hands in front of her and brought blue eyes to meet mine once more. "You have one week."

"One week," Lake repeated. "One week or *what*?"

Lake, I said sharply. On instinct, I held her back, my mind willing her feet not to move, not to carry her into a confrontation with an enemy whose true nature was still, for the most part, unknown.

"One week or what?" Devon repeated. He didn't make a move on Caroline, and it was taking everything I had to keep Lake from ripping out her throat, so I let him press the question in his own way: with a gentle elevation of one eyebrow and an endless, pointed stare.

Caroline took a step back, but I knew by the expression on her face that it wasn't a retreat. She ran the tip of one gloved finger over the inside edge of her jacket, and I saw a flash of silver.

She didn't draw her weapon, but I knew the others had seen it, too.

"I never miss." Caroline said the words simply, the same way I would have said that my eyes were brown.

"Guess that makes two of us." Lake hooked her fingertips through the belt loops on her jeans, a casual gesture completely at odds with the tension in her neck.

"No," Caroline said softly. "You do miss. If the target's too far away, or if the wind isn't right. If you throw knives or take a shot with an arrow, if you line someone up in your sight— sometimes, you miss."

I narrowed my eyes. "And you don't?"

Caroline inclined her chin slightly. "No." A faint breeze caught her hair, and it fanned out like a halo around her head. Beside me, Devon stiffened and took a step forward.

"Can't smell me, can you?" Caroline said, a soft, deadly smile working its way onto her lips. "Call it a gift. Once I leave here, you won't be able to track me. If I'm a hundred yards out, you won't hear me coming."

Her tone was enough to send a chill up my spine, but that was nothing compared to what I was feeling from the others. She was standing right in front of them, and they couldn't smell her. She was armed, and unless they wanted the whole school to see it, they couldn't attack.

"What are you?" I couldn't help asking the question. She looked human, but there wasn't a human on the planet who could sneak up on a Were. There wasn't a hint of fear on her face.

There was no doubt.

She knew what we were, and she wasn't afraid—and *that* was terrifying.

"I'm a hunter." Caroline's smile grew predatory. "It's what I was made for. It's all that I do."

Threat.

The sensation was so overwhelming, so intense that I could feel it as bile in the back of my throat, an incredible pressure at my temples, a knife through my stomach. I let go of my mental hold on Lake, because I needed every ounce of control I had to keep myself from springing forward and tackling this *thing* in front of me to the ground.

She shouldn't have been able to make me feel this way. I shouldn't have taken her words at face value, but it was all too easy to believe that when she took aim, she really didn't miss—that she *couldn't*, that the rest of her so-called family was just as unnatural, just as deadly.

Threat. Threat. Threat.

Predatory grin still in place, Caroline took another step backward, her hands held out to the sides, like she was dancing.

Like she was seconds away from going for her knife.

"You have one week," she said, and then, with every

confidence that not one of us would go for her back, she turned and walked toward the school.

You can't smell me, she'd promised. *You won't hear me coming.*

It's what I was made for. It's all that I do.

I never miss.

"Show of hands," Devon said, breaking the silence. "Who thinks we're screwed?"

CHAPTER NINE

WE CUT OUT ON THE REST OF THE SCHOOL DAY, AND as Chase leapt in wolf form into the back of Lake's Jeep and I buried my fingers in his stiff, damp fur, I had a sinking feeling that none of us would be back.

Not until this threat was taken care of.

Maybe not ever.

For as long as I could remember, I'd attended public school, *human* school, pretending that I could be one of them. That I could be normal. That I had some kind of future outside the boundaries of a werewolf pack. But maybe that was all it would ever be.

Pretense.

One way or the other, I had no business going through the motions of a normal school day while a foreign wolf lay on a bed in Cabin 13. Maybe this was a sign that as much as I wanted to, I couldn't give Maddy homeroom or prom or any typical teen experience to make up for all the things she'd missed growing up.

The five of us were Pack, and we belonged with the others. We belonged at home, not out in the open where a threat could waltz up to us at lunchtime and calmly issue ultimatums we weren't at liberty to respond to.

It was a miracle that none of the Weres had lost their grip and Shifted.

That wasn't a chance I was going to be taking again anytime soon. If Caroline and her "family" wanted a confrontation, they would have to come to us. I had to believe that on our turf, werewolf strength and instinct and the thirst for our enemies' blood would be worth something, no matter what— besides Caroline—the other side had in their arsenal.

Worse comes to worst, you don't have to fight them, the pragmatic part of my brain whispered. *Give them what they want, and they'll go away.*

I didn't want to be the kind of person who could consider that option, but what I wanted wasn't what mattered. Keeping my pack safe mattered. Making sure that no one laid a finger on Katie or Alex or Lily mattered.

But didn't Lucas, with his haunted eyes and heartbreaking wariness, matter, too?

"He really did lie." Maddy's thoughts weren't far from my own, but I knew that this was harder for her, that she'd wanted to believe in Lucas, because she'd seen so much of herself in the things that had been done to him. "Lucas lied."

"No," Lake corrected tersely, taking a turn with all the zeal of an Indy 500 driver. "He didn't lie. He just left out a few key details, such as the fact that the humans who are after him aren't exactly what you'd call run of the mill."

I'm a hunter, the little blonde girl had said. *It's what I was made for. It's all that I do.*

"Caroline might have been exaggerating her abilities." I had to say the words, even though I didn't believe them. There was a tone to Caroline's voice, a look in her eyes that I recognized all too well. "If you can't smell her, you wouldn't be able to tell if she was telling the truth."

Devon glanced at me for a second, maybe less. "You believe her," he said—a statement, not a question.

"Believe what?" I asked. "That she's the perfect hunter?"

The kind you didn't see coming. The kind who never missed.

I shook my head, trying to clear it of unwanted thoughts.

"I believe," I said slowly, "that she's a threat, and I know she's not working alone."

The burn on my skin was fading, but the questions it had inspired weren't going away. We didn't know how big Caroline's family was. We didn't know *what* they were, other than human. We didn't know why they wanted Lucas, and we certainly didn't know the limits of what they could do.

"You think they're like Keely?" Lake asked, gunning the engine the moment she said the bartender's name. "With her ... you know ... ?"

Before Ali had yanked me out of Callum's pack and brought

me to the Wayfarer, I hadn't known there was anything unusual in the world, other than werewolves. I hadn't known that Callum saw possible futures laid out in a complicated web, or that I had an unnatural ability to survive things that would kill a normal girl. I hadn't had a clue that there were people out there like Keely, who could make you spill your secrets just by looking at you a certain way.

In all the time since I'd discovered those things, I hadn't once stopped to wonder what else—or, more to the point, who else—was out there.

"So, what?" I said. "Some people are really scrappy, and some people are easy to talk to, and some people are made to hunt?"

My words were met with silence.

"And what about the other guy?" I continued. "The one I keep seeing in my dreams? That's not just a *knack*. You can't just be born with a knack for *burning people in their sleep*. That's …"

Impossible?

Insane?

"That's not a knack," I said mutinously. "That's magic."

The word felt ridiculous coming out my mouth. I'd grown up around things that would have made normal girls take off screaming, but I'd never once believed in *magic*. Werewolves were just another species. Pack-bonds were connections, as natural as a mother feeding her infant in the womb. Even Callum's seeing the future was something I could write off as …

Quirky.

But this? The symbol carved into Lucas's skin. The foreign presence in my dreams. My pink and sunburned skin.

This was a whole new world of weird.

"I'm going to throttle Lucas," I said, my voice deceptively cheerful. "I mean, seriously? He couldn't have warned us?"

"Maybe he knew that if he told us the truth, we would send him away." Maddy's voice was soft, and in an uncharacteristically affectionate gesture, she laid her head on my shoulder and closed her eyes. "Maybe he doesn't believe that anyone else could ever want to fight for him."

I leaned my head over so that my temple was touching the top of Maddy's head. Behind us, Chase stood up on his hind legs and put one paw on my shoulder and one on hers, huffing into our faces before nudging each of us with a wet, cold nose. The affection he showed Maddy surprised me, and my surprise made me realize that in human form, Chase never touched anyone but me.

"This is all Shay's fault," Devon said from the front seat. "He's the one who gave Lucas to those . . . whatever they are. Shay probably sent Lucas there hoping that he would run to us and bring She Who Hunts to Kill right to our front porch."

That did sound kind of like the type of thing Shay would do. For a few minutes, the five of us were silent. Then Lake pulled into the parking lot in front of the restaurant and slammed the car into park. "So, who wants to share all of this with my dad and Ali?"

"Not it," Devon said quickly.

"Not it," Lake and Maddy chorused. Beside me, Chase let out a small howl, and I cursed under my breath.

"Have I ever mentioned that being alpha sucks?" I said.

"A time or two," Devon replied, but he didn't even have the decency to sound sorry for me.

Sitting there in the backseat of Lake's car, Chase and Maddy close enough that they felt more like extensions of my physical body than members of my pack, I tried to remember what it was like to be a normal teenager, but the next second, Lake popped open the driver's-side door, and a burst of winter wind brought with it the smell of wet fur and cedar trees.

We were home, and underneath the familiar pack scent, my senses registered something else.

Something foreign.

Close.

Still in wolf form, Chase leapt out of the car and came to a halt a few feet in front of us, glancing back over his shoulder, as if to tell us to stay where we were. Undaunted, Lake sauntered forward, Devon on her heels.

"Looks like Lucas is feeling better," Lake said pithily. "Because unless my nose is mistaken, he's not in Cabin thirteen."

Maddy glanced at me and then slid out of the backseat. I

followed, concentrating on my pack-sense and trying to pin-point who among our pack was inside the Wayfarer restaurant and what they were feeling.

Lily. Mitch. Three of the older Resilient kids.

They were in there, with Lucas. The same Lucas who'd lied to me. The one who was currently topping the Not Just Humans' Most Wanted List.

For once, the constant chill on the back of my neck that told me there was a foreign wolf nearby was drowned out by another feeling.

I was now officially pissed.

The first thing I saw when I stepped across the threshold of the Wayfarer was Lucas, his hands wrapped around Lily's tiny frame. The first thing I heard was the three-year-old's scream, shrill enough to shatter glass.

Lily, I thought, my heart jumping into my throat. I was already moving for the shotgun behind the counter when I realized that neither Devon nor Lake was reacting like Lucas was threatening one of ours. A split second later, I registered that on the other end of the bond, Lily wasn't frightened. She wasn't hurting. She was *ecstatic*.

"No, no, no!" she shrieked, trying to escape Lucas's grasp but holding back just enough that she couldn't. "No more tickles!"

In response, Lucas hooked his arms around her body and flipped her upside down.

"She throws up, you'll be dealing with it," Mitch told him, but his lips twitched, like he was trying to keep from smiling at the picture that Lily and Lucas made.

"That dastardly fiend," Devon whispered. "She's never going to wind down in time for her nap."

Lily made a sound halfway between a giggle and a bark and kicked her feet. Beside me, Chase bristled, and I felt the hair on the back of my own neck rising in tandem with his hackles.

Whatever Chase had learned when he went to see Lucas, the feeling I was getting, loud and clear, through the pack-bond was that he didn't trust him, and now that Chase was in wolf form, his instinct to protect our territory was sharper, his bond to the rest of the pack harder to deny and his brain incapable of understanding human thoughts—or recognizing that, red-faced and screaming in the hands of the enemy, Lily was *fine*.

He leapt forward, teeth bared, growling.

I reached out to him with my mind but was met with the uncompromising certainty of the wolf. Lily was *ours*. Lucas was *foreign*. He was touching her, and *the pup was screaming*.

"Chase!" I yelled at the exact same moment that Mitch took a casual step forward and grabbed Chase by the scruff of his neck. Bearing down on him, Mitch forced wolf eyes to meet his, and slowly, Chase sank to the floor.

Lily, seeing further opportunity for mischief, wriggled her way out of Lucas's arms and leapt to land on Chase. "Wrestle!" she declared.

Before I could do a thing, the jumper she was wearing went the way of many play clothes before it. Shifting was simpler for the younger wolves: they melted from one form to another with liquid ease, and all it had taken to trigger Lily was seeing Chase in wolf form.

Now in animal form herself, Lily bobbed her furry head slightly and then grinned, an expression that looked eerie on her puppy face.

Slowly, awareness dawned on Chase. The human part of his brain realized that Lily was fine, that she was happy, and his wolf instincts recognized the unmistakable signal that she was ready to play. In the wild, play fighting was nature's way of preparing wolf pups for the real thing. At the Wayfarer, it was par for the course.

Lily pounced on Chase's paws, and I looked toward the other kids, all of whom were valiantly holding on to their human forms, just to show that they could. Most of our pack were right at that age when they tried very hard not to want to be kids, even though they weren't quite adolescents.

"Go ahead," I told them. "Somebody has to watch out for Chase. Lily's going to decimate him."

For a moment, none of the kids moved, but I flicked my gaze over to them and made it an order, and that was all it took. They were off and running before they even switched forms, and as much as Chase didn't want to leave my side, a silent *please* convinced him to lead them out to play.

Or, more to the point, out of harm's way.

I pulled my mind away from Chase's, but not quickly enough to keep from picking up that while Chase and his wolf would guard the pups, neither wanted to turn his back on Lucas, and neither wanted to leave me there with him.

Luckily, Chase's human half seemed to know that I could take care of myself, and his wolf half knew, on a bone-deep level, that I was alpha, and together, those things were enough to buy me some time alone with Lucas—if *alone* meant "with Lake, Devon, Maddy, Mitch, and Keely standing by."

Lucas took one look at my face, and he knew. I couldn't smell fear, not the way the Weres could, but I knew what it looked like, etched into features that were trying desperately not to show it, and when I took a step forward, Lucas went as still as a corpse. I could see his pulse jumping in his throat, but he closed his eyes and stood there, waiting.

Just like that, I was back in the woods behind Callum's house, my lips bleeding, my ribs cracked. It had taken everything I had not to fight Sora as she came at me again and again. I'd swallowed every instinct, and with each blow, I'd lost a tiny bit of myself, of the life I'd always thought that I'd lead.

I'd broken the rules, Callum had ordered me beaten, and I'd stood there, just like Lucas was standing now.

Pissed or not, betrayed or not, I wasn't going to be the kind of alpha who inspired that kind of fear.

"Maybe we should sit down," I said. On all sides of me, I felt my backup fighting their own internal battles, their wolves crying out for retribution, and their human halves seeing what I saw and thinking that there had to be a way, some way, for it to be different.

Sitting down at a table felt like fitting a noose around my own neck, but I forced myself to do it anyway and waited for the others to do the same. One by one, the Weres came to join me: Devon first and Lucas last, with Mitch, Maddy, and Lake spread out in between.

For a long time, none of us said anything. I didn't press Lucas. I didn't force him to hold my stare. I just waited, and finally, he spoke.

"You know," he said.

"And you didn't tell us," I replied, keeping my voice soft and even and wondering how it was that three minutes after swearing I would be a different kind of alpha than Callum, I could hear the man who'd trained me in every single one of my words.

"Who did they send?" Lucas asked dully. "To tell you?"

"Hey there, boy-o," Devon said, leaning forward slightly. "I think we'll be the ones asking the questions here."

Lucas glanced sideways and slumped lower into his seat. Maddy said his name softly, and after a moment, he nodded.

"Ask your questions," he said, wiping the palms of his hands on denim jeans.

I didn't have to be told twice.

"What are they?"

"Human."

"What *else* are they?"

Lucas took a breath and then he shrugged. "I don't know if there's a word for it," he said. "If there is, I've never heard it. They're just humans who can ... do things."

"Things like what?" Lake asked, and I could tell it was taking everything she had not to make the question any more leading than that.

"All of them are different," Lucas said slowly. "They each have an ... *ability*. One of them gets inside your head. He can make you see things that aren't there, make you feel them. They feed you silver, make you think it's chocolate."

I thought of my dreams: the throbbing in my temples, the tone in Archer's voice—pleasant, but deadly underneath.

"There's a woman, an old woman. She's got a way with animals, a way of making them do things. She likes snakes, and if you're a werewolf, she can force your Shift."

I really, really did not like the sound of that—not that being mentally set on fire was a walk in the park.

"What else?" I asked. Since he hadn't yet referenced someone with Caroline's power, I knew he hadn't told us everything, and I wanted to save my ace in the hole for after

I'd squeezed everything out of him that I could myself.

"There's another woman, her name is Bridget, and she does this…whistling thing. It makes you forget. It's like one second you're there and you're fighting, and the next, you can't fight. You just listen. Even if they're cutting you open, even if you can feel it hurting, you can't do anything but listen."

I waited to see if Lucas would say anything else, trying not to fully digest the horror of what he'd already said.

"They told me that they had someone who's really good at finding *things* when they go missing." Lucas laughed, and it was a miserable, hair-raising sound. "I guess they were telling the truth."

"You came here *knowing* they could track you?" I couldn't help the exasperation in my voice. "And you didn't think it was a good idea to give us any warning that someone might come after you? Even after we specifically asked you who that someone was, you didn't think it might be pertinent to mention that they have about a thousand ways of killing people that normal humans don't?"

You're getting off track, I told myself. *Yelling at him doesn't get you answers. He'll either shut down or expect you to beat them out of him.*

That was what any other alpha would do—except for maybe Callum, who was all the more lethal for how seldom he resorted to using brute force.

Think, I told myself. *What would Callum do?*

My brain wasn't forthcoming with answers, so I decided to focus on my pack's own particular strengths. It was time to bring in the big guns.

"Lucas, would you like something to drink?" The change in tactic took the Were completely off guard. Unbeknownst to him, however, that was more of a by-product than the point.

"Drink?" Lucas repeated dumbly.

"Like a milkshake or a soda or something?"

Mitch caught my eyes from across the table, and it was clear that he knew exactly what I was doing.

Careful, Bryn, he warned. *The other alphas don't know about Keely. If you send this boy back and he ends up tipping Shay off, we could all be in for a world of hurt.*

I knew as well as Mitch did that most alphas wouldn't take kindly to the idea of a human who could loosen lips just by brushing up against someone or looking them in the eye.

She does it all the time, I responded, sending the words from my mind to Mitch's. *And nobody's figured it out yet.*

People—even the kind who turned into wolves on occasion—expected bartenders to be good listeners. Keely just lived up to that expectation—and then some.

"Maybe some lemonade?" Lucas asked tentatively, and I tried to digest that the source of all of this trouble was the type of person who, when asked if he wanted something to drink, requested lemonade.

In Shay's pack, Lucas had never stood a chance.

"Keely?" I called. She'd done a good job making herself scarce, but Keely was a smart woman, and I doubted she'd gone far. She probably knew as much about werewolf politics as I did, and she'd been the human equivalent of truth serum all her life—the moment Chase had taken the little ones out, Keely had to have known that her services might come in handy.

Sure enough, a few seconds after I'd bellowed, Keely sauntered out from the kitchen and leaned across the bar. "You rang?"

"Can we get some lemonades?"

"Sure thing, kiddo." Keely spun glasses out from underneath the counter like a pro, and Devon cleared his throat.

"Don't be stingy with the cherries, Keel," he called back to her.

Obligingly, Keely put a cherry in each of the glasses. I knew for a fact that she could carry four at a time without breaking a sweat, but she opted for carrying one in each hand, a strategy that would allow her to make several trips past Lucas and back to the bar.

Anything happens to her, and we'll be having words, Bryn. Mitch eyed me across the table, his expression deceptively mild. Lake's dad might have been a part of my pack, but Keely and the rest of the folks at the Wayfarer were Mitch's to take care of, the same way the rest of Cedar Ridge was mine.

I did not want to consider the possibility of "having words" with Mitch any more than I wanted to think about something happening to Keely—which meant that I had to play this just right.

"Here ya go," Keely said, bending over to set one of the drinks in front of Lucas, brushing his arm as she did.

"Now that you're all beveraged up, mind telling me how many of these *humans* are after you?" I timed my question perfectly and managed to keep my voice casual and wry.

Lucas never knew what hit him. "There were maybe ten of them total, maybe not even that many, but I don't think I saw them all. Their leader was a woman named Valerie. She and Shay have some kind of agreement, I don't know what exactly, but he did something for her, or she was going to do something for him, and I was just a part of the deal. There was something about a daughter, Valerie's daughter, but I never saw her."

The information was flowing freely now, but I didn't have time to sort through the significance of what Lucas was saying. Keely went back to the bar for two more lemonades, and my next question made its way out of my mouth as she returned.

"How dangerous are they?"

"Very, and they're not exactly fond of werewolves. Something happened a long time ago, and now…sometimes I think the only reason they didn't kill me is because dead dogs don't scream. If I'd stayed long enough, the novelty might have worn off, but it also might not have. I'm not sure if they'll kill to get me back, but if the killing involves werewolves, they probably wouldn't consider it murder any more than one of us would report a fight for dominance to the human police."

Keely made her last trip to and from the bar: two more lemonades, one more question.

"What aren't you telling me?"

It was a pretty broad question, but with Lucas's apparent habit of hiding the truth until it blew up in his face, I had a feeling that the information I most needed to know was probably whatever he least wanted to tell me.

At first, he said nothing, but as Keely leaned over Lucas to pass Mitch a lemonade, the bottom of her arm touched Lucas's shoulder, and his entire body seemed to relax. "I won't go back," he said, his tone conversational, with an iron edge buried layers underneath. "I'd die before going back to those people, and I'd kill myself before going back to Shay. I don't care what I have to do. I really don't, because I'm never going to let anyone do that to me again. When this is over, I'll be six feet under or I'll be free. For good."

Having said his piece, Lucas went very quiet, but his words hung in the air, reinforcing what I'd already deeply suspected.

Sending Lucas back to Shay or giving in to Caroline's ultimatum didn't just mean turning my back on someone who needed my help. One way or another, it meant sentencing Lucas to death, because if the psychotic werewolf-torturers and megalomaniac alpha didn't do him in, Lucas had as good as promised to kill himself.

Between Keely's power and the Weres' ability to smell lies, I had to assume that he was telling the truth.

CHAPTER TEN

THIS TIME, I WAS THE ONE WHO RETREATED TO THE forest—and away from the rest of the pack—to think, and Chase was the one who found me. He'd Shifted back to human form, and I could feel him taking in everything: the way I was standing, the tilt of my head.

"You look like you want to hit something," he observed mildly. "A wall. Possibly a tree. Something hard."

"Lucas is going to kill himself." I didn't sugarcoat it, but my voice didn't exactly reflect the black hole of emotion churning in my gut, either. "If I can't work something out, if we don't protect him from this family and from Shay, he's going to die."

If Chase found what I was saying at all surprising, he certainly didn't show it, and the only thing I felt through his end of the bond was a brief surge of dislike for Lucas, distrust, pity.

"Don't," I said sharply before he could say a word. "Don't tell me this isn't my problem. Don't tell me it's not my fault. There's an answer to this, Chase, and if I don't find it—if I *can't* find it—then whatever happens to Lucas damn well is my fault."

Chase didn't argue, didn't tell me to lower my voice.

"You want to hit something?" he said in an even tone. "Hit me."

I was standing there, yelling at him, and all he did was meet my eyes, his face impassive. How many times had I seen that exact expression, that same control, on Callum's face when I was growing up?

"Go on, Bryn."

Go on, what? Hit him? Hurt him? He was Pack, and he was Chase. I would have died first. Wasn't that the problem? The list of people I had to protect—the ones who mattered—it just kept getting bigger and bigger, and no matter what I did, someone was going to get hurt.

"Shay. Caroline. That guy in your dreams. They're messing with you, Bryn. They're baiting you, and they're hurting you, and if you don't let it out and take a swing at something, you're going to explode. So let's have it." Chase motioned me forward. "I can take it. Promise."

He grinned.

Without even thinking, I swung. Chase ducked, lightning quick and impossibly coordinated, and I swung again, my fist tearing through the air and just missing the side of his cheek.

Again.

And again.

And again.

I didn't lay a hand on him. Not once, but I kept going until the pent-up fury inside me broke and gave way to something else.

I couldn't fight Chase, couldn't match a Were's speed or strength, no matter how hard I tried, just like I couldn't keep Archer or Caroline from entering my dreams and showing up at school. I couldn't make Shay sorry for the things he'd done to Lucas, and I couldn't snap my fingers and make being alpha any easier.

I was what I was. The situation was what it was. It wasn't fair, and it wasn't easy, and maybe Chase was right, and I couldn't save everyone—but I could try. Because that was the kind of alpha—the kind of person—I was.

The pace of my swings slowed, and Chase caught my arms in his. He pulled me close, and I breathed in raggedly, laying my head against his chest, vulnerable, spent. For a few precious seconds, I felt the borders between the two of us give, felt our connection as strongly as I had before there'd been a pack or an alpha or anything but the two of us.

I felt his wolf—animal instinct, undiluted and sure—as if it were my own.

"Thanks," I said finally, pulling back just far enough that I could say the words to his face. "I needed that."

And even though he had to have known, from that split second when we were more like one person than two, that I wasn't backing off this, that I couldn't just take care of myself, no matter how badly he wanted that for me, he nodded, his lips turning up subtly on the ends.

"Anytime."

"Ali, I'm home!"

My words echoed through our cabin, and Ali called back that she was in the twins' room. I took a deep breath and then followed the sound of her voice. Somehow, my ability to adopt a poker face when interrogating werewolves evaporated the moment it was just Ali and me, and I took a few seconds to try to wipe the evidence of the day's events from my eyes, mouth, and brow.

What Ali didn't know wouldn't hurt her—and more to the point, what Ali didn't know wouldn't hurt *me*.

"Hey." I poked my head into the twins' room. For a split second, Ali held my eyes, and then she turned back to folding clothes into the dresser drawers.

"Mitch called." Ali's voice was muted. I couldn't tell what she was thinking—or what, exactly, Lake's dad had told her.

"Oh."

"Yes," Ali replied. "Oh." She shut the drawer and then turned to leave the nursery, gesturing for me to follow.

I did.

When we got to the living room, I expected her to start lecturing, or to go into fierce-and-overprotective mode, but she didn't. She just smoothed down my hair and wrapped one arm around me.

"We'll get through this," she said. "You shouldn't have to be dealing with something like this, but you are, and you have to, and I can't change that. I can't make it go away." Even though Ali's voice was perfectly calm, I knew that saying those words was costing her. Ali had always protected me. She'd stood up to werewolves for me when I was too little to do it for myself. She'd given up a whole other life for me, *twice*: once when she'd left the human world to raise me in Callum's pack, and later when she'd left her werewolf husband and her home in the Stone River Pack to keep me safe.

But now I had responsibilities of my own. I couldn't stay out of this, even if I wanted to—not for Ali, not for Chase, not for anyone—and I loved her for knowing that and for not asking me to, even if a part of her felt like she'd failed me because at sixteen I had the weight of the world on my back.

"I don't know what to do," I said. Admitting that was nearly impossible, but this was Ali, and I couldn't hold the words back. "No matter what I decide, someone gets hurt."

Not emotionally hurt. Not kiss-it-and-make-it-all-better hurt. *Dead.*

"If we don't help Lucas, he's going to die, and if we do..." I searched Ali's eyes. "Did Mitch tell you? About the...*family* of people with...*knacks*?"

"Psychics," Ali corrected absentmindedly. "Humans with special abilities are called psychics."

Somehow, the word *psychic* didn't seem to do justice to the whole "burn you while you sleep" thing, but I didn't see much point in arguing semantics.

"Okay, so there's a family of psychics, and if we don't hand Lucas over in the next seven days, I'm pretty sure they're going to come after us, and even if we can take them, it won't be pretty."

There would be losses, and the idea of digging a hole in the forest and burying Devon or Lake or Chase—or, God forbid, one of the younger kids—was insurmountable.

"It's an impossible choice, Bryn, and if you want me or Mitch to make it for you, if you want us to be the ones who make the call, and you just deliver it . . ." Ali tucked a strand of hair behind my ear, and the casual gesture of affection almost brought me to my knees. "Say the word, Bryn. You have to do this, but you don't have to do it alone."

What kind of alpha was I that her offer tempted me? What kind of daughter was I that part of me would rather have Ali's hands bloodied than my own?

"No," I said softly. There was no getting out of this, no way to un-become what I was.

Ali sighed. "Color me shocked."

"I have to do this, Ali. I'm the reason Lucas is here. I'm the reason Shay beat him down and gave him to a bunch of psychics to use as a pincushion. I'm the one the kids look to, and I'm the one who's supposed to protect them."

Ali folded her arms over her chest. "And who's the one who's supposed to protect you?"

That seemed to be a popular question lately.

"Who's the parent?" she asked. "Who's the wise and benevolent Cool Mom type?"

I cracked a smile—the first in what felt like forever. "I wouldn't go that far."

Ali pretended to be offended. "Are you trying to say that I'm not cool?"

"Fine. You're cool. You're the epitome of cool. Everyone wishes they could have mom hair just like yours."

Ali hooked an arm around my neck. "I do *not* have mom hair," she said, "and you don't have to do this on your own. I know you—you'll look for other choices. Ways to keep Lucas safe without endangering the pack. And I hope to God you find one, kiddo, but either way, deal me in. They're my family, too, and you have no idea how dangerous some psychics can be."

Between Caroline's little demonstration at lunch and the fading burn on my skin, I was fairly certain I did have some idea of what we were dealing with, but I didn't argue with Ali—mainly because my foster mother telling me that I didn't know how dangerous people like this could be meant that for some reason, she did.

"You have experience with psychics?" I asked.

Ali pressed her lips together in a thin line and then wiped her hands on her jeans and nodded. "You could say that."

Her words hung in the air between us, and Ali turned

toward the kitchen. "If they lay a hand on you, I'll kill them myself."

"And how, exactly, are you going to take on a whole *family* of psychics?" I asked, aiming for a light, teasing tone and failing miserably.

Ali shrugged. "For you, I'd find a way, and technically, a group of psychics isn't called a family." Ali started walking toward the kitchen. "It's called a coven."

CHAPTER ELEVEN

THAT NIGHT, I SLATHERED MY SKIN WITH A THICK coat of aloe vera and slept with a fire extinguisher next to my bed. I might have been promised a seven-day cease-fire at lunch, but the psychics would have to forgive me if I was hesitant to take the word of a bunch of superpowered psychopaths who got their jollies from torturing teenage werewolves.

I think you'll find us reasonable, Caroline had said.

"Yeah, right," I muttered, turning over in bed. Despite the risks, I needed to get some rest. A sleep-deprived alpha was nobody's friend.

Closing my eyes, I let my alpha-sense take over, reached out through the bond, and found the others. I let their thoughts and senses flood my own.

Alex. Lily. Katie. Mitch.

Devon, Maddy, Lake, and Chase.

The peripherals at the very edge of our territory. The rest of the kids at the Wayfarer.

We were safe. We were together. We were fine.

The dream started with Callum. He was standing in my old workshop—the one place in Stone River territory that I'd carved out as my own. Callum was watching something, a soft smile creasing a face that had never aged past thirty, relaxed, but leaking power all the same. I followed his gaze and saw myself standing there—a younger Bryn, though not by much, peeling dried glue off her fingertips as she stared with nearly comical concentration at the result of an afternoon's work: a sculpture, maybe, or a mobile. *What* I was working on was fuzzy. It didn't matter.

The look on Callum's face did.

I couldn't put words to the emotion, couldn't describe it, except to say that during the course of my childhood, I'd caught him looking at me that way a hundred thousand times: like I was a puzzle, like I was precious.

Like he didn't want me to grow up, because things would change forever once I did.

As if he could hear my thoughts, the dream Callum turned to look at me—the real me, not the memory of the girl I'd been a year or two before. He moved his lips, but I couldn't hear what he was saying, couldn't make out the words or the familiar tone of his low and steady voice.

I wanted to so badly it hurt.

He took my shoulders gently in his hands, bent down to my

level. I opened my mouth but could not say a word. Everything began to go dark and fuzzy, but I held on, fought to hear what he was saying, wished he could look at me like I was little, like I was his—just one more time. But Callum faded away, to darkness, to nothing, leaving me staring at my younger self, this dream Bryn so caught up in things that didn't matter. She turned, saw me. She pointed.

She smiled.

I glanced down to see what she was smiling at, and that was when I realized—I was bleeding. There were three deep wounds in my side, parallel lines.

The Mark.

I watched in horror as the gashes spread across my torso, leaving me unable to move until the sound of clapping broke me from my stupor. Young Bryn faded away, the way Callum had, and a new form took shape on my workbench.

Archer.

"Bravo," he said. "Encore, encore! The angst. The drama. The symbolism. You're first-class entertainment, little Bryn."

Little Bryn should have sounded like an improvement over *mutt-lover*, but it didn't.

"What?" The trespasser smiled sardonically. "No she-wolf this time?"

I found myself looking for her, even though I didn't want to. The dreamworld shifted on its axis, the workshop giving way all around me to the forest, the snow. My body rebelled against the sudden change, nausea taking me down to my knees. The snow was wet and cold under my fingertips.

It melted under Archer's feet.

So much for a cease-fire.

"Hey now," he said, looming over me and sounding almost offended. "I'm not doing anything unsavory here. This is a dream of your making, not mine, wolf girl. I'm just along for the ride."

Pain chipped away at my temple, like a metal pick striking ice. I fought my way through it, getting to my feet, fists clenched and thirsting for this psychic's blood, but suddenly and without warning, I couldn't breathe.

I looked down and realized with mounting horror that the gashes in my side were still growing—bigger and bigger—and they weren't even bleeding anymore. I could see through them, all the way through my body and out the other side.

Beneath my skin, where there should have been fat and bone and muscle, there was nothing.

No organs. No blood.

I was hollow.

I woke with a start, and in the time it took my eyes to adjust to the darkness, my other senses flared to life. The room didn't smell right. It didn't *feel* right, and the scratching sound of inhuman nails against wooden floor told me that I wasn't alone.

A silver knife was in my hand before I realized I had reached for it. I put my back to the wall and like a wild thing, I crouched slightly, holding my blade at the ready, right next to my ear.

The wolf at the foot of my bed backed up slowly. It took me a moment to recognize him, and a moment past that to push down the compulsion to throw the knife at the spot directly between his light brown eyes.

"Lucas?" I said, trying to process that he was there on my bedroom floor. He made no move to attack, and I returned the favor, but my fingers tightened around the hilt of the blade, ready to buy me whatever time they could.

In human form, Lucas was unassuming. Small. As a wolf, he was scraggly, with ribs poking out under matted fur and eyes that I could describe only as hungry.

"Change." My voice shook slightly as I said the word, and I narrowed my eyes, allowing my own pack's power to flow through me, banishing the kind of fear that the wolf in front of me might be able to smell. "Change, or I'll call for the others, and we'll hand you to the coven wrapped up in a little bow."

At the word *coven*, the wolf went very still, and then I heard the first crack of bone. The shudder that went through Lucas's body in the instant before the Change whetted my own appetite—for running, for hunting, for *something*—but I kept myself from moving, from approaching him.

I didn't lower the knife.

By the time Lucas finished Changing, my own brow was covered with sweat, and my senses were heightened. My heart made itself known with uncompromising force beneath my rib cage, and my ears caught the muted sound of Lucas's ragged breaths. He was hunched over on the floor, but he lifted his eyes to stare just over my left shoulder. The moonlight caught his irises.

He was naked.

Modesty warred with my survival instincts and lost. I knew better than to take my eyes off a predator, naked or not.

"I would never hurt you," Lucas said, his voice breaking. "I needed ... to run ... I needed ... to Shift...." He shivered, eyeing the knife in my hands. "I needed..."

Me.

My mind finished the sentence for him, and I prayed he wouldn't say it out loud.

"I needed to know," Lucas said.

I breathed an internal sigh of relief that the naked boy on my floor hadn't confessed his undying need for *me*.

"Yeah, well, I need you to cover yourself up." I lowered the knife and reached across my body with my left hand to grab the blanket off my bed. I tossed it toward Lucas, and he caught it and did as I asked.

"I also need for you not to show up in my bedroom in the middle of the night." I tried to put this in terms he could understand. "This is my territory. My personal territory, and no one comes here without an invitation."

"I need to know." Lucas was hunched over so far that his broken request was issued more to my feet than my face. "Are you going to hand me over?"

"I don't know." Now my voice was the one breaking. "I'm sorry, Lucas, but I don't know what I'm going to do. I'm hoping there's a way, I'm going to try to find a way, but if you're asking if I'll send my pack to war to keep you safe, when Shay could come in at any moment and demand you back, the answer is no. I can't promise that, and you shouldn't be asking me to."

"There's a lot of things he shouldn't be doing," a low, even voice said.

Chase.

I felt him before I saw him, and my body didn't register even a hint of surprise at his presence. Of course he'd come. Of course he was moving to stand between Lucas and me.

"Lucas shouldn't be here. He shouldn't be asking you to do this. And he shouldn't take it the wrong way that I'm going to give him until I count to three to put as much distance between the two of you as he possibly can."

"Chase—"

Chase didn't let me finish. "He should also be glad that I beat the others here, because I doubt Devon or Lake would be nearly as understanding about this as I am."

Even in the scant moonlight, I could make out the way

Chase's pupils surged until his eyes were more black than blue. There was a part of him—a bigger part than I'd realized—that knew violence, the way he and I knew each other.

He was fighting it, and he was trying, but I could sense his human half wanting to hurl Lucas across the room every bit as much as his wolf wanted to sink fang into flesh.

"One."

As the alpha, I could have made him stop, but I didn't.

"Two."

Lucas took off through the window, the same way he must have come in, and Chase followed him far enough to shut the pane carefully behind him, lock it. He let out a long, even breath.

"He didn't hurt you."

I got the feeling that Chase was talking to himself more than asking me a question.

"He didn't hurt me," I echoed. Now didn't seem to be the right time to point out that I could take care of myself. Instead, I pried my fingers off the knife still clutched in my right hand and massaged my knuckles.

Chase's eyes faded back to their natural blue, and he crossed the room. He ran one hand over my arm and nodded, as if to convince himself that I was fine, that Lucas hadn't hurt me—even though he could have.

"Bryn?"

"I'm fine."

Chase nodded, breathed in my scent.

"He's broken," I said. "The look on his face, it was just..."

"I know," Chase said. "Trust me, Bryn. I—of all people—know."

"But," I prompted, sensing he had more to say.

"I know what he's been through and I'm sorry for it, *but* I don't trust him."

I didn't trust Lucas, either—not by a long shot. He was too unpredictable; he held things back from us too often, too much. But even though I didn't *trust* Lucas, I knew what it was like to be broken, to have to fight through it and find a way to put yourself and your life back together.

And so did Chase.

That was why I needed to do something—because once upon a time, another alpha had done something for me.

"You wanted me to go and talk to Lucas, to form my own impressions, and I did," Chase said, pulling my mind back to the present. "Lucas is desperate. Desperate people do desperate things, Bryn."

I heard him. I believed him—but I couldn't wash my hands of this, no matter how much Chase wanted me to. I couldn't let Lucas down just to take care of myself.

Chase pressed his lips to my temple, and I felt their touch through my whole body.

Your job is watching out for the pack, he'd told me. *Let my job be watching out for you.*

His lips traveled from my temple down to my mouth, his arms pulling me closer—and for a few moments, when it was just the two of us and I could feel him everywhere, it didn't matter that I was alpha, didn't matter that he wanted things for me that I would never be able to have.

I didn't think about Lucas or the coven or the million and one ways this situation could end badly for everyone involved.

All I thought about was us. Chase and Bryn. Bryn and Chase.

Yes.

CHAPTER TWELVE

CHASE SPENT THE NIGHT, AND I WOKE UP THE NEXT morning with my head on his chest and his body curved around mine, like he could ward off the outside world by wrapping my frame in his. I listened to his heart beating in his chest, and burrowed in closer, surrounding myself with the warmth of his body, the scent of his skin.

This was right. *This* was safe. *This* had kept the nightmares away.

And then I heard the sound of someone moving around in the kitchen. My first thought was that Lucas was back. My second was that the coven, unable to send Archer into my dreams, had come to try out their intimidation factor in person. My third thought was the most logical—and the most terrifying.

Ali.

I flipped over onto my side and looked at the digital clock on my nightstand. 10:23.

"Chase." I kept the volume of my voice low but made up for it by shoving him in the ribs.

"Bryn," he said, his eyes still closed, a loopy smile on his face. "Get up."

He must have sensed the urgency in my tone, because the next second, the smile was gone and there was something feral and hard in its place. He moved quickly, pushing me back toward the headboard, crouching in front of me.

I rolled my eyes.

Not that kind of danger, Chase, I told him silently. *You're a boy. In my bed. And Ali doesn't believe in sleeping past ten thirty. Ever. It's a miracle she didn't drag me out of bed to get ready for school.*

In the madness of the day before, I hadn't gotten around to dropping the "no more high school" bombshell. Luckily, Ali seemed to know that there was no margin for error in our current predicament—and no way that any of us should give the psychics an opportunity to divide and conquer.

Still, impending disaster or no impending disaster, the twins had undoubtedly been up for hours, and Ali was probably on the verge of venturing into my bedroom. She was already uncomfortable with the intensity of my relationship with Chase. Somehow, I doubted her finding him in my bed would help matters, even if we did have the mother of all excuses.

You have to leave, I told Chase. *Now.*

He twisted to face me, his posture relaxing, the light, playful smile returning to his face. I was used to the give-and-take between the boy and the wolf inside, but I was still struck by the combined effect of his bed-head and our current situation.

For the first time since he'd come back from patrol, Chase seemed like he belonged here, body and mind—not just with me, but at the Wayfarer. Like this was home.

I should go, Bryn.

His voice was a whisper in my mind, and I wondered if I'd projected my thoughts to him—if *home*, like *Thanksgiving*, was something he'd thought of only in the abstract. Without saying another word to me, silently or out loud, Chase slid off the bed and began walking toward the window, and every instinct in my body said to follow.

Then there was a tentative knock on my bedroom door, and every instinct I had said to cover.

"Just a second!" I called. Ali opened the door, just a crack. Once she had ascertained that I was not, in fact, naked, she pushed it the rest of the way open and came in.

I had never in my life been so grateful for werewolf speed. Chase was gone before Ali's eyes had a chance to register that he'd ever been there. Unfortunately, Ali had the uncanny ability to look at me and know, without a shadow of a doubt, that I was hiding something.

"Sleep well?" she asked, narrowing her eyes.

I had two choices: evade the question and pique her curiosity enough that she'd keep digging around until she figured out what was setting off her mom sense, or distract her with the least damning portion of the truth.

"I slept well this morning, but last night was rough."

"Was it?" Ali asked, glancing around my room and noting the blanket that Lucas had left on my floor.

"Lucas came by," I said. She would have found out eventually anyway; this wasn't the kind of thing I could hide from the pack, and it wasn't the kind of thing I could ignore. Wanting to help Lucas and giving him free rein of our territory were two different things, and I couldn't help that Chase's words had dug their way into my mind. Lucas was a loose cannon. Desperate people did desperate things, and desperate werewolves were a thousand times worse.

Especially when they showed up in your bedroom alone at night.

"I know he's scared," I said, "and it's not like I've been able to give him an answer, but . . ."

"But he broke into a foreign alpha's house and could have killed you in your sleep?" Ali was taking this about as well as could be expected—which is to say, not well at all. "Most alphas would kill him. Callum would cage him."

I knew exactly what Ali thought about the werewolf version of justice. She was the voice in my head telling me that violence—that kind of violence—was never okay.

I shifted uncomfortably on the bed. "I'm leaning more towards asking Devon and Lake to shadow his every move."

Between Lake's trigger finger and Devon's fondness for show tunes, that seemed like a harsh enough incentive to walk the straight and narrow to me.

"Seems reasonable," Ali agreed, "but it might not be a bad idea for you to take on a shadow yourself."

Ali judiciously avoided meeting my gaze as she said those words. In the entire history of my life, I'd never once willingly agreed to lupine bodyguards—not that my agreement had ever been necessary before. In Callum's pack, my refusal had been cause for amusement more than anything else, but now the decision was mine.

"I need you to do this for me," Ali said, and I knew by her tone that it wasn't a request.

Correction, I thought, *the decision is* technically *mine.*

"Fine," I said. "I'll have Devon, Lake, Maddy, and Chase rotate through: half on me, half on Lucas, anytime I'm on the property."

"You planning on leaving sometime soon?" Ali asked. I'd expected her to pick up on that, but I'd also expected her to be adamantly against it. Instead, her voice was guarded, like she knew something I didn't.

Maybe multiple somethings.

"I don't know what I'm planning on doing," I said honestly. "But I'm getting the distinct feeling that you do."

Ali pressed her lips together for a moment and then she spoke. "I called Callum this morning."

Like mother, like daughter—Callum was never far from my mind and never far from hers. The difference was that I'd come to terms with the things Callum had done to set me on the path to becoming the Cedar Ridge alpha, and Ali probably never would. She'd loved Callum, the same way I had, but she'd never cared that he was the alpha. She'd fought him—and me—every time I'd started thinking and acting more Were than human.

He'd promised her once that she'd have the final word on my safety, and in Ali's eyes, he'd broken that promise and then some.

"*You* called Callum?" I asked, watching a bevy of emotions and vulnerability flash across her face until she pressed back against them.

"I was worried, and in his own way, he . . . *cares* . . . about you."

I thought about the Callum in my dream—mute and hovering just out of reach. "Did Callum actually answer the phone, or did he have Sora do it?"

Ali gave me a strange look. "He answered. Why?"

"No reason. Is he the one who told you I needed guards?"

Ali shrugged. "I believe his exact words were 'If she was living in my territory, I'd have half my pack watching her back.'"

Even from a distance, Callum was *still* controlling parts of my life. The fact that he couldn't be bothered to answer my phone calls was just salt in the wound.

I didn't bother to bite back the sarcasm in my reply to Ali. "Did he round out the conversation by giving you cryptic warnings or promising to send you presents with some kind of secret meaning that you absolutely and without question won't understand?"

"No," Ali said, dragging the word out and tilting her head to the side. She waited to see if I would elaborate, and when I didn't, she did. "He did say that it was best if the two of you had no direct contact for the time being, and that he couldn't advise me on how this should be handled or things could go very badly."

"What a drama queen," I muttered, eliciting an incredulous laugh from Ali. "I mean, what's the worst thing that could happen if he helps me out here? The apocalypse?"

"A high probability of civil war," Ali corrected. "Or so says the drama queen."

I just loved it when my worst-case scenario went from bad to horrific. The precarious democracy in the werewolf Senate was a stick of dynamite, waiting to go off. I had no desire to be the one to strike the match.

"So in summation, his only suggestion was putting half the pack on Bryn Babysitting Duty, and he can't do anything to help us directly without inciting a chain of events that might lead to a future he doesn't want."

"If it's any consolation," Ali said in a voice that suggested it wasn't much consolation to her, "I think the part of him that's actually human wishes that he could help. It's just not a very big part. Not anymore."

I wasn't about to touch Ali's Callum issues with a ten-foot pole. "In other not-helpful news," I told her, "I got a visit from one of the psychics again last night."

Ali's entire body went tense. "And you didn't lead with that?" she asked tersely. "Are you okay? What did they do to you?"

In retrospect, I had to consider the possibility that telling Ali this was a mistake. For whatever reason, psychics were a sore spot with her. I should have known she wouldn't take the idea of a nighttime invasion lying down.

"I'm fine. One of them just has a nasty habit of showing up in my dreams. At least this time, he came alone."

"What did he look like?" Ali enunciated each of the words, and I could tell she was fighting to keep her voice from rising in pitch.

"Dark hair. Early twenties. Penchant for sarcasm."

That wasn't exactly a quality description, but at the time, I'd been too busy wanting to kill the guy to take note of his features. Still, the description seemed to satisfy Ali and she let out a breath that I hadn't realized she was holding.

"Early twenties," she repeated.

"College aged," I confirmed. "Maybe a little older, but not much." I hesitated a fraction of a second but then had to ask: "You okay?"

"Yeah," Ali said. "I'm fine. You should be, too. Entering other people's dreams isn't all that different from what people with open pack-bonds can do with each other, and the psychic doing it can't hurt you. He can annoy you. He can frighten you. But that's it."

I decided, for the time being, not to mention that the psychic in question appeared to be able to cross that line with relatively little effort.

"You seem to know a lot about psychics." I let that statement hang in the air, but Ali didn't offer up an explanation, leaving me to wonder if I wasn't the only one dancing around full disclosure.

"I don't know enough," Ali said instead, "and neither do you. I told Callum as much."

"And . . . ?" I knew by the look on Ali's face that there was more.

"And," Ali continued, "he said that it was absolutely crucial for me to tell you that if you go anywhere near this coven, he'd be very displeased. I believe his exact words were that you shouldn't be poking your nose around their affairs and that he *forbids* it."

Forbids it?

Forbids *it?*

I sputtered, "Who does he think he is? I'm not his responsibility, and he's not my alpha. He can't *forbid* anything."

Even when I had been living under Callum's rule, even when he'd been the closest thing to family that Ali and I had, I'd never have let him get away with being that high-handed.

Forbidding me to do something was as good as telling me to do it.

Irritation mounted until I felt like snarling. Slowly, however, common sense intruded on my ire, and a little bell began going off in the back of my head.

Callum knew that telling me specifically not to do something was a surefire recipe for making me want to do it.

He *knew* that.

I glanced at Ali to see if she was thinking the same thing. The edges of her lips turned upward. "Callum's many things, Bryn, but he isn't an idiot. The only reason he'd ever ask me to tell you that something was strictly, absolutely off-limits was if he wanted to ensure that you'd do the exact opposite of what you were told."

When it came to maneuvering around the rules, I'd learned from the master. If the Senate asked, Callum could honestly say that other than telling Ali to keep me at home and under guard, he'd done nothing. He hadn't offered us any advice in his position as alpha, and he most certainly hadn't suggested that if I wanted to find my way out of this situation, I'd need to investigate the coven firsthand.

"Think if I go into town alone, someone will show up to play more mind games?" I asked.

"Most psychics don't have aggressive powers." Ali glanced out the window. "For every person who's good in a fight, there are twelve who are better at messing with your mind. Even if this coven is one of the more powerful ones, if you show up in town without a werewolf escort, someone will show."

I was shocked that Ali was willing to consider the idea of me playing bait—until I realized that she hadn't specified my going into town alone. She'd said that someone was sure to show if I went in without werewolf backup. Given that she and I were the only humans in the pack, it didn't take a genius to figure out that she was planning on coming with me.

Knowing Ali the way I did, though, I was starting to suspect that it was more than that. Ali wasn't just planning on coming with me—she seemed dead set on it, like she wanted to flush out the psychics as much as or more than I did. I could see the drive to do this hidden beneath the almost-neutral set of her features.

Ali didn't just want to come with me. She *needed* to come with me. The only thing that wasn't 100 percent clear to me was *why*.

CHAPTER THIRTEEN

ALI AND I STOPPED BY THE RESTAURANT ON OUR way to town. Living with werewolves meant that everyone would know the second we left the Wayfarer grounds anyway, so there was no point in sneaking around. Besides, Ali needed to drop the twins off with Mitch and check in with the older Resilients to make sure the younger ones were doing okay. There weren't too many kids in our pack young enough to need constant supervision, but the older Resilients—some of whom were just a few years younger than me—had been taking care of the littler kids for years.

In the clutches of the Rabid, they'd been the ones to bear the brunt of the abuse.

If there was one thing that seeing Lucas had taught me, it was how lucky they all were to have come out of it with their minds and spirits intact.

"Where'd you say you're going again?" Mitch asked. His voice was mild, but he was a Were and Ali was female, so the things he didn't say hung in the air between them, heavy and clear.

"We're going to town," Ali repeated, unfazed by the question and the manner in which it was delivered. "Just for an hour or so. Think you can hold things down here?"

"I suspect I can." Mitch paused for a split second and then he turned to me and said, "Bryn, I ever tell you that you and Ali here are an awful lot alike?"

Ali couldn't seem to decide whether to smile or throw her hands up in the air at that, so I saved her the trouble of responding.

"I'm going to assume that's a compliment," I told Mitch. "For both of us."

Mitch shook his head in consternation, and Ali reached up and patted his shoulder, in a motion that I was fairly certain she didn't mean to look nearly as intimate as it did. "We'll be fine, Mitch. If it'll make you feel better, have Lake rustle up a couple of tranquilizer guns. Just make sure they're loaded for humans, not Weres."

Lake wasn't the kind of person you had to ask twice for weapons, so she didn't even wait for her dad to give her a nod before she took off out the front door of the restaurant. I gave it ten-to-one odds that she'd be back with tranq guns in less than three minutes.

Unfortunately, three minutes was all it took for Devon and Chase to show up at the restaurant and innocuously volunteer to shadow Ali and me on our trip to town. Given that the whole reason we were going into town was to flush out people who tortured werewolves for fun, I wasn't inclined to indulge the boys' protective instincts over my own.

"I need you here," I told Devon quietly. "Lucas showed up in my room last night."

I'd expected those words to distract Dev, but he just glanced at Chase and then turned back to me. "I know," he said, and the similarity between my best friend's facial expression and Chase's was eerie.

You told him? I asked Chase silently, torn between annoyance and shock. Chase and Devon weren't exactly friends, and Chase wasn't really what one would call chatty.

"Of course he told me," Devon retorted, even though I knew for a fact he hadn't heard me ask the question. "You can just imagine how thrilled I was to hear it."

I wasn't sure which was worse for Dev: that Lucas had gotten close enough to me that, if he'd wanted to, he could have ripped out my throat, or that Chase had been the one to stop him—and spend the night.

"Dev, I need you and Lake to keep an eye on Lucas. Wherever he goes, you go, and if you can keep him away from the younger kids—"

Devon's eyes glittered. "You don't even need to ask, milady."

The *milady* he tacked on to the end of that sentence was the only thing that reminded me that Dev wasn't usually the type who lived life on the cusp of violence. All of us were on edge.

And, Dev? I added. *If you can keep him away from Maddy . . .*

I didn't allow myself to finish that silent request. It didn't seem right to ask Devon to keep Maddy from Lucas while the rest of our group roamed free. Maddy was a big girl, and if she wanted to stay close to Lucas, to watch him, to figure him out—I couldn't keep her from it, any more than Callum had been able to keep Chase from me.

I knew what it was like to look at someone and see yourself, to need answers, and as off balance as Lucas seemed, I had to remind myself that the day I'd met Chase, he'd snarled at me from inside a cage and told me that I smelled like meat.

You don't have to ask me to watch out for Maddy, Bryn. Devon met my eyes. *And for what it's worth, I don't think you'd have to ask Maddy to watch out for me.*

"Somebody ask for tranq guns?" Lake called, crossing the room in three long-legged strides, ponytail swinging. She handed one to Ali and one to me. "One dart will make a large male groggy or knock out a little bitty human girl."

I assumed from the tone of Lake's voice that the "little bitty" comment referred to Caroline, and that Lake herself would have taken no small pleasure in pulling the trigger. She'd been taught all her life not to attack humans, but knocking them unconscious with tranquilizer guns was more of a gray area.

"Thanks, Lake." Accepting the gun from Lake, Ali turned back to me. "You ready to get out of here?"

I nodded, and Chase echoed the motion. It was on the tip

of my tongue to tell him that he needed to stay here, but Ali shook her head slightly, and I let her speak instead.

"How far away can you be and still sense Bryn?" Ali put the question to Chase and waited for his response. I figured that she was probably planning to tell him to hang back far enough that no one would see him, but close enough that I could call for him if things went bad. I realized a second after Ali asked the question that she probably wouldn't like Chase's answer.

"I always sense her." Chase shrugged, but despite the human gesture, I could tell that the answer was coming as much from the wolf as the boy. *"Always feel her."*

Ali held up one hand.

"TMI?" I guessed.

"Something like that," she confirmed before turning her attention back to Chase. "If you can always sense her, you'll know if she's in trouble, and you'll come. Otherwise, this is kind of a mother-daughter thing."

If there was one argument Chase couldn't counter, it was that.

"I'll wait at the edge of our property," he said, addressing the comment to me, like we were the only two people in the room—like the seven words he'd said to Ali and the heads-up he'd given Dev had tapped out his desire to speak to anyone but me. "You need me, I'm here."

That was what Chase did—whether he agreed with me or not, whether it was comfortable for him or not, he was always *there.*

"I should go." I forced my voice to sound normal and pressed back the desire to close my eyes and remember what it had felt like to wake up that morning with him by my side. "And hopefully, when we get back, we'll have answers."

I didn't bother to enumerate the questions; there were too many of them, and everyone in the room knew each one as well as I did. The only thing the others didn't know was that Callum was the one who'd nudged Ali and me into doing recon on the psychics.

Slipping the tranq gun into the inside pocket of my jacket, I couldn't help wondering what exactly Callum had seen that had caused him to set us on this path.

Time to find out.

"So. You and Chase. How's that going?"

Apparently, this was Ali's version of small talk. I immediately started wishing that the drive to town was a significantly shorter ordeal. Ali had me as a captive audience for at least another ten or fifteen minutes, and this was a conversation I'd been expertly avoiding for months.

"So," I returned evenly. "You and Mitch. How's that going?"

I knew that was a bit of a low blow, but I really didn't want to try to explain to Ali, who'd done everything possible to make sure I had things in my life other than the pack, that as much as Chase and I were just getting to know each other on human terms, there was another part of me—the part that had been raised to think like a wolf—that had known him the second we met.

"I'm not criticizing here, Bryn. I just want to make sure you're careful."

For one horrific moment, I thought she might be on the verge of giving me a sex talk. Luckily, her next words laid that worry to rest.

"Dating means something different to werewolves than it does to humans, and Chase hasn't been one long enough to understand that, let alone control whatever his wolf feels when he's close to you. You're only sixteen, and wolves mate for life."

Casey hadn't.

I didn't say the words, but the second I thought them, I felt like a horrible person. I was the one who'd torn Ali's marriage apart in the first place. I would have preferred biting off a chunk of my own tongue to throwing that in her face.

"I tried to make it work with Casey."

If I hadn't already been silent, Ali voluntarily bringing up his name would have shocked me into it.

"I wanted it to work, but it didn't, because Casey's not human, and no matter how much he thought he loved me, there were always going to be things that mattered more."

I wanted to point out that unlike Casey, whose loyalties had and would always lie with Callum, Chase would never have to choose between his alpha and me. I *was* his alpha. But Ali wasn't done talking yet, and I didn't interrupt her.

"You've seen the way Casey is when he visits, the way he still looks at me, the way he acts when Mitch and I are even in the same room." Ali very deliberately did not elaborate on whether or not Casey had anything to be jealous about. "Whatever I had with Casey is over for me, Bryn, but for as long as I live, it won't ever be over for Casey, and I have to deal with that. I'm a big girl. I can do it, but you've got your whole life ahead of you, and you have no way of knowing what you'll want five years from now, or ten. Maybe Chase is the one. Maybe he isn't. But if you let things get intense now, there won't ever be someone else for him, and you're the one who's going to have to deal with the consequences."

I was beginning to suspect that I would have preferred Ali giving me the sex talk.

"You don't have to worry about me, Ali. Chase isn't like other Weres. He's not possessive. He doesn't expect me to bow down to anyone."

She looked less than convinced.

"And besides," I added, "as *intense* as things are, I have an entire pack inside my head. If it were just him and me, then maybe things would be going too fast, but they're not." I glanced out the window, unsure whether I wanted to say the next part out loud. "Before I was alpha, it was like the two of us were the only people in the world, and now we're not."

Ali had the good grace not to look *too* relieved. "That's not necessarily a bad thing, Bryn."

"I know. And I wouldn't trade the pack, not for anything." I pulled my hair back into a ponytail and looped it over into a loose bun. "Chase wouldn't ask me to—but seeing Lucas, hearing about everything he's gone through, it makes me realize: I think I know more about Lucas's past than I know about Chase's."

Maybe if it had been just Chase and me, we would have talked about his human life more, the way we did in the beginning, but the quiet moments, the ones where the rest of the pack just faded away, were so few and far between.

"People are allowed to have secrets, Bryn." Ali's tone was mild, but the words felt like a reproach. "Even from you."

Ali looked like she was about to say something else, but instead, she killed the engine, and I realized we had made it to town.

Thank God.

I'd take a physical fight over Touchy-Feely Share Time, hands down. Hopefully, though, this wouldn't come to an actual fight.

Assuming Ali's intuitions about the coven were right, once we started making our way down Main Street, our targets would come to us. Based on my previous interactions with Archer and Caroline, it seemed likely that they'd stick to the armistice Caroline had promised—but just barely. If they could get under my skin, mess with my mind, they would.

And then some.

As far as I was concerned, they could try, but I had no intention of letting myself be intimidated. Once they made the first move, I'd know how to counter. Whatever mind games they tried to play would tell me more about who they were and how they operated.

The Callum I knew wouldn't have sent me here otherwise. I hadn't seen him in months, hadn't heard from him, but I trusted that.

Game on.

CHAPTER FOURTEEN

A LIFETIME OF BEING TAUGHT TO WATCH MY BACK made it hard for me to stroll down Main Street without thinking about all the ways I was leaving myself open for an attack. Growing up with people who could turn you into an afternoon snack had a way of giving you an unusual perspective on playing bait. I'd done it before—once—and the effort had ended with me knocked unconscious and tied to a chair in the home of a Rabid serial killer who liked to dress girls up in their Sunday best before making them bleed.

Suffice to say, I was hoping for a better outcome this time—especially since I didn't have werewolf backup waiting just around the bend.

"Mind games," Ali reminded me, her voice muted. "They're all about the mind games."

I was about to ask her why every time she made a statement about psychics, she sounded as straightforward and certain as Lake would have sounded talking about guns, but just as my mouth was about to form the words, I felt something—eyes on the back of my head, a presence cast over me like a shadow.

Step. Step. Step.

The sound of feet treading lightly on concrete was unmistakable—soft, but perceptible to human ears. I glanced at Ali out of the corner of my eye, and she gave a slight nod. She heard it, too.

Step. Step. Step.

And then nothing.

I knew enough about hunting to know when I was being stalked. I also knew, with chilling certainty, that the silence wasn't an indication that the person tailing us had dropped back. She'd wanted us to know she was there, and now she wanted us to know that she could disappear from our radar, that unless she willed it, we would never hear her coming at all.

Caroline.

I kept myself from whirling around. If there was one thing I'd had pounded into my head from day one, it was the necessity of never letting fear show in my posture, the speed of my breath, the weight of my motions.

If this girl wanted to play mind games, I could play them right back.

"Aren't you going to say hello?" I asked, voice casual, eyes pointed straight ahead.

"Hello." Caroline spoke the word directly into my back. She was closer than I'd realized—too close—but I wasn't about to give her the satisfaction of reacting.

"Playing hooky?" I asked, forcing myself to continue facing forward, sending the message, loud and clear, that she wasn't a threat worth facing head-on.

"Mental health day," Caroline replied, her tone light, but lethal. "I'll be back at school tomorrow. You?"

I didn't hear her shifting positions, didn't catch even the slightest sound as she unsheathed a blade, but somehow—instinct, maybe, or my knack—I knew. I reached back and caught her hand seconds before she would have pressed the flat of her knife to my back, just to prove that she could.

"You should stick to throwing knives," I said, tightening my grip and forcing the bones in her wrist together as I jerked upward and spun, bringing myself face-to-face with the blonde with the dead, dead eyes. "Perfect aim doesn't really help you in hand-to-hand."

For a moment, the potential for bloodshed—hers, mine—hung in the air between us, and the part of me that was alpha, the part that had grown up like a Were, wanted it. The coven had come here to my territory and threatened my pack. One of their females had come at me from behind.

That wasn't the kind of thing I was wired to take sitting down.

"Bryn." Ali's voice was mild, but I nodded and dropped Caroline's gloved wrist. We hadn't come here to fight. We'd come for information, and so far, we hadn't gotten much. In fact, the only thing I knew now that I hadn't known before this little melodrama had gone down was that I could take the coven's pint-sized emissary in hand-to-hand—but if she'd had a weapon trained on me from afar...

"I'm Ali." In a surprisingly gentle voice, my foster mother introduced herself to the girl who'd pulled a knife on me.

"Caroline," the girl said shortly.

There was a moment of silence while the two of them appraised each other. Ali had several inches and sixteen years on Caroline, but for a split second, the two seemed disturbingly well matched.

"We didn't know the wolf girl had human friends," Caroline said.

Ali shrugged. "I didn't know your coven was on good enough terms with the people in town to risk pulling a knife on someone in broad daylight—unless, of course, you have someone running interference, showing them something else."

Caroline blinked once when Ali said the word *coven* and once when my foster mother called that Caroline probably hadn't come here alone. It wasn't much of a stretch to think that if Archer could enter my dreams, the coven might have someone who could make the rest of the people in town think they were seeing something they weren't.

"You have no idea what you're up against," Caroline said, and for a second—a single second—she sounded almost sad. "Don't tell me the two of you would die for one of *them*. Don't tell me they're worth it. They're monsters, and you know that, same as me."

A reply was on the tip of my tongue, but before I could press Caroline to tell me how she could call my pack monsters, given what her coven had done to a battered teenage boy, a single note, haunting and low, made its way to my ears, and suddenly, whatever I was going to say didn't seem nearly so important.

Caroline turning and walking away didn't seem important.

Nothing did.

Objectively, I knew that another person might describe the sound as a whistle, compare it to the product of blowing a steady stream of air into a hand-carved woodwind. But to me, it wasn't just a sound. It was a song.

It was paralyzing.

I knew what was happening, knew that there was a person making this sound, and that when she'd made it for Lucas, he hadn't been able to move or scream or even care that he was being tortured.

I knew, I knew, I knew—and I didn't care.

My hands fell to my sides. My lips parted slightly, the tension evaporating from my face and jaw. All my other senses receded, because nothing mattered as much as the sound.

The sound.

On some level, I realized that Ali had gone still beside

me, her muscles as liquid and useless as mine. I saw people approaching, recognized Archer, noted the old woman standing beside him, looking every inch the storybook grandmother but for the snake coiled like a scarf around her neck. And then there was the third in their little trio, the one whistling that one-note song that snaked its way through my brain, around my limbs, in and out of my blood, my skin, *everything*.

Archer and the old woman closed in on me from either side, the snake slithering from Grandma's neck down her shoulder, poised to strike.

For a second, a split second, the sound stopped as the woman who was whistling took a breath, and I had a moment of clarity, a moment when I could think and move and realize exactly how bad this situation was, before the sound started again.

A feeling, alien and familiar all at once, crackled through my body. The *sound* pushed back against it, willing me to relax, to forget, to just stand there and let the psychics have their way with me, but this time, I heard a lower sound, an older one, a whisper from the most ancient part of my mind, from my gut, from the core of what it meant to be me.

Threat, threat, threat, it seemed to be saying. *Survive.*

My body was relaxed, my limbs frozen in place, but that single word was enough to free my mind. My vision blurred. Darkness began to close in from all sides, and even before I saw red, I tasted it, the color tinny and electric on my tongue.

This was what it meant to be Resilient. The taste, the color, the rush of adrenaline into my bloodstream. The fury and power and uncompromising need to *escape*. To *fight back*.

To *survive*.

Instinct took over. One second I was standing there, and the next, the roar inside me was deafening, drowning out anything my external senses had to offer. I leapt forward, the world colored in shades of black and blood, blood-red, and by the time I came fully back into myself, the sound had stopped, and everyone who wasn't me and wasn't Ali was on the ground.

I couldn't remember how they'd gotten there, or what I'd done, but whatever it was must have sent a message, because as they climbed to their feet, the woman who'd been whistling kept her mouth closed, and the other two kept their distance.

"Easy there, mutt-lover. If we wanted to fight, you'd be dead right now." Archer gave me a genial smile. Like he knew me. Like we were friends. "I'm not much of a fighter, but even I could have slid a knife between your ribs in the time it took you to fight off Bridget's hold."

Having said his piece, Archer glanced pointedly to his left, at the old woman, who was stroking her snake's triangular head like it was a kitten. The suggestion was clear—if Grandma had wanted me dead, her pet could have seen to that just fine.

"You should know what you're up against." Bridget's speaking voice was absurdly plain compared to the sound she'd made before. For some reason, that didn't surprise me, but the note of kindness in it did. "If we fight you, really fight you, there will be casualties on both sides, but we *will* win. Your people will fall, some of them"—she glanced at Ali—"without ever realizing there's a battle they should be fighting."

Bridget's warning sank in.

Being Resilient meant being resistant to dominance and having a knack for escaping even the direst situations. If I could fight my way through Bridget's hypnotic hold, chances were good that Chase, Maddy, and the other Resilients could do the same.

Eventually.

I tried not to think about what the rest of Bridget's coven could do in the time it took us to combat her ability. I tried not to think about the fact that Ali, Mitch, Devon, and Lake might not be able to fight it in the first place.

Lucas hadn't.

"You've seen Caroline," Bridget continued softly. "You know what she can do."

Darkness flecked across Bridget's eyes when she said Caroline's name. Fear, thick and uncompromising, with a life of its own.

For a moment, the same expression descended over the others' faces, like Caroline was their bogeyman as much as she was ours.

Archer recovered first. "This shouldn't be your fight, Bryn," he said softly. "Sometimes, backing down is the right choice.

The smart one." Archer reached out to tweak the end of my hair, but Ali caught his hand in hers.

"You don't talk to my daughter," she said. "You talk to me." She looked from Archer to Bridget to the old woman cooing at the snake. "Is this how your coven operates? You send a child out to issue your threats? You torture teenagers and play mind games with little girls?"

I hadn't been a little girl in a very long time, but Ali on a rampage was a thing to behold, and far be it from me to interrupt.

"You make me sick." Ali spat out the words, and Archer faltered, his smile replaced by something uncertain, some measure of loathing for himself and what he was doing, but as quickly as the emotion had come, something else replaced it.

Anger.

Bloodthirstiness.

Disgust.

The same expression overtook the whistler's face and the old lady's, as potent as the fear they'd shown at Caroline's name. The emotions writhed beneath the surface of their flesh, so vivid it looked like it might at any moment take on a life—and an agenda—of its own.

"Did Lucas do something to you?" I asked, floored by the depth of their hatred, but unable to keep the doubt that Lucas was actually capable of doing anything more than annoying them out of my tone.

"He's a werewolf," Archer said finally, his voice venomous, but somehow dull. "They're animals—all of them."

The woman with the snake shook her head. "Not natural," she murmured. "Not animals. Worse."

I bristled. Nobody knew better than I did what a werewolf could do, if he chose to cross that line. I'd spent my entire childhood aware that my life could have been forfeited the minute any one of them lost control. If Callum hadn't made my safety a matter of Pack Law, I might not have survived to adolescence, and I still dreamed about the sound human flesh made when canines tore it apart.

But that kind of werewolf was the exception, not the rule. Alphas didn't allow their wolves to run wild. We killed our own if they hunted humans. We weren't—my family and friends, *they* weren't monsters.

Werewolves were people, too.

"You've had a run-in with a Rabid," Ali said, judging their reactions. "Your coven has lost someone."

Her words were met with steely silence, and I braced myself for another attack as Ali kept pushing at it, kept pushing them.

"He or she must have been very important. You must have loved whoever it was very much."

Bridget quivered like a rabbit facing off against a fox and then snapped. Her hand connected with Ali's cheek with a loud crack. I was already in motion, retaliating, when Ali smiled. She'd gotten a rise out of them, and for whatever reason, she was happy about it.

Trust me, Bryn. It's a good thing. That was the first time I'd ever heard Ali through the bond she shared with my pack, and I went into a state of immediate shock, stopping all onslaught. Being human allowed Ali to keep her bond shut, the way I had for most of my life in Callum's pack. That she'd opened it, even for a second, told me it was crucial that I keep calm and let her continue playing her current game.

"You must have loved him," Ali repeated. "Whoever it was that you lost. It makes me wonder, though—if a werewolf did that to someone you loved, if you hate their kind so much, why would you trust one to give you a gift? Why make a deal with the devil?"

Ali's words didn't permeate the loathing the trio wore on their faces, as permanent and striking as some kind of tattoo, but I registered their meaning instantly.

Shay had sent Lucas to the coven.

Lucas had said it was part of some kind of deal.

So what had the coven given Shay in exchange? And why would they have agreed to give him anything in the first place?

"We should probably be heading home," Ali said, tucking a strand of my hair behind my shoulder, in a maternal gesture that would have been a lot more appropriate if the two of us had been out shopping. "We've been standing here awhile, and unless one of you is still actively blocking it, I think we've probably put on enough of a show for the rest of the town, don't you?"

I glanced around and realized that more than one shop owner was watching our exchange with feigned disinterest, and a couple of people were gawking in a way that suggested they might have seen me lash out and put the newcomers on the ground.

In retrospect, it was probably a very good thing that I'd already decided to withdraw from the local high school.

"Nice meeting you all," Ali said in a tone that suggested it was anything but.

Archer was the one to reply, and despite Ali's warning, he directed the words at me, not her.

"Six days."

I turned. Ali turned. We walked back to the car in silence. I knew what we were up against now, better than I had before, knew at least part of what they had in their arsenal. I'd marked the way they looked at and interacted with each other. It didn't take a rocket scientist to figure out that they considered Caroline to be the biggest threat.

I climbed into the car. Ali climbed into the car. We shut our doors.

If anything, this recon mission had assured me that my earlier assumptions were correct. If we fought the coven, there would be bloodshed, and a large portion of it would be ours. If we gave in to their demands and let them have Lucas, he would be better off dead.

Six days.

I had less than a week to decide between two evils. Less than a week to find out what kind of deal the coven had made with Shay.

CHAPTER FIFTEEN

THE RIDE BACK TO THE WAYFARER WAS SIGNIFI-
cantly quieter than the ride out. Ali seemed calmer somehow,
like the interaction, which had sent a rush of adrenaline surging through my veins, had sedated whatever worries she'd
been holding on to all day.

Instead of thinking about Shay, or the coven, or the partly
unhinged werewolf waiting for me to save him from both of
the above, I thought about Ali and the way she was handling
all of this. We'd been hypnotized. A natural hunter had pulled
a knife on me. Violence had been promised and there was
every indication that this group, family, coven, *whatever* could
deliver.

Ali was taking it in stride.

She'd pushed them and prodded them and borne their
presence in her mind without so much as blinking. She hadn't
shown any sign of weakness, any sign of fear.

Any surprise.

People are allowed to have secrets, Bryn. Even from you.

The words Ali had said in our conversation about Chase came back to me with a vengeance. Ali was handling this well—too well—and I couldn't shake the feeling that she was keeping secrets from me, the same way she'd never bothered to mention that Callum could see the future.

The same way I hadn't told her when I went off to hunt the Rabid.

The same way I probably wasn't going to tell her that I already had plans to go on a second recon mission. Alone.

The coven had a deal with Shay. I needed to know what it was, and I wasn't going to find out by letting my foster mother ask the questions. For whatever reason, she knew psychics, but I knew alphas, and I couldn't imagine Shay giving Lucas to the coven without asking for something in return.

I also couldn't imagine that the werewolf Senate would be happy to find out that one of the pack alphas had made some kind of alliance with a group of werewolf-hating humans. Once I found out what the deal was, once I had proof, I might actually have something to hold over Shay's head. And if I had the backing of the Senate, I might be able to convince the coven to back off.

"What are you thinking?" Ali asked. After ten minutes of silence, I was surprised to hear her voice.

"I'm thinking about secrets." I leaned the side of my head against the window and watched the mounds of snow pass by as we drove. "Yours. Mine."

"If you want to know something, Bryn, just ask."

People were allowed to have secrets. Being alpha didn't mean I had to know everything—I didn't need to know how Ali felt about Mitch, or what she was planning to do about Casey, or why she would never consent to running with the pack.

But I needed to know everything I could about psychics, so I had to ask. "You handled that well."

"That wasn't a question," Ali commented, her tone completely neutral.

"You knew what to expect. You knew how to read them. And I can't shake the feeling that you got more answers out of that little exchange than I did. Am I wrong?"

"No." Ali pulled the car over to the side of the road and slid the gearshift into park. She left the key in the ignition and the heat blasting, but unbuckled her seat belt and turned to face me. "Did you see the look in their eyes whenever they talked about werewolves?"

Hatred, undiluted and pure. "Hard to miss," I said.

Ali inclined her head slightly. "Did you happen to notice the size of their pupils?"

I was used to watching Weres' eyes for hints of the Change, so it only took me a second to walk my way back through the scene and pinpoint the moment Ali had referenced.

"Their pupils got bigger."

"And when do humans' pupils dilate?" Ali asked me.

How was I supposed to know? I couldn't even diagnose the full meaning of eyelash batting.

"A human's pupils dilate when they walk into a dark room, when they're attracted to someone, or when they're under some form of external psychic influence." Ali paused, and I saw her weighing her next words very carefully. "I spent most of my childhood with dilated pupils."

Somehow, I didn't think Ali was suggesting that she'd spent her formative years in the dark.

"It's not the kind of thing most people notice—at least, not at first. Most *knacks*, to use your expression, are like Keely's—subtle enough that even if you know what to look for, you don't realize what's happening. It's like . . . Imagine that for every natural ability in the world, there's a spectrum, and on one side of the spectrum, you have all of the people who are really bad at that thing, and on the other side, you have all of the people who are really good at it. And occasionally, once every ten million or fifty million or however many people, you'll get someone who's *really* good at it."

I nodded, afraid that if I said a word, she'd stop talking and wouldn't start again.

"My mother was like that, with emotions. She always knew what everyone was feeling, and whenever she smiled, it made you want to smile, too. If she was sad, I was sad. If she was angry, I was angry. I loved her *so* much, because she was my mother, and because she wanted me to."

Ali's eyes were completely dry, but mine were stinging, because I knew already that this story wasn't going to end well. Ali had cut off contact with her human family to join Callum's pack and take care of me. It hadn't ever occurred to me that she might have had other reasons for leaving her old life behind.

"When I was six, a group of people came through town, and one of them realized what my mother could do. They told her she was special. They offered to train her. They took us in."

I digested that information. "You grew up in a coven?"

Ali nodded. "Until I was twelve."

I tried to process, but couldn't keep up with her words.

"There were twenty or thirty of us, lots of children, and everybody fell at that far end of the spectrum—the gifted end—except for me. It would have been hard, growing up with other people poking around in my dreams and my head, sneaking up on me, playing cat and mouse with me even when I didn't want to play, but my mother wanted me to be happy, so I was happy."

Suddenly, I could understand why Ali had always kept her pack-bonds closed. Why she'd never let the others in, never risked losing herself to the pack mentality and—up until I'd broken with Callum's pack—encouraged me to do the same.

"We used to move around a lot. One person with a knack is subtle. A couple dozen aren't, and one day, when I was twelve, we'd been staying at an RV camp near the Kansas-Oklahoma border, and I went out to run an errand someone had told me to run. When I came back, everyone else was gone. It took a couple of days for my head to clear. I used to get these headaches, and these nosebleeds, and I remember looking in the mirror at social services and seeing my pupils, and they were small enough that you could tell that my eyes were hazel and not just brown.

"I don't think I'd ever actually seen my eyes look like that before. I was twelve years old, and that was the first time I could ever remember being able to feel something just because it was the way I felt. I went through eight foster homes in six years, then I went to college, and one of the girls I'd kept in touch with from one of the group homes disappeared. The rest of the story, you know."

"You went looking for the girl and found a pack of werewolves," I said.

"And the pack's alpha had just taken in a little girl, a human girl, and he told me that she'd need somebody to take care of her, because the rest of the pack would always be bigger, and they'd always be stronger, and she'd be alone."

To someone who'd grown up as the only normal kid in a coven of psychics, Callum's words must have really hit home. My whole life—or at least Ali's part in it—suddenly made so much more sense. She'd loved me and protected me and taught me to be my own person because no one had ever done that for her.

"The coven in town. Is it the same one you—"

"No." Ali didn't even wait for me to finish the question. "I thought it might be. That's part of the reason I went with you today, but I didn't recognize any of the people we just saw, and if I had to guess, I'd say this coven is much smaller than ours was. Their knacks are ones I've seen before, but that's to be expected. For every million people who have a way with animals, there's one who can influence them; for all the people who can sing lullabies that put babies to sleep, there are a handful who can put normal people into a trance. Entering dreams just means you're really good at getting inside other people's heads, and I'd lay ten-to-one odds on this coven having an empath, because the hatred the three in town felt when they talked about werewolves wasn't just theirs. Their pupils were the size of marshmallows."

I hadn't been paying attention to pupil size, but I'd seen an alien depth to the emotion and recognized it as unnatural, dangerous. On some level, I'd felt the same thing when Bridget had spoken about Caroline. If someone was manipulating the psychics' emotions to make them hate werewolves, it seemed like a fair assumption that the same person might be nudging them into being scared of Caroline.

Or at least *more* scared than they otherwise would have been, given the whole "I was born to hunt" thing.

"You said that most powers are just extensions of natural abilities—like the way Keely is really easy to talk to, and the way that people like me are . . . *scrappy*." I paused. "But you heard how quiet Caroline was when she was tracking us. She got within an inch of us without me hearing her, smelling her, anything. At school yesterday, none of the Weres could catch her scent, and she says she has a way with weapons, that once she takes aim, she never misses a shot. That she *can't*." I decided to stop beating around the bush. "She feels like a predator, Ali. That's not just a knack, and it really doesn't seem that mental. Even the other psychics are scared of her. So is she one of them, or is she ... something else?"

I really was not ready to deal with a *something else*. Psychics and werewolves, and mind games from both, were more than enough for me, thank you very much.

"She's a psychic," Ali replied, "but knacks with physical manifestations are rarer, and having a set of skills, instead of just one, isn't what I would call common."

Whole lot of good that did us.

"In most covens, the person with the most power is usually the leader."

I heard the stress Ali put on the word *usually*, and responded, "And when they're not?"

"Then they're the odd one out."

The same way a normal human would be. The same way Ali had been. I thought of the way she'd introduced herself to Caroline, the way she'd accused the adults of using a child to do their dirty work. The rest of the coven had approached us as a group, but twice now, they'd sent Caroline after me alone.

They talked about the things she could do like she wasn't quite human.

In the werewolf world, the easiest way to get information on any pack was through the peripherals. That was why we kept the Wayfarer restaurant open to people passing through from other packs, and that was why step two of my reconnaissance plan might involve trying to get the coven outsider alone.

Again.

A plan began to form in my mind, and it occurred to me that maybe I'd been a little hasty in swearing off my human education forever.

CHAPTER SIXTEEN

THE BEST THING ABOUT HAVING FRIENDS WHO KNEW me as well as Devon and Lake did was that they recognized from the moment I told them my plan that trying to talk me out of approaching Caroline was futile.

The worst thing about being alpha was that on some level, all three of us knew that even if they hadn't been inclined to go along with the plan, I could have forced it.

Forced them.

I wouldn't have done it, but the fact that I *could* seemed so much more noticeable now. Hierarchy was like breathing: the only time you thought about it was when something went wrong. With the presence of an outside threat, every instinct we had was amped up to the nth degree.

I couldn't help thinking that did not bode particularly well for Caroline, hunter or not.

"Ali suspect anything?" Devon asked once he, Lake, and I had put sufficient distance between us and the Wayfarer.

"Does she find it highly suspicious that the three of us are going back to school when there's a psychic army looming threateningly in the background?" I leaned back in my seat. "Of course she does. But given that she helped me play psychic bait yesterday, she can't really complain about us doing the same thing today. Besides, Callum *forbids* it."

Devon and Lake snorted in unison.

"Bryn Rule number twenty-three," Devon intoned, "whenever someone tells you to do something, make it a point to do the exact opposite."

"I'm not *that* bad."

Lake grinned. "Plausible deniability is a girl's best friend."

"Rule twenty-seven?" Devon guessed, wrinkling his brow, deep in the throes of mock thought.

"Fourteen," Lake interjected. "If I remember correctly, Bryn Rule twenty-seven involves the evils of werewolf bodyguards."

"Present company excluded, of course," Devon added, eyeing me reproachfully.

"You guys aren't here as bodyguards," I said, eyeing him right back. The last thing I needed was for Devon or Lake to feel obligated to throw down with Caroline in front of our Weston High fan club. "Shay made a deal with the coven. Caroline's mother is the head of the coven. Ergo, we need Caroline to start talking."

Lake smiled.

"We need her to start talking *of her own volition*," I clarified. "No violence. No scenes. No 'but I've been watching *NCIS* reruns and I think I'm really getting a hang of this interrogation thing.'"

And no Keely, I added to myself. If anyone could recognize her knack for what it was, it would be another psychic, and we couldn't risk word of Keely's knack getting back to Shay.

"No interrogation? Why don't you just come right out and say 'no fun'?" Lake grumbled.

I shrugged. "No fun. The coven gave us one week to hand over Lucas. Today is the third day. The last thing we want is to prod them into early action."

"So if we can't threaten Caroline, and we can't interrogate her, how are we supposed to get her to say a darn thing?" Lake's question was a good one, and I didn't reply—mostly because my plan didn't have much nuance beyond "poke it with a stick and see what happens."

Luckily, this situation seemed to fall under Devon's area of expertise, and he obligingly picked up the mantle. "Now, don't shoot me, ladies, but I'm going to go out on a limb here and guess that you two, as lovely and endearing as you are, might not be terribly well versed in the art of making friends and influencing people."

Lake snorted. "And you are? Seems I remember *you* wanting to rip Miss My Family Can Be Very Patient's aorta out her nose, same as I did."

Devon executed a delicate shrug of his massive shoulders. "The thought might have occurred to me once or twice, but you know what they say, Lake—you catch more flies with honey than with vinegar."

I could feel Devon's *Gone with the Wind* impression coming on, but since it seemed to be a step in the right direction compared to disembowelment, I decided to let it slide.

"You should have seen the way the other members of the coven talked about this girl, Lake." I paused, letting my words sink in. "They're scared of her—the kind of scared that involves pupils twice as big as they ought to be."

Lake gave me a look that said I wasn't doing a very good job of convincing her that playing nice with Caroline was the answer.

I tried again. "Maybe I'm wrong about this. Maybe we'll try to talk to her and she'll shut us down, but my gut is telling me that she's used to living on the fringe. She's used to people being afraid. She might even like it, but deep down, she has to be lonely or angry or bored."

If watching Ali assess the trio the day before had taught me one thing, it was that you didn't need supernatural powers to play off other people's emotions. Whatever Caroline was hiding beneath that unbothered, uninvolved exterior, I was willing to bet that it ran deep, and given that she'd explicitly threatened the lives of everyone I loved, I wasn't going to feel guilty about using that.

Using her.

It took me a moment to realize that Lake had stopped

driving and that both of my friends had gone still beside me. It was several seconds more before I realized that if my alpha status had been noticeable before, I was practically bleeding dominance now.

Pack was what mattered. *Protecting* them. *Destroying* threats.

For a few seconds, I stayed there, in that distinctly alpha frame of mind where nothing and no one else mattered but protecting my pack, and then, like a drowning man coming up for air, I managed to pull myself back. We were just going to talk to Caroline, try to get some answers.

That was all.

Devon in full-on charm mode was a terrifying thing. Caroline must have thought so, too, because she avoided him, evaded him, and glared brutal, bloody murder in his direction right up until the moment the three of us sat down at her table at lunch.

"Mind if we join you?" Devon slung one arm over the back of his chair and stretched his legs out, looking for all the world like some kind of larger-than-life male model smoldering on the side of a city bus.

"It's a free country." Caroline met his eyes with an unnatural, absolute calm. "You can sit wherever you want."

Most people's bodies telegraphed their thoughts in ways that run-of-the-mill humans never noticed, but Caroline was like a blank slate. She wasn't hiding her fear. She wasn't deliberately communicating that she wasn't afraid. She just sort of *was*.

There was some chance that this was going to be harder than I'd thought.

"You left before the real fun started yesterday." I kept my voice casual, all too aware that the rest of the student body was watching the four of us like we were their soap opera of choice. "Your family is just a bucket of laughs."

Caroline bared her teeth, and it took me a moment to realize that she was smiling with her mouth but not with her eyes. "The others are very friendly. Have you given any more thought to what we talked about on Monday?"

"I have." Devon leaned forward in his chair, staying out of her personal space, but bringing the full force of his blue eyes to bear on hers. "I don't know about the girls, but I'm having some, shall we say, *doubts*."

"Doubts," Caroline repeated.

Devon grinned. "Doubts. I could tell you that I'm devilishly handsome, have an impeccable sense of style, and am much, much stronger than I look, but I could also claim to be the reincarnation of Humphrey Bogart." He lowered his brows slightly and played his *here's looking at you, kid* face for all it was worth. "How's a girl like you supposed to know who or what to believe?"

For the first time, I saw a chink in Caroline's otherwise

emotionless armor: she raised one eyebrow, ever so slightly, and turned to me. "Is he serious?"

"Almost never," Lake replied. "But the boy has a point. It's one thing to breeze into town and *say* you can do something. It's another thing to put your money where your mouth is and prove that it's true."

"Are you suggesting that I'm *not* the reincarnation of Humphrey Bogart?" Devon gave Lake a disgruntled look. "I'm hurt."

"And I'm going to finish my lunch outside." Caroline slid her chair back and stood up. "I'd give you all a demonstration, but Bryn's already gotten a hint of my tracking skills, and to show you the rest, I'd have to ask one of you to play the target. I doubt there'd be any volunteers."

Devon stood up. "Where do you want me?"

"Devon." At times like this, I really wished he had an aversion to his full name so my saying it could carry the same weight as his calling me Bronwyn.

"What?" Dev said, the very picture of innocence, all six foot five of him.

I wasn't buying it. *This is how you make friends and influence people, Devon?* I asked. *By volunteering for target practice?*

He shrugged. *What did you expect me to do, Bryn, compliment her shoes? She's a trained killer who issues ultimatums on behalf of an entire coven of psychics. I don't think we'd get very far with girl talk, and besides, have you seen her shoes?*

I had to admit that there was a twisted kind of reason to his logic. To get any information out of Caroline, we'd have to talk her into spending more than three minutes at a time in our presence. If challenging her to show off her skills gave us more time to work our way in, it wasn't the worst idea in the world— except for the part where Devon volunteered to be the target.

"You want me to demonstrate my skills on you?" The neutral set of Caroline's features gave way to a small, self-satisfied smile.

Devon straightened his lapels. "I'd love for you to demonstrate your skills on me."

Beside me, Lake groaned. *Forget Bogart,* she told me. *He's channeling rakish bad boys 101. Don't know about you, B, but I think I'm gonna be sick.*

I was right there with Lake on that sentiment. I was used to seeing Devon hop from one role to the next, but nine times out of ten, I was the target of his shenanigans, and he reverted to form the second I smiled.

But Caroline wasn't smiling anymore. She was smirking, and I was only about 90 percent sure that Devon was playing, because as the four of us walked outside, he didn't say a single word to me—not out loud and not in my head.

Dev, I really hope you know what you're doing, I told him as Caroline jumped the parking lot railing and headed for the forest, the three of us on her heels.

Bronwyn, dearest, have you ever known me to charge into something blind or without a plan?

Yes, I replied immediately.

Devon's eyes flitted from Caroline's form to mine. *Something that* wasn't *your idea?*

It was possible that in the history of our friendship, I'd gotten Devon into more trouble than I'd gotten him out of. It was also possible that if the roles had been reversed, Dev would have had my back, no matter what.

Fine, I told him. *But if you get hurt, I'm going to kill you.*

"You're sure you want to do this?" Caroline asked. For the first time, I could sense something beyond cold detachment in her voice. She wanted Devon to say yes. She wanted to shoot him.

She wanted to hunt.

I recognized her desire. Lake recognized it. Dev had to have recognized it, too, but as he went radio silent on the other end of our pack-bond, I took the message loud and clear. I was going to have to trust him to take care of himself on this one, and I was going to have to stop thinking about the reasons this was a bad idea and start thinking about ways to make it work.

Chances were good that Caroline would assume that Devon would have the same reaction to silver that most werewolves did. Chances were also good that she wouldn't go for a kill shot. We still had four days left on her mother's ultimatum, and Caroline didn't seem like the type to kill on a whim.

No matter how badly she wanted it, no matter how strong

the instinct to hunt down her prey was, she was still human. She wasn't Rabid. She wasn't out of control. She was scarily in control, and while I had no doubt she could kill, my gut said that she wouldn't until she had orders.

I'd spent enough time skirting Callum's dictates to recognize when someone else had had following orders pounded into her for years.

About a hundred yards into the woods, Caroline stopped. In a slow, deliberate movement, she bent down and unsheathed a dagger strapped to her side. She turned and the weapon left her hand before I even realized she was preparing to throw it. It whizzed past Devon's left ear, slicing through the air and making it sing, a deadly sound that stopped only when the blade cut down a bird, mid-flight, pinning it to a tree half a football field away.

"I don't miss. You can either take my word for it, or you can start running."

Devon grinned—and then he ran. Caroline didn't bother tracking his movements. She didn't move to pull out a weapon. Instead, she turned to me.

"It's your call," she told me. "Do I aim for him?"

No. Absolutely not. Never.

"Aim for his hair," I told her. "He's been going for a little more volume lately, and if you're as good as you say you are, you should be able to give him a trim."

Caroline nodded. She reached into her jacket and pulled

out an arrow, tipped with silver, and a small crossbow, sized to fit perfectly under her jacket without being seen. The sheer number of weapons she had managed to conceal within seemingly ordinary clothes defied the laws of physics.

Devon was still visible in the distance—well outside the range in which I could have hit him, but not so far gone that she didn't stand a chance.

"Move," she whispered. "Run."

Hearing her words, despite the distance, he turned at a ninety-degree angle and began running in a line perpendicular to the one on which Lake, Caroline, and I stood. His pace and motions were erratic and unpredictable.

He was fast.

Caroline didn't lose a moment. She didn't pause to get a feel for the wind. She didn't narrow her eyes. She just lifted her arm and turned her head to face me, and without even looking at Devon, she fired.

This was a mistake.

I knew that when I saw the look in Caroline's eyes: certain and satisfied and a little bit sad, like there had never been any question in her mind that she would hit him, and like she wished, on a gut-deep level, that there was.

"You got him." Lake tried very hard to keep the admiration out of her voice. "Right where it hurts—in the hair gel."

Dev? I didn't have the benefit of Lake's eyesight, and I needed to know for myself that he was okay, that Caroline hadn't missed her target by a fraction of an inch in the wrong direction.

I'm fine, Bryn. Not quite as pretty as I was a few seconds ago, but fine.

All things considered, he was taking it well, but for some reason, Caroline wasn't.

I assessed her reaction. "Are you upset that you hit him, or upset that it was only his hair?"

Caroline's eyes flashed. "I don't get upset," she said. "I don't lose control."

"That the difference between you and a werewolf?" I asked.

Caroline took a step forward, closing the space between us. "I'm nothing like you." Even though her tone never changed, the way she spaced her words did, each one issued with the weight of an entire sentence. "Any of you."

I caught her gaze and held it. "You hunt. Werewolves hunt. There's a part of you that likes it. You're a predator. You may not go furry on the full moon, but you're not any more human than they are."

"Maybe not." That wasn't the response I'd expected. "But if there weren't people like you, the world wouldn't need people like me. If I'm a monster, you made me that way."

"Is this the collective 'you' we're talking about here?" I asked, pushing her that much further, that much harder.

Caroline's right hand lashed out, but unlike the woman who'd hit Ali the day before, she didn't strike me. She brought her fingertips to the edge of the glove on her opposite hand, and she tugged.

There was a part of me that expected an explosion of power the second her skin hit the crisp winter air, but there was nothing: no sound, no smell, no foreboding sense of things to come.

And then I saw the scars. They were puckered and white, and they drew my eyes to the skin around them. The skin that was there.

The skin that wasn't.

"Werewolf attack," she said. "When I was seven."

I shook my head. "Unless you're hiding a lot more scars somewhere, you're mistaken."

Werewolves didn't attack to maim. Under the Senate's rule, they didn't attack at all, and when a wolf went Rabid, he didn't care about anything but the hunt. He certainly didn't let a seven-year-old girl walk away after taking a single chunk out of her arm.

"I shot him, right between the eyes."

"Were you shooting silver?" Lake asked quietly.

"No." Caroline issued the word like it was a challenge. "But it was enough to slow him down. Enough for me to get away." She pressed her lips together into a thin white line. "Not enough for my father to get away, too."

Bullet or not, there wasn't a werewolf on the planet who would let his prey get away with nothing more than a sizable love nip. When werewolves attacked, they attacked to kill—and the only people who didn't die as a result were the kind who could survive things that normal people couldn't.

Caroline wasn't Resilient—I would have known in a heart-beat if she was, the way I'd known from the moment I'd seen Chase that we were *the same*, the way the Rabid—who'd been Resilient himself—had known exactly which kids could survive being Changed.

We just *knew*—and Caroline didn't engender even a spark of that recognition.

"You thinking what I'm thinking?" Lake asked me.

I glanced away from Caroline, just for a second. "I'm think-ing she got away because he *let* her."

One second, I was standing and talking, and the next, I was on the ground, and Caroline's foot was wedged under my chin, holding me down, pushing my head back.

There was a slight chance she was better at hand-to-hand than I'd given her credit for.

With Caroline's foot bearing down on my trachea, I couldn't breathe, but I didn't panic. I didn't fight her, and I managed to keep Devon and Lake from responding to the action.

"Nobody *lets* me do anything," Caroline said, her eyes slits in an otherwise cherubic face. "I do what has to be done, and if that means shooting silver, to make sure that what I put down stays down, then that's what it means."

My lungs rebelled inside my chest, and I knew that the

second things started going hazy, the familiar blood-red haze of my survival instinct wouldn't be far behind. In a matter of seconds, Caroline would be the one on the floor, and I would have lost the only advantage that mattered right now: she was talking.

"Werewolves are animals. God made me a hunter. You do the math." Having had her say, Caroline lifted her foot off my trachea, and I fought down the urge to put her in the dirt, to show her *my* mettle.

"Do we look like animals to you?" Devon asked, coming up behind me. With a sizable chunk of his hair now missing, he looked more like a disgruntled eighties pop star than an animal of any kind. "Whoever attacked you deserved the bullet, and if you'd been shooting silver, he would have deserved that, too, but unless the wolf in question was a pup at the time, it wasn't Lucas. It wasn't Lake. It wasn't me."

"Did they tell you that our pack is mostly kids?" Lake asked, looking Caroline straight in the eye. "Our age or younger. Some of them aren't much older than you were when you got those." Lake gestured to the scars on Caroline's arm. "You attack us, and you're no better than whatever took a bite out of you."

"You're not human." Caroline's voice went cold. If I hadn't been watching for it, I might not have noticed the way her pupils surged, covering her irises like ink spreading slowly across a page. "I won't feel bad for you—or for them."

My eyes on hers, I climbed to my feet, wondering if she

knew her feelings weren't entirely her own. "I'm human," I said softly.

Her pupils constricted.

"If you were really human, if there was any humanity left in you, then you would understand. They aren't like us. They'll never be like us."

I wanted to tell her that there was no me and her, no *us*, but there was a part of me that didn't want to know whether those words would smell like a lie.

A werewolf had killed my father, too.

I pushed down that thought. "If your coven is so convinced that werewolves are animals, then why would you make a deal with Shay?"

"Shay?" Caroline repeated.

"Lucas's alpha."

Either the words weren't ringing a bell, or Caroline had an even better poker face than I'd given her credit for.

"Big guy, kind of looks like me?" Devon kept his tone casual, and my heart sank for him, for what it cost him to acknowledge any similarity to the brother he barely knew.

"Shay," I said sharply, expounding so Devon didn't have to. "The guy who gave Lucas to your coven? Sadistic, kind of smarmy? About yea tall?" I raised my hand over my head. "Probably asked you guys for something in exchange for loaning out his favorite punching bag?"

Caroline stopped looking at me like I was the enemy and

started looking at me like I was insane. "No one *gave* us Lucas. We caught him. He doesn't have a pack or an alpha. He's on his own, and if he hasn't killed yet, he would have eventually. Lone wolves always do."

"Not always," I countered, "and it's a moot point, because Lucas isn't a loner. Right after he showed up on our land, I got an email from his alpha, demanding him back."

"This is the first we've heard about it," Caroline said tersely.

"It's the first *you've* heard about it," I corrected. "But Lucas said Shay made some kind of deal with your mother, and whether or not the rest of the coven knows a thing about Shay, I can promise that he knows about you."

Caroline didn't reply. She just turned on her heel and left—but not before I caught sight of the darkness that spread across her eyes the moment I mentioned her mother.

CHAPTER SEVENTEEN

I CONCLUDED THREE THINGS BASED ON OUR INTER-
action with Caroline.

One: she hadn't exaggerated her skill with weapons. She'd
taken a chunk out of Devon's voluminous hair—from a hundred yards away. That wasn't the kind of shot a normal person
could make. That was military-sniper-level good—with a
crossbow.

Two: whatever deal her mother had made with Shay,
Caroline—and quite possibly the rest of the coven—had been
left completely in the dark. She genuinely believed that they'd
captured Lucas, and just talking about werewolves sent enmity
surging through her veins, deadly and cool.

The third thing, I said out loud, since it was the one that
might have passed Devon's and Lake's attention. "Caroline's
mother is the coven's empath. She's good with emotions, she's
the leader, and she's the one who programmed them to go full
throttle on the hatred scale anytime werewolves come up."

It was probably also safe to conclude that the empath was

the one who'd given Bridget a psychic push to feel a rush of fear when she thought about Caroline, and that made me wonder.

What kind of mother wanted people to be afraid of her own kid?

"So what now, oh fearless leader?" Devon ran a hand through what was left of his hair.

"Now we figure out a way to get close to the person pulling the strings." I exhaled slowly and worked out the logic of our situation as I spoke. "If the rest of the coven *wanted* to take on an entire werewolf pack, their leader wouldn't have to amp up their desire to fight. And that means that if we can get close enough to said leader to knock her out of commission, we might be able to reason with the rest of them—especially if we can convince them that Caroline's mother made some kind of deal with Shay."

I hadn't been around any of the other psychics enough to judge, but I was positive that Caroline would take that news—once she believed it—about as well as I'd taken finding out that Callum had spent most of my life lying to me about what had happened to the werewolf who killed my parents.

I knew what that kind of betrayal felt like. For that matter, I knew what it was like to remember, every single day, the look and sound and *feel* of a monster tearing everything you loved to shreds.

Next time Caroline mentioned that a werewolf had killed her father, I was going to have to tell her to join the club.

"How, pray tell, are we going to get anywhere near Caroline's mother?" Devon cocked one eyebrow heavenward, and Lake mimicked his quizzical expression.

"I doubt she's going to throw out the welcome mat, Bryn. The whole coven hates werewolves, and if Caroline's any indication, they don't play all that well with other humans, either."

I thought back to what Ali had said about the coven she'd grown up in: that they'd moved from town to town, never staying in one place long enough for the ordinary humans to grow suspicious. Ali had been the odd one out, and when she'd gotten old enough, they'd left her like trash on the side of the road.

The only way to get into a coven was to be psychic yourself, and I said as much out loud.

"Keely could do it," Lake said, chewing on her bottom lip before continuing. "Assuming my dad would let her."

I wasn't a fan of that idea. Keely had already put herself on the line for us once, getting answers from Lucas. If Shay came to call, she might have to do it again. I couldn't ask her to waltz right into the lion's den, too—especially when there was another option.

"Keely's not the only one with a knack." I waited for my meaning to register with the two of them, sure that they wouldn't like where this was headed. "I'm Resilient. Some of the psychics have even seen me go into Survival at All Costs mode. If all it takes to join a coven is to be human and have some kind of supernatural ability, then technically, I meet the qualifications."

My words were met with deafening silence, followed by the unmistakable sound of growling inside my head.

I knew they wouldn't like where this was headed.

"If the coven wanted me dead, they would have already made their move." I tried to keep my voice calm and even, willing my friends to push down their instincts and hear the very human logic of what I was saying. "Instead, they've been playing with me: stalking my dreams, letting me feel the heat. Literally."

Most alphas wanted two things: territory and the power to protect it. I had to wonder if it was that different for psychics. Something had compelled Caroline's mother to make a deal with Shay, and whatever that something was, she'd chosen to keep it a secret.

Just like she'd chosen to let Caroline do her dirty work.

Just like she'd chosen to make the others fear what Caroline could do.

When I'd asked Sora what I could do to save Lucas, she'd told me that the only way to get a wolf away from an alpha who didn't want to let go was to give the alpha something he wanted more. Maybe the same logic applied to the coven, only instead of wanting females or territory or the kinds of things that mattered to Weres, their leader might be after something different.

Me.

The larger the pack and the more powerful its members, the stronger that pack's alpha became. Given that Caroline's mother seemed to have a way of manipulating people into doing what she wanted them to do, I had to assume that she'd welcome the chance to bring a powerful Resilient into the fold, especially if the Resilient in question had an entire werewolf pack at her beck and call.

If the coven could control me, they'd get my entire pack as a bonus. I doubted Caroline's mother would be able to ignore the potential for that kind of payoff. At the same time, though, I wasn't sure if I could take that kind of chance. Putting myself in the line of fire was one thing, but betting the entire pack's safety on my ability to shake off psychic holds was risky.

Unfortunately, the only option that wasn't risky involved sentencing a boy who'd come to me for protection to death.

There has to be a way to go in myself but minimize the risk to the pack, I thought fiercely, willing it to be true.

"Lake, should we perhaps lock Bryn in a closet?" Devon kept his tone light, but his eyes were deadly serious. "I'm thinking we should perhaps lock her in a closet."

Lake tilted her head to one side, clearly considering the option. "You really think you can do this?" she asked me.

I didn't bother tiptoeing around the truth. "I don't know."

Lake nodded, and for a second, she was the spitting image

of her dad. "When you figure it out, I suspect you'll let us know?"

That was Lake-ese for "deal me in or die a slow and painful death." She wanted a promise that I wouldn't run off behind their backs, that I wouldn't do anything until I had a plan, and that once I had a plan, she and Dev would be the first to know.

"Bryn?" Dev parked the car, and his voice broke into my thoughts. The part of me that was alpha wanted to respond, to tell them both to back off, to take a lifetime of friendship and turn it into something else.

I ground my teeth and shook my head.

The three of us had always watched out for each other. *Always.* I wasn't going to let what I was change that, change me. Our pack wasn't like other packs. I wasn't like other alphas.

That was it.

The idea came to me fully formed, like it had been in my head all along, and I just hadn't unearthed it until now.

"Hey, Lake?"

She grinned. "Would I be right in thinking that you've got everything figured out?"

"Yup."

"And you really think you can do this?"

"Yup."

"By Jove," Devon said, reading between the lines of my one-word answers, "I believe the lady has a plan."

For the first time since Lucas had shown up at the Wayfarer, I really felt like I did.

This time, I was the last one to the clearing. The moon wasn't full. The pack was sleeping, and those of us who weren't hadn't come here to run.

"Our pack isn't like other packs." My words appeared as wisps of white in the night air and echoed through the forest. The moon provided scant light, but even in the darkness, I could make out every detail of each of their faces.

Waiting.

Ready.

"We chose each other. When it counted, when the stakes were high, when no one else was there, you three had my back. You all gave up another life, another future, a hundred thousand things that might have been, and you did that for me, without even thinking, without questioning, without batting an eye."

For a time, after I'd broken off my connection with Callum's pack, but before we'd had our standoff with the Rabid, it had been just the four of us: Lake, Chase, Devon, and me. Later, there were others, and no matter where I went or what I did, the others' names would always be etched into my soul, their well-being my first priority—but in the beginning, before we knew what it meant or what any of us were on the cusp of doing, there were four of us.

And there was no alpha.

"If something happens to me—tonight, tomorrow, five years from now, I know that you guys will take care of the others." I met Dev's eyes for a second and then closed mine. "You'd take care of each other."

"*Nothing* is going to happen to you." Devon was the one who said the words, but I felt the intensity with which he'd issued them emanating from all three. It should have been suffocating, but instead, it warmed me, held me, sent a charge racing along the surface of my skin.

The whites of Chase's eyes caught the moonlight just so, and for a moment, I felt something animal and raw staring back at me.

I met his gaze head-on. I felt it down to the tips of my toes.

"Nothing is going to happen to me." I repeated Devon's words. "Because no matter what, the three of you would never let anything happen to me. It's not supposed to work that way, because I'm the alpha, and that means that I'm supposed to be the one protecting you."

My chest tightened, and the cold air cut into my lungs with each breath. I could sense their wolves, just below the surface. I could see the tension in their neck muscles and feel the adrenaline snaking its way from vein to vein.

"I'm not like other alphas." The words slipped off my

tongue almost as a confession, rather than a statement of pride, but I wasn't here looking for absolution. I was here to make what I was—and what *they* were to me—work for us, instead of against us.

They wanted to protect me. They would always want to protect me, and admitting that I might need their help, that I might need to be protected, didn't have to mean giving up the idea that I could keep the rest of the pack safe.

It just gave me another way to do it.

In the past six months, I'd learned that being alpha meant knowing everything about everyone. It meant that at any second on any day, I could tell you where every last member of my pack was, what they were doing, what they were feeling. I didn't push them. I didn't pry. But I was always there: in the things Chase would never tell another living person, in the way Maddy felt the first time she saw Lucas, in the quiet moments when Lake did nothing but run.

They could speak to me silently. I could make myself heard in their minds, but our pack-bond wasn't exactly a two-way street. I was the alpha and they were my pack, and nature hadn't designed werewolves to know their alpha the way he knew them.

She, I corrected myself silently. I wasn't male. I wasn't a werewolf, and there was nothing in the rule book to say that I couldn't make it a two-way street.

I stepped forward, my head bowed—not in submission,

but in something closer to prayer. I brought one hand to Lake's cheek and another to Devon's. I brushed the side of my face against Chase's neck. I closed my eyes, and I let go.

For this moment, in this private midnight congress, I didn't have to be alpha. I didn't have to be the strong one. Chase had tried telling me that. So had Ali. For the first time, I could almost believe it—believe that I didn't have to fight this battle alone.

I felt their breath on my skin. Heat leapt from their bodies to mine, and for all the perfect silence of the forest, the sounds inside my head rose.

I let out a ragged breath, pushing down the animal desire to howl. The scars on my hip bone felt like lines of liquid fire against my skin, but I didn't fight it. I didn't try to control the bond.

I let it control me.

I let them in.

I didn't say anything to them. I let them see it for themselves: everything I thought, everything I felt. I let them sift through my mind, and with the part of me that was alpha screaming, I forced my body still, until the muscles in the back of my neck melted away, leaving my head lying on Chase's shoulder, the way it had when he'd spent the night.

Devon nuzzled my right palm. Lake brought the tips of her fingers to touch my face. My mind and my body and every part of my being were so full of the three of them—what they were and what we were together—that there wasn't room for anything else.

Anyone else.

Being alpha meant always being inside everyone else's heads and never letting them inside yours, protecting the pack and never needing their protection—but it also meant that if the coven got inside my head, they'd have free access to everyone else's.

Not anymore.

"When Chase spent the night, Archer couldn't find me in my dreams." I heard the words as I whispered them, felt the soft sound wrapping its way around each of their bodies. "If we're lucky, having the three of you inside me will be enough to keep all of them out."

And what if it's not, Bryn? I recognized Lake's voice in my mind, and for a split second, I saw an image of the two of us when we were eight or nine, suntanned and skinny-limbed and laughing.

I brought my hand to Lake's and pressed my nails into the skin of her wrist, dragging them softly downward, leaving my mark.

You're going to protect me, I told her, *the way you always have, and if it doesn't work, you're going to protect the pack.*

It wasn't an order, but it wasn't a question, either, because I knew them, and they knew me, and there wasn't a single one of us who didn't already know how this was going to end.

Lake met my eyes, her own blazing, and then left her mark on my palm. The exchange was symbolic, the kind of formality our pack had never observed, but somehow, my dominance spreading among the four of us, their inner wolves as much a presence in my mind as theirs, it seemed appropriate.

Devon.

Chase.

Two more times, my fingers laid marks into someone else's skin. Two more times, marks were laid upon me. When we finished here, I'd go into the lion's den to take out the lion, knowing that I wasn't alone, that if something happened to me, my friends would take care of our pack, even if it meant hurting me.

With the wind whipping through my hair, I knelt and lifted my head to the waning moon. I breathed. They breathed. And when they Shifted, and I felt the rush of wild power, bittersweet and pure, I wondered if this time, they felt me in the same way I felt them.

If being a part of me made them just a little bit more human.

I was still alpha. I always would be, but the constant rhythm in their minds as I buried my hands in their fur wasn't *alpha*. It was *Bryn*.

CHAPTER EIGHTEEN

⌒

I SHOWED UP ON THE COVEN'S FRONT PORCH LOOK-
ing every inch the runaway. My hair was a tangled mess, my
clothes still smudged with forest dirt. My teeth were chatter-
ing, and I had a duffel bag slung over one shoulder.

Ali was going to kill me.

Waltzing straight into the belly of the beast wasn't exactly a
mother-approved kind of plan. In a few hours, when Ali woke
up and found me gone, there would be hell to pay, and I was
seriously glad that I wouldn't be the one around to pay it. I was
only about 60 percent sure that Lake and Devon would be able
to keep her from charging in after me—and only the fact that
my friends had open access to my mind and would know the
second things went south made me rate their chances that high.

This is what Callum foresaw, I thought, willing the words to
be true. *I'm supposed to be here. Ali will understand that.*

My friends snorted inside my head in stereo. I wasn't convincing anybody here—not even myself.

Feeling as if my body weren't entirely my own, I lifted my

right hand, fisted it, and knocked on the wooden door. The coven had set themselves up on the far side of town, in a falling-down farmhouse that had been abandoned for years. I lifted my fist to knock again, but the door opened before I could repeat the motion. I shivered, half from the cold and half because the wolves lurking in the corners of my brain didn't like the looks of the woman staring me directly in the eyes.

She was older than I'd expected. Werewolves aged slowly, and most of them never looked much older than their thirties, so seeing eyes that were worn around the edges and lips that had thinned with age was an unusual experience for me, especially when the owner of those eyes and lips felt alpha in a way completely at odds with the fact that she was human.

"Bryn." She said my name like she'd been expecting me, like everything up until this point had been her way of luring me in.

"Hello." I didn't give her more than I had to, and I watched her face for some clue as to what was going on inside her head. "You're Caroline's mother."

She smiled, and for a moment, it was easy to picture her as one of those PTA soccer moms.

"Please," she said. "Call me Valerie."

The expression in her eyes never changed, but I felt it the moment she reached out to my mind, like a cube of ice sliding down the length of my spine. Her smile was gentle and warm, and just looking at her made me want to smile, too.

But I didn't.

Instead, I concentrated on the shiver that ran through my body and the sound of wolves breathing heavily in my head.

Lake and Devon and Chase.

Valerie's smile deepened. Her eyes glittered, and without another word, she moved aside, gesturing for me to step across the splintered threshold into the house.

She'd tried to get inside my head, to push me to trust her or fear her or whatever it was she'd had in store for my emotions, and she'd failed. She knew I wasn't really there to join them. I knew that she knew, just like I was fully cognizant of the likelihood that she would keep trying to find a way into my head. The two of us were dancing, playing chess.

I stepped across the threshold.

"I was wondering how long it would take you to come to me," Valerie said, her voice soft, comforting. "Bridget and Archer told me that you had an episode in town. It's only natural that you'd have questions about what you are. What *we* are."

The way she said the word might have made me feel like there really was a *we*, but for the unwavering certainty that I was already part of something bigger.

"I've done a pretty good job figuring things out for myself," I said. "Good enough that all three of your people ended up on the ground."

"You're a fighter." The edges of her lips tilted up in amusement. "No control. No forethought. Things go red around the edges, and you start cutting people down. It's hardly surprising."

"Because I was raised by werewolves?"

Valerie didn't as much as blink at the word. The other members of the coven might feel blind fury whenever the species came up, but she wasn't bothered by it.

Odd, considering that a werewolf had killed her husband.

"No, not because you were raised by werewolves, though I shudder to think of the effect that might have had on some with your natural proclivities." Valerie reached forward and brushed a strand of my hair out of my face, a gesture so maternal—and so familiar—that I felt like I'd been slapped. "Most psychics require practice to hone their craft. The more you practice, the stronger you become."

For a single, jarring second, I could feel her again, coming at me from all sides—pressure at my temples, the slightest hint of a suggestion: *confusion, loneliness, yearning.*

Yeah, right.

Valerie's eyes narrowed. "People with your particular gift tend to be a bit more . . . *feral* about things. Reining it in won't make you more powerful, but it will give you choices, about when and how your ability manifests itself."

My heart pounded in my ears, and when she stepped forward and took my chin in her hands, the only thing that kept me from going into fight-or-flight mode, from throwing her to the ground and giving in to the desire to *escape*, was the calming sound of other hearts, beating in other chests.

Chase's eyes.

Lake running in a blur of white-blonde fur.

Dev.

They pulled me back from the edge. I brought one hand to my hip, laying my fingers over the scars underneath my clothes and feeling the light scratches on the surface of my hands.

"You've known other Resilients?" I asked calmly.

After a long, considering moment, Valerie let go of my chin. "Resilients?"

"People like me."

"You sound surprised." She tilted her head to the side, and her voice went from honey sweet to ice sharp in a moment. "Surely you didn't think you were one of a kind?"

I couldn't keep myself from snorting out loud. One of a kind? Me? Any human who'd ever survived a werewolf attack major enough to trigger the Change was, by definition, Resilient. As it happened, I had an entire pack of them back at the Wayfarer. I had no illusions whatsoever about being unique.

Of course, no one outside our pack knew that the secret to making new werewolves was to choose your victims very carefully. Shay didn't know what separated the Changed Weres in my pack from the ones who'd been born that way, and he couldn't tell Valerie what he didn't know.

Advantage: us.

"As it so happens, there's a man in our coven who shares your gift," Valerie said.

I ingested that information, absorbed it, and kept my

surprise from showing on my face. I'd met other Resilients, but by the time I'd met them, they'd already been Changed. I'd never met a human like me. I'd never even considered that there had to be others.

"His name is Jed," Valerie continued. "He might be able to teach you a thing or two about control—that is, if you plan to stay?"

Of course I planned to stay. Just like I planned to learn everything I could about the coven, to choose my moment, and to use the tranq gun hiding in my boot to knock Valerie out long enough to put the rest of them through emotion detox.

"Will I be safe if I stay here?" I asked, knowing I might get more information out of what she didn't say than what she did.

"I don't make a practice of attacking my own kind, Bryn. We generally consider that type of thing to be a last resort."

Her eyes flickered to my right, and I followed her gaze and realized that Caroline was standing there, a shape in the shadows, her arms at her sides. This time, I felt more than a chill as Valerie pushed at my emotions.

Threat.

I'd always felt it in Caroline's presence. Valerie wanted me to feel it more. She wanted me to look at Caroline and think *last resort*. She wanted me to wonder who else Caroline had attacked at her mother's request.

Even as I fought back against Valerie's interference, I couldn't help noticing the icy calm on Caroline's face, the absolute readiness, the blackness that bled outward from her pupils as she stared at me, set her sights *on me*.

Lake and Chase and Dev. Pack.

Whatever entry Valerie had found into my subconscious, the others pushed her out, prowling the halls of my mind like creatures on the hunt.

"I'm staying," I said.

Valerie smiled. "I was hoping you would." She glanced toward the shadows and lifted one eyebrow. "Caroline will show you to your room."

Caroline moved silently, each step measured, not a single hair falling out of place. She walked past me, and I saw a glint of metal as the lamplight caught the blade concealed in her left hand just so.

Lake.

Devon.

Chase.

I could do this. I *would* do this.

As Caroline and I began to climb up the battered staircase, Valerie's voice drowned out the sound of creaking wood. "Sleep well, Bryn."

I think everyone in the room—and those guarding my mind—knew that Valerie meant the words as a threat.

CHAPTER NINETEEN

THE SUN DIDN'T RISE UNTIL SEVEN THIRTY, SO I had hours to kill, ensconced in a faded denim comforter and all too aware that the moment I went to sleep, my Keep the Psychics Out of My Head plan would be tested to the limit. There was a part of me—a sizable one—that wanted nothing more than to keep my eyes and ears open and my back to a wall, which was probably Valerie's intention all along. She wanted me tired, off my game, and out of it enough that I'd stop resisting her assaults on my emotions.

She wanted me scared.

I closed my eyes and allowed my breathing to slow. Sleeping in their house—if I could manage it—would be like staring another alpha straight in the eyes.

I'm not scared of you, I thought as the rest of my mind went blank. *You have no power over me.*

For the longest time, I didn't dream. I just lay there, my body relaxed, my senses perfectly attuned to the world around me, and then a dam broke somewhere in my mind, and in a rush of color and sound, I was gone.

Back in the forest, dressed from head to toe in white, I waited. One by one, my friends came out from behind mounds of snow and tree trunks the color of black cherries, the pads of their paws skating lightly over the frozen ground.

Lake and Devon and Chase.

Anyone else would have gone stiff with terror the moment they saw the three of them, teeth gleaming in the moonlight. I knelt on the ground and waited, unable to shake the feeling that someone else was supposed to be here.

Someone or something was missing. It took me a moment to realize what—*who*—I was looking for: the wolf from my other dreams, the one I could never quite catch.

She wasn't there.

The world around me flickered, like someone was trying to change the channel on an old-fashioned TV. Within the span of a single heartbeat, I was surrounded on all sides by muscles and fur. They kept their backs to me and their eyes forward. My lip curled, baring my useless human teeth.

Archer's trying to get in, and he can't, I thought, buoyed by that realization. Still, I turned—wary, ready—taking in a three-sixty view of the forest.

Silence.

Pressure built at my temples. Sweat rose on the surface of my skin. I held my position, and as my friends circled around me, their wolf eyes scanned the darkness for signs of life.

Bryn. Bryn. Bryn.

My guards held the perimeter, my name a constant hum in their animal minds.

Somewhere in the distance, I heard a wolf—*the* wolf—howling, and the sound resonated with me, blood and bones and bittersweet longing. Just when I thought I couldn't take it any longer, I woke up.

"Good morning."

The words took me by surprise, but I had enough presence of mind not to go for my knife. Years of dealing with frustratingly stealthy werewolves had equipped me with an excellent poker face, and I refused to let a human—particularly this human—know that he'd gotten the drop on me.

"Anyone ever told you that watching a girl sleep is pretty much the textbook definition of creepy?"

Archer inclined his head slightly, acknowledging the point. "You were blocking me. I was curious. Shoot me."

"That an invitation?"

Channeling Lake was second nature, and I felt a snuff of agreement in my head. Both Lake and her wolf approved of the threat, though her wolf half would have preferred if I'd delivered the threat while digging my fingernails into the fleshy part of the intruder's throat.

"Don't be ridiculous," Archer replied, completely unbothered. "If any teenage girl is going to put a bullet in me, it's going to be Caroline when Valerie finds out that all I got out of your dreams last night was two smells and a sound."

He waited for me to ask him to elaborate, but I didn't.

"Wet dog, pine needles, and howling." He shrugged, but his eyes went cold, and he clenched his jaw. "Werewolves."

I snorted. "You're scared of Caroline. You hate werewolves. Your pupils are on steroids. Shocking." I paused, letting my words sink in. "You do realize that those emotions aren't really yours, right? That Valerie's messing with you?"

Archer's pupils spread outward, blocking the color of his eyes altogether. Just like that, it was as if the words I'd spoken were completely uninteresting, like my warning that Valerie was messing with his mind was the most boring thing he'd ever heard. Ignoring me, Archer reached for his back pocket. As a matter of reflex, I went for my knife and wrapped my fingertips around its hilt, but instead of pulling out a weapon, he brandished a piece of charcoal and turned to the wall.

I watched as he began to draw, and after a moment, I let go of the knife. Based on the size of his pupils, I was going to go out on a limb and guess that Valerie had programmed him to disregard anything she didn't want him to hear, and I forced myself to remember that the man who'd infiltrated my dreams, stalked me, hurt me, and called me a mutt-lover wasn't the real enemy here.

Archer was just a symptom. Valerie was the disease.

I'd come here to find out what I could about Shay's connection to the coven and to take Valerie out of commission long enough for the rest of the coven to clear their minds. I hadn't come here to fight Archer, make him bleed.

Just a taste? Lake asked plaintively. *Wouldn't hurt to show him that messing with you is about as far from a good idea as ideas get.*

Lurking in my mind, Devon wasn't as opposed to violence as he otherwise might have been, and Chase was even more bloodthirsty than Lake—which, as a general rule, was really saying something.

If he touches you, I will kill him.

Coming from Chase, the thought wasn't a threat as much as a statement of fact. If Archer was smart, if he had any common sense whatsoever, he wouldn't keep his back turned on a Were.

Human, I reminded myself. *You're human.*

"You're not one of them, little Bryn." Archer's tone was completely conversational. "Do you wish you were?"

I didn't reply, and he turned to face me, stepping aside so that I could see the image of a wolf staring back at me from his makeshift canvas. I recognized her instantly: larger than some, but not full grown, light fur giving way to darker markings around her face.

"I may not have gotten into your dreams this morning, kiddo, but I've been there before. You flashed back to a memory of the werewolf who raised you, and the marks he left on your body were suddenly larger than life. You ran with your pack, and then you dreamed about a female wolf—a wolf that forever hovers just out of reach. If I recall correctly, you've even dreamed that you're hollow inside. I'm not Freud, but I'd say that has some pretty disturbing implications, wouldn't you?"

Apparently, keeping Archer out of my head was no protection against more mundane mind games. Even though I knew he was trying to get to me, I couldn't help staring at the image on the wall and wondering if he was right.

"Admit it, little Bryn—they've done a real number on you. Not a werewolf, barely human. They took you and they raised you and they used you. You're just a kid, and you never even had a chance."

I wasn't entirely sure how to reply. *Blow me* and *screw you* both seemed like strong contenders, but the peanut gallery in my head appeared to be favoring castration.

To his credit, Archer seemed to sense that it was time to retreat. "Breakfast's downstairs in five, wolf girl."

This time, I couldn't help hearing the words *wolf girl* a little differently, but I pushed the thought out of my head and concentrated on the business at hand. If Archer was Valerie's version of a wake-up call, it was probably safe to assume that breakfast was a thing to beware.

"Good morning." Valerie smiled. Needle-sharp pinpricks bombarded the base of my skull—but this time, Valerie's attempt to manipulate my emotions wasn't my biggest problem.

Gathered around the kitchen table were the handful of psychics I'd already met and several I hadn't. The old woman whose knack allowed her to influence animals was feeding part of her muffin to a snake. A pair of college-aged girls were engaged in some kind of staring contest, their eyes bloodshot and their irises ink black.

"Valerie, could I have a word with you? Alone?" I was tired of skirting the issue, tired of pretending that I'd come here to join the coven when both of us knew I'd come here to test my mettle against hers.

Valerie's smile broadened, cutting through the smattering of wrinkles near the edges of her lips. Her eyes zeroed in on mine, and I felt a stab of loneliness, confusion, rage—before the sound of snapping teeth and a guttural growl pushed her back out.

Sooner or later, she'd get tired of testing me, tired of losing. I needed to make my move before that happened.

"What would you like to talk about?" Valerie asked, moving around the kitchen table to pour herself some tea.

"Shay."

Her stride broke, just for a moment, and I knew I'd hit my target.

"Whatever you have to say to me you can say in front of everyone. We don't have secrets here, Bryn." Her tone sounded genuine, but her eyes were steely, merciless, hard. There were six other people at the dining room table and more coming into the room the longer I stood there, and in unison, their pupils surged.

The old woman whispered something, and her snake began writhing its way slowly toward me. The girls in the staring contest suddenly turned those fathomless black eyes on me.

"Was there something you wanted to say, Bryn?" Valerie sipped her tea.

There was a lot I wanted to say to her—once I managed to get her away from her little army of marionettes.

"Go ahead, Bryn. Say it."

There were too many eyes on me, too much power in this room. I felt trapped, and things began to go red around the edges. The instinct crept up on me, dark and sure, and for a second, it was more of a presence in my mind than Devon, Lake, or Chase.

Trapped. Trapped. Need to escape. Survi—

"Easy there." A strange hand clapped me on the shoulder, and without thinking, I grabbed the hand and the attached arm and moved to flip the owner onto the kitchen floor. To my surprise, the hand's owner ducked out of my grasp and took a step back, palms held up, facing me. "I come in peace."

His delivery of that line sounded so much like Devon that I almost smiled, and that cleared my mind enough that I was able to really look at him. My opponent was much older than I'd expected: sixty-five if he was a day, and though his eyes sparkled, I could see each one of those years literally carved into his skin.

He had more scars than anyone I'd ever seen.

"I'm never quite myself before my morning walk," he told me. "I'm sensing maybe you're not much of a morning person, either. Care to join me?"

It was on the tip of my tongue to say no, but annoyance flashed across Valerie's face the moment the man extended the invitation, and that made me reconsider.

"Maybe that's a good idea," I said.

"Maybe it's not." Caroline stepped out from the shadows and made her presence known. I wasn't the only one who turned to track her progression into the room. In fact, the only two people who didn't react that way were Valerie, whose eyes were locked on mine, and the old man, whose weathered face softened the moment Caroline appeared.

"Rule nineteen, Caro," he said, his voice gruff. "And for that matter, twelve."

I got the feeling that unlike the facetious "Bryn Rules" my friends like to reference, Caroline and the old man really did have a numbered list.

"Rule seven," the girl in question countered.

The man rolled his eyes. "Fifty-three."

That, apparently, was something Caroline couldn't argue with, and my companion turned his attention back to Caroline's mother. "Don't worry, Val," he said, brown eyes shining against white-scarred skin. "I'll bring our little visitor back. Scout's honor."

With those words, he put his hand on my shoulder again and guided me to the door. This time, I didn't resist—not because of the way he'd handled Valerie and Caroline, but because the moment he touched me, I felt a familiar sensation, like I knew him.

Like we were the *same*.

He's Resilient, Chase whispered from his place in my mind. *Like you. Like me.*

Like us.

I tried to remember what Valerie had told me the day before, but all I could remember was the man's name—Jed.

The two of us walked in silence, each taking the other's measure. Once we were out of earshot of the house, Jed spoke. "Came close to flashing out in there, didn't you?"

"Flashing out?"

He strung his thumbs through his belt loops and kept walking. "It's what happens when people like us get backed into a corner. Smart girl like you must realize that woman was backing you into one on purpose."

I knew other Resilients. The majority of our pack was Resilient. But this was the first time I'd met another human whose gift was being scrappy and stubborn and coming out unscathed when other people would be dead.

"I wasn't going to lose it," I told him.

The man grunted.

"I'm better at keeping my head than people give me credit for."

He grunted again. "I shouldn't have grabbed you, but she was pushing the others, and if you'd flashed out, they would have attacked."

"She doesn't want me dead—not if there's a chance she could turn me into one of her little sock puppets instead."

My use of the phrase *sock puppet* seemed to throw Jed for a loop, but only for a moment. "If Val can't get inside your head, she won't have any other use for you. Lucky for you, woman's not the type to accept defeat. She's been trying to get in my head going on eleven years now. Most of the time, I shake her off. Doesn't put her in the best mood, but as long as I keep my mouth shut about it, 'bout what she's doing to everyone else, she lets me be."

As I processed Jed's words, I realized that I was talking to the one person in the entire coven who was able to insulate his emotions from Valerie's influence. From that, I concluded two things: first, that even without the others in my head, I might be able to do the same; and second, if I wanted to figure out what was really going on in this coven, my current companion would be a good place to start.

"Eleven years—is that how long you've been with the coven?"

Jed shook his head. "That's how long *she's* been with the

coven. She showed up on our doorstep, same way you did, with a little blonde moppet in tow. Cutest kid you'd ever seen—real solemn, except when Valerie wanted her otherwise. Two months after the two of them showed up, Valerie married Wes."

"Wes?"

"He was a good kid," Jed said. "Great leader. I'd been with him since he was seventeen. He was the one who talked me into finding others like us. He found them, saved them, made them family."

Your coven has lost someone. You must have loved whoever it was very much. The words Ali had used to spur the psychics into showing their hand echoed in my mind.

"He's the one who got killed by a werewolf?" I said. Doing the math, I hit a snag. "He wasn't Caroline's father?"

"Not by blood."

That shouldn't have surprised me. I knew better than anyone that blood wasn't what made people family.

"Valerie was with us three years when Wes died. By that time, it seemed natural to most folks that she'd be the one to take over."

"Most folks," I repeated. "But not you."

He shrugged. "Never wanted to lead much myself. Filling Wes's shoes would have been tough on anyone, but Valerie took to it." He paused. "I always thought she took to it a little too well."

It was on the tip of my tongue to ask him why he'd stayed.

It couldn't have been easy, watching Valerie work her way into everyone else's emotions, making them feel what she wanted them to feel—about her, about their former leader's death, about Caroline. But before I could even ask the question, I had my answer, because in the brief exchange I'd seen between Jed and Valerie's daughter, there'd been shades of Callum and me.

Everything I've done, I've done for you.

Now was not the time to get caught up in memories—not with company in my head and a slew of questions Jed might be willing and able to answer.

"Valerie had Caroline give me an ultimatum—either I hand over a Were under my protection, or your coven is going to attack my pack." I measured Jed's response. Nothing I said surprised him, but his jaw tightened when I mentioned Caroline, scars jumping to life on his face as the muscles underneath them tensed. I pushed harder, further, testing my intuition that Jed's weakness, the whole reason he'd stayed with the coven, was the girl. "How do you think Caroline is going to feel if her mother uses her to murder a bunch of little kids?"

Jed reached out, lightning quick, and grabbed my arm, his fingernails digging into my flesh and sending my pack-mates into a defensive roar in my head.

"I know what's at stake here," Jed said, his voice surprisingly quiet given his viselike grip on my arm. "Know it better than you, so if you've got questions, ask them, but don't play with me, Bryn."

He had one of those tones—one that said that I was a kid and he wasn't and he'd been waging wars since before I was ever born.

"Fine," I said. "Question: why does the coven care so much about getting Lucas back? What's he to Valerie?"

Jed let go of my arm. "I'm no expert on the workings of that woman's mind, but if I were a betting man, I'd say that odds are that one teenage werewolf is not what she's after. She's just using him to get the others all riled up, same as she'll use you."

It had occurred to me that Valerie might not want Lucas—that she might want me—but I'd never thought, even for a second, that maybe neither one of us was the point. That if I met Valerie's ultimatum, she might find something else to demand, some other reason to set her coven against my pack.

"If I gave Lucas back, she'd just find another excuse to fight us."

"That a question?" Jed asked, looking amused.

I crossed my arms over my chest. "Should it be?"

He grunted.

"I'll take that as a no."

The realization was strangely liberating. I'd spent all this time thinking that I had to choose between my own pack's safety and sending an innocent to be tortured by people who blindly hated his guts, when in reality, there'd never been a choice.

On the downside, that meant we had no safety net, no backup plan, no options.

Ask him if he knows anything about the deal, Chase suggested quietly. He, Lake, and Dev had been so quiet that I'd almost forgotten they were there.

"Lucas said that Valerie made some kind of deal with his alpha," I said, searching Jed's features for some kind of reaction. "Shay gave Lucas to Valerie. Any idea what he asked for in return?"

"Well, I don't know," Jed replied facetiously. "This Shay guy got any reason to want anyone in your pack dead?"

I could practically feel the blood drain out of my face. Shay had reason to want anyone who stood between him and the Changed females dead—including, but not limited to, *me*.

"Thought so." Jed ran a scarred hand roughly over his neck. "Going after your pack is a risk, and Valerie's not in the habit of risking something for nothing. The question you should be asking isn't what Shay wanted Valerie to do—it's why she's doing it."

My mind was reeling. Shay sent Lucas to the coven. They tortured him. Lucas escaped and came running straight to me. Shay had to have known that Lucas would go for help— maybe he'd even asked the coven to let him escape conveniently close to my territory so that I would be the obvious choice. Then, when Valerie came after our pack, she could use Lucas as an excuse—a focal point for her coven, an excuse to keep me from figuring everything out.

From the outside, it would appear that the coven had their

own reasons for fighting us—reasons that weren't Senate business in the least.

Somewhere, in Snake Bend territory, the Snake Bend alpha was sitting back on his haunches and watching a group of psychics fight the battles that Senate law wouldn't let him fight. Shay couldn't challenge me. He couldn't fight me, and he couldn't take what was mine, but technically, he wasn't.

He was letting someone else do the dirty work for him.

Why would Valerie agree to something like that? What could Shay have possibly offered her to justify the risk? And more importantly, now that I knew that giving Lucas back wouldn't change our situation, what exactly could I do to stop this from turning into an all-out war?

"If we take Valerie out," I said, disturbed by how easy it was for me to ask the question, "does everyone else go back to normal?"

"You a killer?" There was no condemnation in my companion's voice, and I got the distinct feeling that if he'd gotten any of his scars fighting, his opponents probably hadn't lived long enough to scar.

"No," I said. "I'm not a killer, but I do have a tranq gun, and we could keep her unconscious for a good, long time."

"Val uses her own daughter to keep the others in line. She's convinced the entire coven that Caro is a remorseless, soulless killer. Kid even believes it herself. If undoing that were as easy as knocking Val out, I would have done it myself, years ago." Jed stared me straight in the eye. "Doesn't matter if she's unconscious. There's a part of her mind that doesn't sleep, and once a suggestion is implanted, it's in there good. Killing her might work, but it also might not."

He watched me, waiting for some indication of whether or not I was up to the task. Whether I could kill just because it *might* break Valerie's spell.

I had a knife.

I had the training.

We have a problem. Dev's voice broke into my thoughts, sparing me from answering the question. *You need to come home, Bryn. Now.*

"I have to go," I said, and Jed nodded, like that answered that.

"Go on, then," he said. "But don't be surprised if Valerie moves up her little game. You came here, to her house. She's likely to answer in kind."

I would have liked to ask Jed other things—what sort of knacks the other members of the coven had, how many of them there were, what we could do to defend ourselves—but I didn't get the chance, because whatever the problem back at the Wayfarer was, it was a big one.

Lake, Devon, and Chase pulled out of my head at once.

CHAPTER TWENTY

I MADE IT TO THE EDGE OF THE PSYCHICS' PROPERTY, running at a solid and furious pace, my skull pounding with the sudden withdrawal of my guard. I could still sense them— Lake and Devon were at the Wayfarer; Chase was on his way here; and all three of them were on edge, like someone had shot a flare directly into the heart of our pack, but the two-way street that I'd opened for them was closed.

Something had snapped them out of my mind and back into their own.

Someone want to tell me what's going on? I made it to the road and sent the question out to anyone who might feel compelled to listen.

Chase answered my call. *Four peripherals, Bryn. At the Wayfarer.*

Through the bond, I could feel Chase getting closer, moving faster, and I realized—belatedly—that Lake had loaned him her truck.

"Peripherals." I said the word out loud and let the ramifications wash over me. I ran harder, faster, every inch the alpha determined to get back to her pack. The road was deserted, the morning sky giving way to what looked to be another gray afternoon. My limbs were human-heavy, my pace too slow.

I needed to be there. With them. Now.

Forcing myself to calm down, I kept my eye on the road and tried to focus on logic over instinct. There were peripherals at the Wayfarer, and they'd arrived unannounced. When the Wayfarer had been at the edges of Callum's territory, that might not have been nearly as much of an insult, but it was the *center* of ours—our base of operations, our home—and four peripherals coming this far into our territory without permission was on par with an act of war.

Whose peripherals are they? I sent the question to Chase, possibilities dogging me at every step. Maybe Callum had broken his hands-off policy and sent me backup. Maybe Shay had gotten tired of waiting for the psychics to do his dirty work and had launched another attack.

Maybe—

I heard the truck before I saw it. Chase slammed on the brakes and threw open the door. "Ours."

He didn't bother repeating the question, didn't say more than that one word, but it was enough to make my entire body relax. Shay wasn't attacking. Callum hadn't foreseen some fuzzy future I couldn't combat without him. The members of our pack who lived at the border of our territory—the ones Chase visited when he was running patrol—had simply come home.

"All four?" I asked.

"Jackson, Eric, Phoebe, and Sage." The way Chase said their names told me something I hadn't realized before—that the peripherals weren't peripheral to him. They were the loners, the outsiders, the ones who could keep their distance and survive.

They were what Chase would have been if it hadn't been for me.

"Are they okay?" I asked.

Chase shrugged. "They're not bleeding."

"But...," I prompted.

"But they need their alpha." Chase waited for me to get in the car, then turned it around and accelerated. "Jackson and Sage haven't said a word since they got here. Phoebe was still in wolf form when I left."

"And Eric?" I asked. He was the oldest of the peripherals, a college freshman who'd been attacked by the Rabid when he was thirteen.

"Eric said that the Snake Bend Pack is closing in."

Our territory was adjacent to three others. One was Callum's. One was Shay's. The third was irrelevant—at least for the moment.

As I got closer and closer to the Wayfarer, it was all I could do to keep from extracting the information from the peripherals' brains with all the finesse of a person attempting to rip a phone book right down the center. The only thing on the surface of their minds was a mixture of sensations and emotion—confusion, adrenaline, hunt-lust, fear.

No details.

No explanations.

Devon met me at the door to the restaurant. Behind him, I could see Eric, lanky and in need of a shave. Phoebe lay in wolf form in the corner, her head on her paws, and Jackson and Sage both took a step toward me, my presence washing over them like a wave across the sand.

Alpha. Alpha. Alpha.

I was there. They were safe. We'd get through this.

The part of me that had been lying dormant since I invited my friends into my head—the alpha part—began to rise inside of me like smoke. Beside me, Dev ran one hand through his freshly trimmed hair and gave me a small smile, one that told me he understood—and reminded me that in order for me to be fully alpha, he'd had to willingly step back into his role as number two.

"It's okay," Dev told me, reading me, the way he always had. "You let us in. You let us protect you. You, Bronwyn Alessia St. Vincent Clare, actually admitted that you needed help, and I think we all know that's a minor miracle in and of itself." He cleared his throat. "And now it appears as though someone else needs your help."

Eric stepped forward. He was tall, though not as tall as Devon, and had not gotten a haircut the entire time I'd known him. I hadn't seen him in months, but he still smelled like Cedar Ridge: like pine needles and fresh snow, like *us*.

Eric bowed his head as he approached me, an instinctive gesture that made me reach out and place my fingers underneath his chin and bring his eyes back up to meet mine.

"Welcome home," I said.

He closed his eyes, breathing in deeply. As loud as it must have been for him here, as disconcerting, I recognized that on some level, it was also a relief.

"Two days ago, I was coming back from a dorm party," he said, taking his time with the words. "And I felt something—like the world was turning itself inside out, like everything was wrong. I thought maybe I'd had too much to"—Eric cast his eyes around, looking for Ali or Mitch—"drink, but then I smelled it—sour and sweaty, like vinegar, only stronger."

Eric's upper lip curled as he spoke. Peripheral or not, he still had the same reaction to the scent of a foreign pack. "I tracked it back to the border between our territory and Snake Bend, and there they were."

"How many?" I asked.

"At least fifteen men," Eric replied, his hair falling into his face. "Older than me. A *lot* older, I'd guess. They claimed not to have crossed over to our side of the border, but there were so many of them, the scent was so thick—I couldn't tell for sure whether that was a lie."

Maybe it was. Maybe it wasn't. Either way, it didn't take a rocket scientist to figure out that if Shay had fifteen full-grown Weres camped out along our northwest border, they were there for a reason.

Biding their time.

I looked past Eric, toward the others. Phoebe lived a good hundred miles north of Eric; Jackson and Sage lived farther south.

"Was it the same for you?" I asked them.

Phoebe inclined her head, then Shifted out of wolf form, the cracking of her bones providing a sound track to Jackson's answer. "There were more than fifteen where I am," he said. "Twenty, at least, spread all up and down the border."

Sage just nodded, and for a moment, I saw things through her eyes, saw the men standing a hundred yards away from her, tracking her progression with hungry, lupine eyes.

I swore. Vehemently. And so loudly that Eric actually blushed.

Technically, Shay wasn't breaking Pack Law. He couldn't invade my territory without explicit permission to do so, but there was nothing to stop him from playing the intimidation card. From lining his troops up along our borders. From letting them make my wolves feel like they weren't safe.

"He wants us to know that if we fight him, he'll win."

Devon's voice was sharp enough to maim, and there was no question in my mind whose blood he wanted—just like there was no question that someday Dev would go alpha. "He's playing with you, Bryn."

My fingers worked their way into a fist, my fingernails digging into the skin of my palms. "Like he was playing with us when he made a deal with Valerie to have her coven attack us on his behalf? Like he was *playing* when he let them cut and tear and burn Lucas into ribbons and ash, for no reason other than needing a victim to bait me into a confrontation?"

"If it's any consolation," Devon said, his voice low and comforting, "I'm going to kill him."

"Dev—"

"Maybe not today. Maybe not this year. But five years from now, or ten, or fifty, or however long it takes for me to do it right, Shay is going to die. Maybe it will be long and brutal. Maybe it will be short and sweet. Maybe I'll hate myself for it, or maybe I'll enjoy it, but I *will* kill him for doing this to you. To them."

I wondered what it said about my life that I could listen to my best friend calmly discussing dispatching his brother to the great beyond, without having any emotional reaction other than an acknowledgment, deep in my gut, of the fact that Dev could do it, would do it, was probably *meant* to do it.

According to Pack Law, if Devon killed Shay, he'd be the alpha of the Snake Bend Pack. He'd have to transfer packs first, and Shay would have to accept him, but given Shay's ego and what Devon meant to me, Shay would probably allow it. For a moment, I almost felt like Callum, looking over the years to come and seeing the likelihood play out, right before my eyes.

Someday I would lose Devon.

Someday Dev would kill Shay.

Right now, however, thinking that far ahead was a luxury I couldn't afford. The coven had us in their sights, and Jed's warning that Valerie would repay my visit to her house in kind meant that I needed to be prepared for some sort of attack. Not five days later. Not after the deadline had passed.

Now.

Worse, if Shay wanted what I had badly enough to make deals with humans, I wasn't entirely certain that Senate Law and the threat of Callum's reprisal would be enough to keep him—and his men—on their side of our invisible line.

The phone rang, jarring me out of my thoughts and sending my heart pounding. Keely answered it, then turned toward me.

"It's for you," she said, holding the phone out across the bar. "It's Shay."

"I sent you an email."

Of all of the things Shay could have opened with, that wasn't one I'd expected at all.

"Does this email happen to explain why the entirety of the Snake Bend Pack is playing peekaboo across the border to my territory?"

Shay laughed, and it was a horrible, genial sound that made me want to put a fist through his trachea and pull out his spine. "I know you're new at this," he said, condescension and sly, understated viciousness fighting for control of his every word, "but there is a simple explanation for this kind of thing."

He paused, and I pushed back the urge to bang the receiver into the wall over and over again until there was nothing left of either one of them.

"My pack goes where I go—within my own territory, of course. We've been in our current stronghold a long time, and quite frankly, I've been considering a move. To decrease the chance of exposure, of course."

"Of course," I replied dully. Shay's picking up and moving his entire pack to the border between our territories could not possibly bode well for us, but there was no law against it.

He's doing this by the book, I thought. I wasn't sure whether the realization was comforting or not. The Senate wouldn't be fond of the idea of an alpha aligning himself with a coven, but it wouldn't give Callum the kind of justification he'd need to take Shay out of the picture *without* declaring himself the alpha of the entire North American continent. There was nothing in Pack Law to say that Shay couldn't abuse his own subordinates, nothing to say he couldn't bat me around like a cat with a mouse. But there was a law that said that Shay couldn't step a foot on my territory without asking permission, and just like that, I knew why he'd called.

"Do you actually think I'm going to agree to let you and the little foot soldiers you've got peppered up and down my border cross over into Cedar Ridge territory?"

He had to be actually, clinically insane.

"Of course not," Shay replied smoothly. "If you read the email I sent, you'll see that I only requested passage for myself and one guard to assess the situation with the Snake Bend wolf you're currently holding at your compound."

He made it sound like I was keeping Lucas hostage.

"I think you'll find that the other alphas consider my request to be quite reasonable. A few of them may have even chimed in to say as much. You've had the boy for days. Whatever justice you were going to impart on the trespassing matter should have been carried out immediately. *Indecision*," he said, savoring the word, "is a sign of weakness."

"Cut the crap, Shay," I said, only I didn't use the word *crap*, and I didn't call him Shay. There were so many other names that seemed more appropriate. "You don't want Lucas."

I could practically hear him smiling on the other end of the line. "Do you?"

He'd backed me into a corner, and now he was dangling a carrot just out of reach. I recognized the tactic. There was only one person at the top of a werewolf pack—good cop, bad cop all rolled into one.

"Are you saying you'd consider cutting ties with Lucas?" I couldn't keep myself from asking the question. Before I'd gotten bogged down in psychics and conspiracies, getting Shay to relinquish his claim on Lucas had been the goal. I hadn't been within a hundred yards of Lucas for almost forty-eight hours, but I could still see him kneeling on that bed, baring his scars.

I could hear him telling me that if I couldn't help him, he wanted to die.

"I'm willing to entertain the idea," Shay replied, "if you'll give me a little something in return."

"I'm not giving you any of my wolves."

"Pity," Shay said. "I do think the boy actually believed you could save him, that you *cared*."

I didn't rise to the bait, but knowing he was doing it on purpose didn't take the sting out of his words. I wanted to help Lucas, and I couldn't. If a loophole existed, I hadn't found it.

I'd *lost*.

"I also hear you've got yourself into a sticky situation with a coven of psychics." Shay reverted back to bad-cop form. "If you could be persuaded to part with one or two of your little ones, I might be able to help you with that, too."

"The answer is no."

"No, you won't consider my offer, or no, you really don't care about the safety and longevity of your pack?"

I hated Shay—hated him more than I'd thought I could hate anyone.

"I will not, under any circumstances, give you any of my wolves." My voice echoed with more than my sixteen years of experience, and I wondered if this was what it felt like to issue a decree as an alpha, the kind of promise I couldn't have broken even if I'd wanted to.

"Well, if you're not open to the idea of a trade, perhaps you'd prefer a wager?"

I would have preferred Shay be abducted by aliens and vaporized at the molecular level—but if Shay was telling the truth, if the other alphas were backing his request for entry into my territory, I couldn't imagine that they'd react well to my holding Lucas much longer.

Across the room, Chase met my eyes, and I didn't need the pack-bond to know what he was thinking.

Sometimes, at the end of the day, you had to take care of yourself.

"No wager?" Shay said, and I tore my eyes away from Chase's. "In that case, bring Lucas to the border—unless you'd prefer to give me your permission to come collect him myself. There's a thing or two I'd like to say to the boy, and I believe the psychics want a word as well."

While Shay blathered on, I used the bond to ask Devon to

check my email. Dev confirmed everything Shay had told me and informed me that in the time that Shay and I had been talking, another alpha had replied, asking that I either permit Shay access to my territory or send Lucas back to Shay.

That might not have sucker punched me the way it did but for the fact that the alpha was Callum.

Time was running out. I had to make a decision, but the only thing I could think about was Callum, teaching me how to throw a knife. Callum, running a hand over my hair. Callum, trading away a portion of his territory to save Marcus, who hadn't deserved it.

I knew then that I couldn't do the safe thing. I couldn't hang Lucas out to dry, not if there was a chance—even a small one—that I could save him without endangering the rest of my pack.

I knew what Callum would do, and I had to try.

"Shay, you, and only you, have permission to come into my territory for exactly three hours." The moment the words were out of my mouth, I could feel Devon on the other side of the bond, sending an email to the other alphas that said the same thing.

The email was time-stamped. The clock was ticking.

"Am I coming to retrieve my wolf, or am I coming to play you for him?"

I wasn't sure of the answer to that question, so I responded by hanging up the phone. If Shay was as close to the border as he'd claimed, he'd be here in a little over an hour, and I needed time to assess the situation.

To decide.

What do you expect me to do? I knew things were dire when I started having pretend conversations with Callum in my head. *You sent that email. I did what you wanted me to do, what you would have done. What now?*

There was no answer—not from pretend Callum, and not from anyone else. As I sat there, the countdown already under way, I was sure of only one thing.

If Shay and I wagered anything—and that was a big if—it would be on my terms. Not his.

CHAPTER TWENTY-ONE

I STOOD WITH MY BACK AGAINST THE POOL TABLE, one ankle crossed in front of the other, waiting. The restaurant was eerily quiet, and as I felt Shay drawing nearer, twin urges—one to shudder and one to growl—fought for dominance in my mind. All around me, my backup seemed to be fighting the same battle, but they faded into the woodwork, letting me take the lead.

Before we could fight as a team, I had to meet Shay one-on-one, alpha to alpha.

Foreign. Wolf.

Threat.

I was familiar enough with Shay's type to know that he wanted me to feel him coming. He wanted me to feel his presence washing over my body like thick, syrupy oil. He wanted me to shudder, to growl, to make one wrong move after another after another.

Shay wanted the advantage. Considering that we were on *my* land, surrounded by *my* wolves, that wasn't going to happen. Shay could puff up his chest and leak pheromones until the cows came home, and I still wasn't going to respond like he was a threat—even though all my instincts were telling me that he was. I wouldn't let him get a rise out of me, wouldn't let him see me scared. No shuddering. No growling. As the door to the Wayfarer opened, I didn't bat an eye. I didn't straighten to my full height. I just stayed there, leaning against the pool table, using the knife in my right hand to clean the fingernails on my left.

"You look well."

Judging by Shay's words, you would have thought the two of us were old friends, but I suspected that he meant them more as a complaint than anything else. For a fragile little human lotus blossom, I had an annoying habit of coming out of things unscathed. Shay probably would have preferred to see me in pieces.

Glancing down at my fingernails, I took my time responding to his greeting. "It took you an hour and fifteen minutes to get here. Presumably, it will take you an hour and fifteen minutes to go back where you came from, which means that the permission I granted you to be here expires in half an hour."

I wasn't going to let him get a rise out of me, but I didn't have to sit there and exchange niceties, either.

"Very well," Shay replied, strolling through the room like he owned the place. "This shouldn't take long."

I ran my fingertips over the worn felt of the pool table and met his eyes as if they held no more significance to me than a speck on the wind. He returned my stare, his face as blank as mine.

Alpha. Alpha. Alpha.

The familiar call of my pack took on a different tone in my head. I was alpha, Shay was alpha, and there was a subtle suggestion in the air all around us, a whisper in my ear, telling me that there was only ever meant to be one. Werewolves weren't meant for politics. Shay and I weren't meant to be exchanging *words*.

"I appreciate your hospitality."

My only clue that Shay was feeling the undercurrent, same as I was, was the way that even as he was coating his words with sugar, his chest rose and fell at a quicker pace. It was all too easy to imagine him in wolf form, breathing jaggedly over my corpse.

Alpha. Alpha. Alpha.

Shay brought his gaze to meet mine. I felt him let go of his hold on the instinct to dominate, and I let go of mine.

I imagined my eyes boring twin holes in Shay's body. I stared at him, and I smiled, because from the moment he'd engaged in this little staring contest, there was a way in which he'd already lost. Every second I held Shay's gaze, every moment that I was able to stare back at him—the way very few werewolves probably ever had—was an insult.

I was human. I was a girl, and I was mocking him.

"How do you like that?" Devon said.

Shay turned toward the sound of his brother's voice, and a rush of adrenaline flooded my body like water bursting through the holes in a dam.

Shay had looked away first.

Logically, I knew he'd been distracted, but no amount of logic could override the bodily sensation that I'd won something, that I was *more*. At the very least, I hadn't lost—and even a draw felt like a win against a werewolf as powerful as Shay.

With a glint in his eyes, Shay took a step toward Devon, each of them a distorted reflection of the other. Dev was a fraction taller. Shay was broader through the shoulders. They had the same cheekbones, the same jaw, but while Devon's features were in constant flux and motion, Shay's face had an unnatural stillness to it, like he was incapable of smiling or frowning or displaying real human emotion of any kind.

"How do I like what?" Shay asked in a tone that would have been more appropriate for talking to a toddler. He was wasting his breath. Dev was the only werewolf in existence with a fondness for the Metropolitan Ballet—he'd been immune to all forms of mockery for years.

"Knowing that you looked away first," Devon clarified with a pointed grin. "How do you like *that*?"

Shay didn't answer Devon. Instead, he turned slowly back to me, and though I could sense an animal rage building inside him, his tone never changed.

"Are you sure you wouldn't reconsider a trade?"

I didn't catch Shay's exact meaning until he elaborated.

"You keep the runt. I'll take my brother."

Devon? Shay wanted Devon?

I hadn't been expecting that. To my left, Devon managed to force his features into a mildly bemused expression, but not before I saw the flicker of hunger and violence cross his face.

If I sent Devon with Shay, there was no way things would end without bloodshed. As much as I wanted to believe that Devon could take his brother, I wasn't sure of it. I had doubts, and I told myself that was the reason I was going to say no.

It had nothing to do with the fact that sending Devon with Shay would mean losing him. It had nothing to do with the way that losing Dev would feel like cutting off a part of my soul.

"No."

"No trade?" Shay repeated. "Pity. A wager, then? Or should Lucas and I just be on our way?"

He said Lucas's name in a cold and careless way, and I tried not to think of the bruises, the scars, the haunted eyes too timid to look me straight in mine.

"What kind of wager did you have in mind?" I asked evenly.

Shay met my eyes. "Before we talk wagers, show me the boy. I assume you're keeping him close by? He's a bit of a runner and more than a bit of a coward. I'd hate for you to wager something dear only to find out that the prize you were after had drowned himself like a kitten."

"He's close," I said, not wanting to call Lucas out, because I couldn't trust myself to look at his face the moment he saw Shay and still do what was best for my pack.

"Define 'close,'" Shay said, his tone demanding an answer I wasn't willing to give. The silence that stretched between us was charged, and I could feel the need to challenge him rising again.

"Here." The word came from the vicinity of the kitchen, where I'd told Lucas to wait, but he wasn't the one who said it. Maddy stalked into the dining room, looking like some kind of Valkyrie come to gather the souls of the dead. There were dark circles under her gray eyes, and her lips were swollen.

Freshly kissed.

"Lucas is here." Maddy's voice was quiet, but there was something regal about the set of her chin, and I knew, maybe even before she did, what she was going to say next. "If you let him stay here, I'll go with you."

Her words felt like lightning going off in my brain. She knew what she was saying. She knew what it would mean. She wasn't asking permission.

She was sure.

"No." I didn't raise my voice, but Maddy's pack-bond pulled her closer to me, forced her head down. "Not going to happen, Maddy."

"Making the decision for her, are you? And here I thought you weren't *that kind of alpha*." The emphasis Shay put on the phrase told me that he'd been watching us more closely than I'd realized.

"I'm whatever kind of alpha I need to be." Saying the words made them true, and suddenly, I knew that I could do whatever was necessary to protect my pack.

"Bring me the boy." Shay issued the words like an order, like he had a right to come here to my territory and demand anything. I moved forward, my steps slow and even, my hands loose by my sides. I walked up to him—right up to him—stood on my tiptoes, and blew in his face. It was a childish, human insult meant to emphasize that Shay was being insulted by just that: a human. A child.

For a moment, I thought he was going to hit me. I hoped that he would, because if Shay attacked me based on little more than an insult, my pack would be justified in fighting back. But instead of hitting me, Shay moved in a flash toward Maddy. Our entire pack flew into motion, but almost too late, I realized that Shay wasn't going after Maddy.

He was going after Lucas, who'd come to stand by Maddy's side, and there wasn't a thing I could do to stop him.

Shay caught the smaller boy roughly by the neck and pulled him out from behind Maddy. I knew the second before Maddy leapt for Shay that she'd lost it, but it was too late for me to pull her back through the bond. Luckily, Lake was close enough and fast enough that she was able to take Maddy down before she could lay a finger on Shay.

"Maddy. Madison. Mads." Lake had her pinned, but Maddy wouldn't stop struggling against her hold, writhing on the ground like someone was shooting electric shocks through her body with the voltage set to high. A sound like thunder and the cracking of wood brought my eyes back to Shay, just in time to see Lucas go down.

Standing over Lucas's prone body, Shay brought his eyes up to mine. I'd pushed him to the edge, hoping to goad him into attacking me, and instead, he'd turned on the only person here that he could, by Pack Law, beat to a broken, bloody pulp.

This is your fault, Shay's eyes told me. *The boy. The coven. The bloodshed.*

It was all for me, and for a split second, there was something in Shay's eyes that made me wonder if hatred was all he felt when he looked at my face.

"Bryn—" Lucas managed to choke out my name before Shay's foot connected solidly with his ribs, popping the bones like bubble wrap.

Shay was going to kill him. Right there, right in front of us, with Maddy watching and Lake holding her down.

"Touch him again, and I won't even think about your wager." My voice was so steady it surprised me, and I could hear a hint of Callum in my words. "Damaged goods."

Shay took a single step away from Lucas, but before he did, he leaned down and whispered something in the younger boy's ear. "Stay."

It was a direct command from Lucas's alpha—one he'd be physically unable to disobey.

"Now that that's taken care of, would the alpha of the Cedar Ridge Pack rather choose the game we're betting on or the stakes?" Shay asked, his pupils dilated with an appetite I recognized all too well.

Violence. He wanted to hurt me. He wanted to hurt all of us.

"The game or the stakes?" I repeated.

I shouldn't have been surprised that Shay had offered me a choice, but I was. He wanted to be able to say that this had been a fair wager, aboveboard, completely legitimate. He didn't want anyone to be able to say that he'd strong-armed me into doing this.

He wanted me complicit.

"Game or stakes," Shay confirmed. "One of us sets the stakes—that would be what we're betting and, specifically, what you're willing to lose if I win, since we've already established that my side of the bet is"—he waved his hand in Lucas's direction—"that."

He paused, just long enough for Maddy, still pinned to the ground, to start fighting against Lake's hold again. "Whoever doesn't set the stakes gets to choose the game on which we'll lay them."

I had only a few precious seconds to decide whether I'd rather choose the game we were betting on, or what I was willing to give Shay if I lost. It was a lose-lose situation. If I let Shay chose the game, he'd choose something I'd never have a chance of winning. If I let him choose the stakes, he could demand I put my entire pack up for grabs.

"If I choose the stakes, what's to stop me from betting a napkin?"

"Good point," Shay said. "Let's say that whatever you put up as your half of the wager has to be a person. A wolf for a wolf. If you set the stakes, you get to choose which wolf. If you choose the game we're betting on, the choice of prize is mine."

I wasn't sure whether he meant them to or not, but as Shay spoke, his eyes lingered on Lake's body, and a lump rose in my throat. For years, she'd been the only eligible female of the species in our entire world. Living under Callum's protection, she'd been safe. Off-limits. Forbidden.

When we'd discovered the Rabid's pack of Changed werewolves—seven girls among them, all of whom were now Cedar Ridge—I'd thought there might be safety in numbers, but Lake had been the ultimate prize for too long, and now she didn't have Callum to protect her.

All she had was me.

No, I thought, the word rising up from my gut. I couldn't do it. Not to Lake, not to Mitch, not to Callum and everything he'd raised me to be.

I'm sorry, Maddy, I said, sending the words to her across the bond, feeling her heart break like it was my own. I couldn't bring myself to look at Lucas, couldn't rid my mind of the sound of popping bones.

"Choose the game, Bryn." Lake said the words out loud, even though she could have passed them quietly from her mind to mine. She eased herself off Maddy's body and stood up.

She wanted Shay to know she wasn't afraid.

She was a liar.

She must have seen the refusal on my face, because she repeated the words she'd said out loud silently, for my ears only. *Choose the game, Bryn. Let him choose the stakes.*

I narrowed my eyes. *Lake, I'm not going to let him force me to bet* you.

Lake didn't even blink. *Sure you are. You're going to bet me, and you're going to bet on me, and we're going to win.*

I glanced from Lake to the pool table, from the table to Lucas, and from Lucas to Maddy, who had eyes only for him. The floor was smeared with blood.

I can do this, Bryn, Lake said. *I've done it a million times before with a million other Weres.*

Lake had been hustling pool since she was ten. I was pretty sure she hadn't lost since she was twelve.

I've never asked you for anything, Lake said, the intensity of her voice pushing out every other thought in my head. *Not since we were kids, and I'm asking you now, as your friend, as* Maddy's *friend, to let me do this.*

Without thinking about it, I glanced over at Dev, but there was no counsel in his eyes, only violence, anguish.

"Do we have a bet?" Shay asked, his own face an emotionless mask.

Lake caught my gaze and held it, and after a long moment, I nodded.

"Choose your stakes," I said roughly. "The game is pool."

CHAPTER TWENTY-TWO

LAKE DIDN'T SO MUCH AS LOOK AT SHAY AS SHE walked over to the pool table and chose her cue. She just ran her hands over the length of the wood and murmured something under her breath. I could see her lips moving but couldn't make out the words, and I wondered if she was talking to the cue, the way she sometimes did her guns, or if the words were just another part of the performance she was putting on for Shay's sake.

On Thanksgiving Day, I'd watched Lake teaching a bunch of twelve-year-olds how to hustle pool. She'd told them that the trick was to look completely helpless so your opponent would underestimate you. Now my friend's entire future was riding on her ability to put her money where her mouth was and practice what she preached.

Lake could do this. She could.

I wanted to believe it. I wanted to tell myself that Lake really was *that* good, and that I wouldn't have been any kind of friend at all if I'd kept her from trying, but I couldn't, because despite everything we'd been through together, despite what she and the others had done for me the night before, I couldn't shake the feeling building up inside me, the one that said that *I* was supposed to be protecting *her*.

"Take me instead." My voice was low and guttural—a foreign thing in my own throat.

"Excuse me?" Shay raised one eyebrow, and for a single second, he looked so much like Devon that it hurt to look at him.

"The game hasn't started yet. You can still change the stakes." I ignored the low rumble of the others inside my head.

I ignored Chase, who'd gone ashen beside me, the unreadable look on his face masking the flash of horror and denial I could feel through the bond.

"Are you suggesting that if I win, you'll abdicate the rule of your pack to your second-in-command and willingly transfer into mine?" Shay sounded vaguely amused. I thought of everything he could do to me, everything he *would* do to me, and then I nodded, unwilling to let myself feel even the smallest bit of fear.

Unwilling to let him smell it.

"That's exactly what I'm suggesting."

Devon could take care of the pack once I was gone, he could be their alpha, and I could put my life on the line to save Lake.

Shay's face hardened, amusement morphing into something darker. I recognized the emotion from places in my memory I didn't want to go. The blood, the screams, my human parents. The smell of mildew and bleach as I backed myself farther and farther under the kitchen sink. Even dead, the Rabid still haunted my dreams, and I *knew* that Shay wanted that. He wanted me to cower, wanted to wear my blood and taste my human screams.

"You think highly of yourself," he said, his eyes pulsing with bloodlust, and the muscles in his jaw tense with the effort it took to fight it back. "But at the end of the day, you're human. You're frail, you're weak, you're breakable. You're *meat*. This one . . ." Shay turned to look at Lake, and through the bond, I felt her conflicting desires to lash out and shrink back from his gaze. "*This one* is strong."

Shay didn't come right out and say that Lake would make a good incubator for his future children, but he might as well have, and no matter what I did, I couldn't shake the image of Lake running, running, running and never getting far enough away.

Bryn, if we lose, I'm going with her. Dev met my eyes from across the room as the silent words passed from his mind to mine. If I'd been capable of feeling anything other than the animal need to answer Shay's innuendos with fury and blood, I might have taken a moment to consider what it would mean to lose Devon and Lake at the same time.

What it meant that he would leave me to go with her.

Instead, I gritted my teeth and nodded. *If we lose, Dev, I want you to go.*

Shay flicked his eyes from Devon's to mine, unable to hear our words, but aware that something had passed unspoken between us.

"So the stakes aren't changing." Lake tossed her hair over one shoulder and twirled the pool cue absentmindedly in her hand. "Now that we've got that over with, you want to break, Shay, or should I?"

Lake threw out the challenge, looking cocky and young and like the type of person who would rush into a bet like this one without thinking things through, but I knew better. Her bravado was a familiar mask, a special brand of fearlessness that she could put on at the drop of a hat.

She was smart. She was strong. She could do this. I repeated that to myself over and over again.

"You can break." Shay walked past her and picked up the longest pool cue, twirling it lightly. "I spent most of the fifties in pool halls. If I broke, you'd never even get the chance to shoot."

Shay might as well have taken a page out of Caroline's book and pronounced himself incapable of missing a shot.

Unperturbed, Lake racked up the balls and walked the perimeter of the table, her hips swinging with forced carelessness, her eyes registering every angle, every contour, every ball. She placed the cue ball just to the left of the table's center and leaned over, lining up her first shot. Numbness worked its way up my body, inch by inch.

Lake relaxed her grip on her stick.

Shay smiled.

And then she took her first shot.

The cue ball ricocheted off its target, and the rest shot outward, like an explosion had gone off at their core.

I felt, rather than saw, the first ball drop into one of the center pockets, and I forced myself to breathe.

There were too many of us in this room. There was too much riding on this moment, and it went against every instinct I had—as an alpha, as their friend, as a person who knew what it meant to fight for survival every second of every day—to just stand there, watching and willing Lake to sink one ball after another after another.

It hurt to hope.

It hurt to breathe.

Lake moved around the table with the precision of a surgeon, mid-operation, and the more shots she took, the closer the mask of fearlessness on her face came to slipping.

She wanted this.

She was fighting.

She was scared.

I ground my fingernails into the palm of my hand until red half-moons dotted my skin. I couldn't feel the pain, couldn't breathe, couldn't do anything but wait for Lake to sink the next ball.

And then she missed.

With a sickening grin, Shay leaned down to the table, lined up his shot, and sent two balls ricocheting into opposite pockets with the ease of a pro. He worked his way around the table, shot after shot after shot.

I could feel Lake on the other side of the pack-bond, feel her insides shattering like glass as she tried *so hard* not to be scared. Seeing the bravado on her face nearly brought me to my knees.

Shay only had three balls left.

Then two.

Then one.

I knew then that I never should have let Lake risk it, never should have put her in a position where a game of pool could cost her everything, *everything*.

It's going to be okay, Bryn. Whatever happens, it'll be okay. Chase met my eyes, and for the first time in memory, I felt like I was looking at a stranger. If Shay won, if he took Lake, nothing would be okay. Not now, not ever. If Chase didn't understand that, he didn't understand *me*.

"Call your pocket." Lake's voice was steady, and she thrust her chin out, like she could make him miss by sheer force of will.

"Back left corner."

My eyes went immediately to the pocket in question. If Shay made this shot, he'd win—the bet, Lake...

I saw the eight ball hit the corner of the pocket. Saw it hover there. Saw it fall in.

Protect. Protect. Survive.

As my Resilience rose up inside me, I could barely make out the world around me. I could barely see Lake, shutting down and shutting out the fear. I could barely see Shay, moving slowly toward her from one side, or Devon, cutting across the room from the other.

But I did see the cue ball as it bounced off one corner and rolled slowly toward another. My eyes tracked its progression, my fight-or-flight instinct taking control of my body even as they did.

Survive. Survive. Survive.

An instant before I completely lost it and gave in to the desire to do to Shay what I had done to the psychics on the street, the cue ball disappeared off the table, falling into one of the side pockets. Something gave inside me, and the blood-red haze began to fade.

Shay had just scratched.

On most shots, it wouldn't have mattered all that much, but I was familiar enough with pool to know that scratching on the eight ball meant forfeiting the game.

Shay had lost.

I was still trying to process this when Shay froze in his stride toward Lake.

Devon turned back toward the table. Lake grinned.

"Well," she drawled, setting her own stick down, "that has to hurt."

Lake had always been a horrible winner, and it took me a moment to find the naked, vulnerable relief underneath her gloating.

Shay scratched, I thought, letting myself believe it this time. *He lost.*

Beside me, I felt Chase reaching out, on the verge of saying something through the bond, but he must have decided against it, must have known how I would have taken it, because all there was between us was silence.

Relief painted my body with an unearthly, adrenaline-fueled glow. Lake was okay. I was okay. We were all okay—including Lucas, who Shay had just officially lost.

"Your permissions expire in a little over an hour," I told Shay. "I expect you to retract your claim on Lucas and be off my land before then."

I could feel Callum in the set of my jaw, the ease with which the words rolled off my tongue.

Shay snapped his pool cue in two, as easily as he could have—and would have—snapped my neck if it weren't for Callum and the Senate. He stalked over to Lucas and lifted his limp body like a rag doll. Shay held him with one hand and flexed the fingers on the other until they began to take on the appearance of claws. He slashed his not-quite-human nails across Lucas's face, and I felt the world shifting around us.

This was how pack transfers—the official kind—worked. The first alpha retracted his claim, cut off all mental ties, leaving the second alpha free to instate his—or in my case, *her*—own.

As I watched, unable to tear my eyes away, Shay wrenched his mind out of Lucas's with all of the delicacy of a dentist using pliers to pull teeth.

"You are nothing to me," he said, the words coming out more like a growl than any I'd ever heard spoken out loud. "I am nothing to you. If you step foot on Snake Bend territory again, I will kill you."

With that, Shay dropped Lucas back onto the ground, and the younger Were's back arched so hard and fast that I thought his body would snap in two.

"Lucas." Maddy was by his side in an instant, and as the panic cleared from Lucas's eyes and he met hers, I saw the contours of his face the way she did, felt his hand on hers as if it were mine.

Lone. Wolf.

My pack-sense trembled with the realization that Lucas didn't feel foreign anymore—that now that Shay had released his hold, Lucas felt like something else altogether.

"He's yours if you want him." Shay kept his comment short and sweet. "But he'll bring you nothing but trouble."

That sounded more like a promise than a threat, and I thought of the psychics and everything Lucas had already led—however unwittingly—straight to our door.

"I doubt the Senate will be pleased when they find out you've been making deals with psychics." I tossed the words out like they meant nothing, but I saw the moment they hit their mark. "I may be new to all of this, but I'm fairly certain that bringing the outside world into Pack matters is frowned upon."

Shay recovered before I could fully register how deep my threat had cut. "The Senate would want proof," he said, "and without my help, I doubt you'll be alive to give it."

Without his *help*? I snorted. Shay had orchestrated all of this. He'd forced my hand to allow him entry to my lands, he'd strong-armed me into wagering one of my wolves against one of his, and now that he'd lost, he was trying to *offer me help*?

"Your pack has one adult male, fewer than a dozen teenagers, and a handful of children. You can't expect to face down a coven of psychics on your own."

To my left, Devon's eyes glittered. "Would this be the same coven of psychics who are attacking us at *your* request?"

Shay shrugged, the human gesture completely at odds with the feral glint in his eyes. "The *why* and the *how* don't matter. If I were you, I'd be more concerned with the *when*."

Jed had warned me that Valerie might call an end to the armistice, repay my visit with one of her own now that she had a better idea of what I could do. Now, Shay seemed to be promising that Jed's words would prove true.

"You have hours." Shay began walking backward toward the door, each footstep falling like a gavel. "At most, you have a day. If and when you come to your senses, say the word, and the Snake Bend Pack would be more than willing to cross into your territory and fight on your side."

Fight on our side? He was the one who'd set them on us. Maybe if I hadn't realized that, I would have taken his offer as mercurial, but given everything I knew, it seemed absurd.

"You're offering to fight on our side?" I asked. "Couldn't you just tell them to back down?"

Shay smiled. "Invite us into your territory," he said, "and I will."

Every time I thought I had Shay's strategy figured out, I peeled back a layer of his machinations and found another one underneath.

He'd sent Lucas here so he'd have a reason to come to my territory. He'd made a play for Lake, and just in case that failed, he'd lined his pack up along our borders and sent the coven after me so that I'd have reason to invite his people in.

"The answer," I said, the words working their way up from the pit of my stomach, uncompromising and sure, "is no."

Backing me into a corner was a mistake, and someday, Shay would pay for it. Maybe not today, but eventually he'd regret every trap he'd laid for me and mine. I took a step toward him, this foreign alpha who didn't belong here, and the rest of my pack moved in tandem, all eyes on Shay as we closed in.

He didn't have my permission to be here any longer, and I wasn't asking him for help.

Not surprisingly, given Shay's pedigree, he didn't flinch.

He didn't blink. He didn't even shrug. Instead, he lowered his voice to a whisper that crawled up my spine. "Funny, isn't it?" he said. "You're in danger, I'm here, and Callum's not."

The statement hung in the air, and without another word, Shay Shifted effortlessly into wolf form, and in a blur of timber-colored fur—his markings a perfect match for Devon's—he was gone.

CHAPTER
TWENTY-THREE

I KNEW BETTER THAN TO LET SHAY GET UNDER MY skin, but still, his parting shot hit me hard. I'd almost lost Lake—and Dev. I'd been threatened and burned, and another alpha was circling my territory, just waiting for an opportunity to swoop in.

There was a good chance the psychics were planning an attack.

And where was Callum?

Not here. He hadn't even taken my phone call.

"If the psychics are planning to attack, we need to set up a defense." I looked at the others, one after another: the peripherals, Lucas, my inner guard. "Able-bodied fighters need to be ready to fight. Earplugs are a must. Dev, tell Ali to get the younger kids together. They're going on a field trip. Lake?"

Leaning back against the pool table, Lake preempted my next request. "Weapons?" she asked, all business.

"Anything that will help us secure the perimeter. I'm thinking some strategically placed explosives wouldn't hurt."

Some people lived for the phrase *strategically placed explosives*. Lake was one of those people.

"On it."

I turned to Chase. "Help Maddy with Lucas," I said.

Lucas's bones were probably already healing, but he still hadn't picked himself up off the floor. I couldn't be sure how much damage Shay had done when he'd pulled out of Lucas's head, so despite being free to claim him, I held back, uncertain if Lucas could take that kind of mental assault at the moment.

Besides, I had bigger fish to fry.

"Meet back here in half an hour," I said. Just enough time for the others to finish their jobs and for me to get on with mine.

I didn't know the coven's plan of attack. I didn't know the extent of their knacks. I didn't know their weaknesses, or if killing Valerie would remove the emotional suggestions she'd planted.

But I knew somebody who probably did.

Callum might not have been omniscient. He might have seen the future as a complicated web, with possibilities branching out like leaves on a thousand-year-old tree. He might have been limited by distance, but chances were good that he'd know something.

More than I knew, at least.

Now that Shay was technically out of the picture, Callum's sharing what he knew couldn't be considered a political alliance. The coven wasn't a part of our world, their safety wasn't a Senate concern.

"You're going to answer," I said, willing the words to be true. "You have to."

I picked up the phone. I dialed.

"Hello."

One word. Just one—but the moment I heard Callum's voice, I had to sit down.

"This is the alpha of the Cedar Ridge Pack," I said, my voice shaking with the things I wasn't saying. "We have a situation with some humans, and from one alpha to another, I need some advice."

"Bryn." That was all he said—my name—but it was enough to make me feel absolutely naked, like he could see the expression on my face, like he could see inside me, no matter how far away he was.

"Callum." A hint of steel crept into my voice. This wasn't a social call.

"Did you get my gift?"

"Yes." I paused. "I don't suppose it means that the key to the coven's destruction is *horses*."

Callum made a choking sound, and I wondered if I'd actually managed to surprise a laugh out of him.

"This is serious, Callum. We have kids here. Katie. Alex. A half dozen others under the age of ten. Ali's packing them up as we speak."

"And where are you sending them?"

There was only one place I could send them, one person I could trust with their safety. Callum had to know that.

Had to know that it was him.

"I'll get them out of the line of fire however I can." I danced around the truth.

"And how many escorts will you be sending with your little ones?" Callum did a passable job of sounding curious, but I wasn't fooled. He wasn't asking for his benefit.

He was asking for mine, and I realized almost immediately that I couldn't send the kids off by themselves—and that I didn't have many guards to spare. Counting the peripherals, and me, we had ten able-bodied fighters—eleven if Lucas could heal enough to fight by our side. I couldn't spare more than one or two to escort the kids, and that wasn't good enough, not when the coven—or, if he was up for risking the Senate's wrath, Shay—could feasibly intercept them along the way.

"I'll send the kids into lockdown here," I told Callum, thinking out loud. "If we fight the psychics, there'll probably be casualties, but to get to the kids, they'd have to take us all out, and I don't think they have that kind of manpower, knacks or not."

"Who do you think they'll kill?"

If I hadn't known Callum, hadn't spent my entire life reading meaning into his most indecipherable tones, I would have thought the question was facetious, but it wasn't.

He wanted names.

"You'd know better than I would," I said, my voice catching in my throat.

Callum didn't respond. I couldn't even hear him breathing on the other side of the line, but werewolf hearing probably meant that he could hear the beating of my heart, the sound I made each time I swallowed.

"There are eleven of us," I said, "assuming the wolf I just won from Shay can fight." I didn't mention that this assumption was stretching it, given Lucas's current condition—and his previous experience with the psychics. "Chase, Maddy, and the peripherals are ... *scrappy*."

Like me, they had a way of surviving things that should have killed them dead.

"Devon's Dev, and I don't even know how old Mitch is."

That left Lake. I'd already almost lost her once.

To Shay.

Thinking of the way Shay had looked at her, the expression on his face, made me remember exactly who and what Lake was. She was a female Were—one of very, very few, even with the addition of Changed Weres in my pack. Shay wouldn't want her dead. If she died—if any of the females died—the hope that any of the alphas would be able to get their hands on them— now, a year from now, a hundred years from now—died, too.

"They won't kill the females."

I measured Callum's response to my words.

Silence.

"The psychics have a deal with Shay," I said, working through the logic out loud. "And Shay would want the females alive."

The number of people Shay wanted dead was probably relatively small: me; Mitch if he got in the way; depending on Shay's mood, maybe Devon…

"This isn't war," I said softly, unsure if I was talking to Callum or myself. "It's a hit."

Slowly, the layers of Shay's plan crystallized in my mind. He'd set the psychics up to attack us. He'd offered me help, hoping to gain access to our territory, and when I'd refused…

"You could die, Bryn." Callum confirmed my thoughts, and for the first time, I heard emotion in his words. It was faint, but it was there, and though I had to strain to hear it, once I did, something inside me, something broken, began putting itself back together again, bit by bit by bit.

"I could die," I repeated. "If I do, Devon will go alpha."

There was no doubt of that in my mind; with Dev, it was only a matter of time.

"Devon could die," Callum said softly.

"And if Devon died . . ." I forced myself to imagine it. I was the alpha; Dev was my second-in-command. If we were both dead—

"There's not an obvious third," I said.

There were two ways to become alpha: as a member of a given pack, you could challenge and kill the current alpha and take their rank, or, if the alpha was killed by an outsider, you could be strong enough that there was never any question that you would be next in line. Mitch was too peripheral to lead. Lake, Chase, and Maddy—they all had their natural strengths, but the hierarchy between them was far from clear, and unlike most Weres, my pack wouldn't jump straight to fighting it out for supremacy.

In the time it took for them to reach a consensus, they'd be easy targets.

Sitting ducks.

Open.

"Senate Law forbids taking another alpha's wolf," I said slowly. "But if there's no alpha, then technically, there isn't a pack."

If the psychics killed me, if they killed Devon, there would be an opening, however brief, for someone else to come rushing in.

I thought of Shay's wolves, lined up and down the edge of our border. Waiting.

"Dev can't fight," I said, coming to a conclusion that crept under my skin and hung in the air all around me. "If I fight, Devon can't, and I *have* to fight."

Callum didn't respond, but he didn't have to. I was the alpha, and an alpha couldn't run and hide, couldn't send the pack off to fight, die on their own. The pack needed me there, the same way the peripherals had needed to see me when they'd arrived at the Wayfarer, the same way the others looked to me for the signal to run on the full moon.

"In the end," Callum said, his voice soft, gentle, "it all comes back to you. You protect them, you love them, you live for them, and someday, you die. That's what it means, Bryn-girl, to be what we are. It's lonely. It's impossible. It's all-consuming."

It is what it is.

Callum didn't say it. Neither did I. But it was there, between us. And it was true.

"Okay," I said, fighting for acceptance the way a drowning man tries for air. "Devon can't fight. I can't risk sending the kids away, because someone could intercept them before they get to you. During the actual confrontation, the coven will be gunning for me, and they'll be under orders from Shay not to kill any of the female Weres."

Granted, Callum hadn't *said* any of that. He'd just sat there, on the other end of the line, asking questions and letting me come to it on my own.

"Now I just need a plan for neutralizing the coven as quickly as possible," I said. "Any idea if taking out their leader will free up the others' minds?"

Callum didn't respond.

"Callum? Words of wisdom? Cryptic hints? Anything?"

Nothing. No answer. Silence.

And that was when I realized he'd already hung up.

CHAPTER TWENTY-FOUR

⁓

AS I STALKED OUT OF THE HOUSE AND BACK TOWARD the restaurant, my mind jumped from one thought to another, a never-ending medley of the things Callum had said, the promised confrontation with the psychics, and Jed's suggestion that the only way to stop Valerie was to kill her. I thought of the carving Callum had sent me, and remembered all the times growing up that I'd seen him with a piece of wood in his hands. I remembered "borrowing" his knife when I was eight, trying to carve something myself. If Ali had been the one to catch me unsupervised with the sharp object, she would have freaked, but Callum had just sat down behind me and pulled me onto his lap. He'd put his hands over mine, guiding them, ready to catch the blade if it slipped.

Was that why he'd sent it to me? To let me know that even now, he was doing the same thing? Or was the message really that he couldn't do that anymore, that this time, if the knife slipped, I'd bleed?

Hurt.

Die.

"You okay?" Chase fell into step with me, and I felt his presence the way I always did, in my flesh and bones: a flash of similarity, a desire for the space between us to disappear.

This time, I kept my distance.

"Lucas is healing. He seems a little more . . . *present* now. Maddy's with him." Chase paused, and I could feel him debating whether to continue. "He's asking for you."

Getting out of Snake Bend had been only half of Lucas's goal; he'd said from the beginning that he wanted to be a part of our pack, and now, with Shay out of the way, there was nothing to keep me from giving Lucas his wish.

Except, of course, for the fact that the psychics might pick any moment to descend.

"It can wait," Chase said, and even though I'd been thinking more or less the same thing, coming from him, it chafed—maybe because I couldn't help remembering that he'd used that same soft, quiet tone to tell me that even if we lost Lake, it would be okay.

It wouldn't have been okay. And neither would I.

"Shay wants the females alive." I changed the subject—out loud and in my head. "That's the good news."

"You'll make the girls our first line of defense, then." After my one-sided conversation with Callum, Chase actually answering me made for a pleasant change of pace. "If Maddy, Lake, Phoebe, and Sage take the perimeter, then the psychics will have to work their way back to the rest of us with less than lethal force. It's a good plan, Bryn. It buys the rest of us some time."

"Not all of us."

"The bad news?" Chase guessed.

I nodded. "I'm going to ask Dev not to fight."

I expected Chase to ask why. He didn't.

"He won't say yes." Chase didn't—wouldn't—look at me, but even from this angle, I could see that his expression had gone carefully neutral.

"Devon won't be happy about it," I corrected. "But he'll do it."

Maybe that was the difference between Chase and Dev. Neither one of them wanted to see me hurt. They both would have died for me, the same way I would have died for them. They felt an animal need to protect me, and always had—but at the end of the day, Dev felt that way about other things, too. He would have gone to Shay's pack to protect Lake. He'd stand down on this fight for the good of the pack.

"Dev will do it," I said, taking a page from Chase's book and staring straight ahead. "But you wouldn't."

"Bryn," Chase said, reaching for my arm, his touch light against my skin.

"Would it even matter," I asked him, feeling that touch to my core, "if I told you it was what I wanted? If it was what needed to happen for us to know that the pack was going to come out of this okay?"

To his credit, Chase didn't hesitate before he answered. He didn't sugarcoat it. He didn't tell me what I wanted to hear. "No."

"Well," I said roughly, "then I guess it's a good thing I'm not asking *you*."

Chase's hand tightened, ever so slightly, his touch turning to a hold. He stopped walking, and I turned to face him.

"If it came down to me or the pack," Chase said, his face giving away nothing, his mind calm and cool on the other end of the bond, "what would you choose?"

I tried to process the fact that he was even asking, that from his perspective, in his mind, that was even okay.

"You'd choose the pack," Chase said. He moved his hand from my arm to my chin, angling my eyes gently toward him. "I know that, Bryn. I'm okay with it, and I will *never* ask you to choose."

I searched his eyes, wishing that I could smell the truth on him, the way he could on me.

"If it ever comes down to a choice between me and the pack, I want you to choose them. Don't think about it, don't second-guess it, don't feel guilty after the fact. I know you, Bryn. *I know you*, and I am not asking you to change." His lips curved upward in a slow, sad smile, and I thought about what Callum had said about being alpha—it was lonely, it was impossible, it was all-consuming.

Chase brushed a strand of hair out of my face. "But at the end of the day, Bryn, if *I* had to choose between you and the pack, I would choose you—every single time, no questions asked. You need to know that, because that's who *I* am, and it's not going to change. Not now, not ever. For me, it will always, always be you, even if deep down, you wish I could be something or someone else."

Standing there, looking at Chase and listening to him say something I hadn't even allowed myself to think, I knew objectively that I wasn't being fair. That I couldn't expect the pack to matter to him the way it did to me. That he had accepted what I was, even though it meant that he would never be my number-one priority, the way I was his.

I knew it wasn't fair to him to expect more than that, but with everything that had happened in the past few days—with everything that was on the verge of happening even now—I couldn't convince myself that mattered.

I would always choose the pack. Chase would always choose me—and I wasn't sure I could accept that, fair or not.

Unable to think, to breathe, I brushed my lips lightly over his, pretending for a moment that the two of us were the only people in the world, and then I turned and ran for the Wayfarer, where we weren't.

"Are you actually asking me to let you go out there and fight the coven alone?" Dev's voice was surprisingly pleasant. He shifted his gaze from me to Chase, who'd followed on my heels, and raised his eyebrows in a look meant to convey that I was crazy.

Ignoring said look, I tried to stay focused on the task at hand. "The coven is working for Shay. Shay wants our females, so he set the coven up to take me out of the picture without irreparably damaging the girls. Once I'm gone, you're next in line for alpha, Dev. Think about it. Shay would have taken you in exchange for Lucas—is he really that sentimental, or do you think he just wanted you out of the way?"

"Touché," Devon said. His mother had beaten me unconscious at Callum's command. His brother had tortured a wolf under his care. The Macalisters weren't really a family known for their sentimentality.

"Dev, if you stay and the coven kills both of us, Shay will sweep in and pick the females off one by one. Is that what you want for Lake? For Maddy? For Katie and Lily and—"

"Enough." Devon held up one palm in a gesture that looked so choreographed, I almost smiled. "You've convinced me that only one of us can fight."

"So you'll take Ali and the kids and hunker down somewhere safe until the threat has passed?"

Dev snorted. "Not for all the tea in China. Not for front-row seats at Fashion Week. Not for a featured role on *Glee*."

I snorted right back at him. "Tell me how you really feel, Dev."

"You're the alpha. That means that you have to come first. And like it or not, you're human, and that means you're—"

"Breakable?" I suggested, the word Shay had used dripping sarcastically from my own lips. "I'm also Resilient. What happens when Valerie starts messing with your emotions? Or when Bridget whistles a little ditty that turns you from teen wolf into a sitting duck? Lucas said one of the psychics can control wolves. What happens if you can't fight her off?"

Devon's jaw snapped shut, and for once, he was absolutely silent. I waited, my eyes locked on his, his locked on mine, and after a long moment, he nodded. He wouldn't say it, wouldn't admit that there was even the smallest possibility that I was right, but he would take the younger kids and go, because I'd asked.

He would do what had to be done, even if it killed him. Even if it killed me.

He'd do it for the pack.

"Well, this is nice and cozy."

If the circumstances had been different, it might have been gratifying to see the way the boys jumped then, given that I'd spent most of my life with werewolves sneaking up on me, but the person who'd gotten the drop on them was standing with her back against the opposite wall, a gun in her hand, blonde hair concealing the left half of her face.

"Caroline."

She shrugged, like my saying her name was an accusation—one to which she was completely indifferent.

"Did you come here to *warn* us?" Devon asked, putting melodramatic emphasis on the word. Swooping in to issue her mother's ultimatums was more or less Caroline's MO.

"I don't know why I came here," Caroline said, looking down at the gun. "But if you want to take it as a warning, that works. My mother won't be able to hold the others back much longer."

"Hold them back," I repeated. "Yeah. Right."

"You couldn't make it easy," Caroline said, ignoring my sarcasm. "You couldn't just give us that thing and walk away."

"That thing as in Chase?" I asked, following her gaze to my left, where Chase was eyeing Caroline with detached objectivity, even as his lupine nature became more apparent in his posture, his expression, the feel of his mind.

"Or that thing as in Lucas?" I continued. "Maybe you'd like my baby sister? She's not quite a year old yet, but she's a holy horror when she doesn't get her way."

"You're like them," Caroline told me, her pupils beginning to bleed outward as she stepped away from the shadows. "You're just like them."

"No," I said, aware that Chase was close—very close—to Shifting. "*They're* just like you. Did you know they used to be human—Chase and Maddy and the rest? They were human, just like you. They were attacked, just like you. They survived. For that matter, so did I." I thought about what Jed had said about the man who'd led the coven before Valerie. "My parents didn't."

My words seemed to snap Caroline out of it. She stopped moving forward. Genuine emotion overrode whatever psychic push Valerie had left in her daughter's head, and I saw an instant of doubt, vulnerable and raw, in Caroline's blue eyes, a single moment during which she wanted desperately to believe that she wasn't alone.

That she wasn't a monster.

That someone, *anyone* else could understand.

"Do you really think this is about Lucas?" I asked her. "You really think that your mother is willing to go up against an entire pack of werewolves just so she can squeeze out a few extra days of torturing one? Valerie wants to fight. She wants you to want to fight, and I think we both know that your mother has a way of getting what she wants."

Uncertainty danced around the edges of Caroline's features, but the mere mention of her mother was enough to make her pupils pulse. I thought of Ali's description of her own childhood, growing up under the constant influence of an empath.

If she was sad, I was sad. If she was angry, I was angry. I loved her so much, because she wanted me to.

Caroline wasn't angry. She wasn't sad. I wasn't even sure she loved her mother, but whatever she was feeling, she felt it irrevocably and intensely, and the emotion had a mind of its own.

She glanced down at the gun in her hand and then back up at me. I had a single second to process the realization that if Valerie wanted me dead, she didn't need a whole coven to do it.

"She didn't send me here," Caroline said, turning the gun over in her hand. "I came on my own, but it doesn't matter. None of it matters." She closed her eyes, then opened them again, lifting the gun. "What I want doesn't matter. What you want doesn't matter. This is what I was made for. It's what I'm good at. It's what I do."

I felt a flare of energy the second before Chase Shifted. Caroline switched her gaze from me to him, and my heart jumped into my throat when I realized that a girl who'd been programmed to hate werewolves was standing there, watching him Shift, her hand on a gun.

Caroline's knuckles went white. Her blue eyes bled black again. She turned her attention from Chase to me, and she raised the gun.

Bryn. Mine. Protect.

Chase's thoughts. Before I could process them—or what the wolf was about to do—he leapt, straight for the gun pointed at me.

Straight for Caroline's throat.

Devon jumped forward, Shifting in midair faster and more

fluidly than any Were I'd ever seen. His body slammed against Chase's, and the muted sound of flesh hitting flesh was drowned out by the snapping of teeth and a low, vibrating growl.

Almost instantly, Dev was back on four feet, and he whirled around, bringing the full force of his massive size to bear on Caroline, matching Chase's growl with one of his own. The message was clear, even to an outsider: Devon had saved her, but if Caroline gave him reason to, he'd kill her himself.

Caroline's eyes went suddenly blue, her pupils shrinking to pinpoints as she stared at Devon in wolf form. For whatever reason, seeing him had knocked out the effects of Valerie's interference, and for a split second, I relaxed.

Then Caroline's finger tightened around the trigger. With no warning whatsoever, she took aim and fired—but not at me.

In her right mind and of her own volition, she put a silver bullet straight through Devon's heart.

CHAPTER
TWENTY-FIVE

YOU CAN KNOW, OBJECTIVELY, THAT YOUR BEST friend isn't allergic to silver. You can be fully aware that, setting the silver issue aside, most werewolves can take a bullet to the heart and come out of it okay. You can *know* it, and it doesn't matter.

The second I saw the bullet pierce Devon's chest, I was on the floor beside him, saying his name out loud, calling to him through the pack-bond, willing him to be okay. My hands warm and sticky with his blood, I felt the Change ripple through his body as he Shifted back to human form.

"Dev. You're going to be okay, Devon. You're going to be fine."

He said something—softly. I couldn't make it out, couldn't get my human ears to decipher whatever he was trying to say.

You're going to be okay, Dev. You're going to be fine.

If I could have made it an order, I would have. I would have *ordered* him to be okay, but I didn't get the chance, because he spoke again—silently this time—and I heard what he said just fine.

Caroline.

I felt a pulse of rage go through my body, and all around me, the rest of the pack felt it, too.

The smell of Devon's blood brought the rest of the pack straight to us, and as a unit, they turned their attention on Caroline. She moved quickly, quietly. Mitch caught her roughly by one arm, but an instant later, he was wearing a dagger through his bicep, and she was gone.

She dove out a window, straight through the glass.

The pack wanted to follow. They wanted to tear her open, hunt her down, make her bleed the way Devon was bleeding now.

Prey. Prey. Prey.

With their animal instincts beating a constant rhythm in my mind, I could feel the desire rising in my own body: tears in my eyes, a tightening in my throat, and the thrum of my heart and theirs all around me.

"Could be . . . trap," Devon wheezed.

The second I heard his voice, I let out a breath I hadn't realized I was holding. Appreciating his meaning took me a second longer. Caroline had just taken out one of our strongest fighters *and* whetted the pack's desire for blood. Every instinct they had, every instinct *I* had said to chase her.

But what if that was what she wanted?

I couldn't rule out the possibility that Valerie had sent her daughter here to lure us out, even though the memory of Caroline's eyes—blue and completely her own—and the expression on her ashen face as she'd leveled the gun at Dev made me think that none of this had been planned, that she hadn't come here to kill anyone, that shooting Dev after he'd saved her life had been . . . personal.

Time was passing. Precious seconds, and once Caroline was out of eyesight, she was impossible to track. The pack wanted to go after her. *I* wanted to go after her. But I couldn't take the chance that it was a trap.

I couldn't take any chances, because if there was one thing the blood on my hands had hit home, it was the reality that from here out, we were playing for keeps.

"She's not prey," I said out loud. "Not yet. We're going to let them bring the fight to us."

Beside me, Devon groaned. With no small amount of ceremony, he lifted his right hand, dug his fingernails into his chest, and ripped out the bullet.

"Well, there goes that manicure," he muttered.

"Somebody bring me a med kit," I said, my voice the only sound in the room. "Mitch, I'll need you to weigh in on a couple of things. Lake, bring me up to speed on the explosives. And will somebody *please* get Devon some clothes?"

My hands soaked in my best friend's blood, I prepared

my pack for war. Now that the course was set, now that we'd passed the point of no return, I felt an odd sense of calm rolling over my body, a whisper in the back of my mind.

I could practically taste the red haze of Resilience, hovering just out of reach.

We waited for the attack at the edge of the forest, where we had the benefit of cover and our attackers would not. Lake, Maddy, Phoebe, and Sage took the front line; Devon and the kids were hidden safely away. Our perimeter was lined with explosives, and I was ready and willing to use them.

If Caroline tried to set up some kind of sniper's nest and pick us off one by one, she was going to be very unpleasantly surprised.

I felt detached from what we were about to do, but my heart was pounding, feeding my brain adrenaline, fueling the pack's appetite for blood. This was a *hunt*. We were hunters, and the air was heavy with the things a werewolf pack, backed into a corner, could do.

Would do.

I could see the expression on Caroline's face as she took in Devon's wolf form, pulled the trigger. She'd shut down emotionally, but as I played the moment over and over again in my mind, I caught wisps of fury, vulnerability, fear.

Pack. Pack. Pack.

I didn't want to kill her, didn't want to kill any of them, but if it came down to our lives or theirs, if Caroline started shooting, I'd put her down like a rabid dog—the same way I was going to go after Valerie and end this once and for all.

Alpha. Alpha. Alpha.

My chest tightened and a ball of energy exploded inside me, pushing me forward, *willing* me to force my way to the front of the pack—in front of Lake, in front of Maddy. Every instinct I had said to face this threat head-on.

"Bryn."

My eyes were so focused on the horizon that I didn't see Ali until she'd made her way back to the point in the forest where I stood. Briefly, I wondered what she was doing here, but then I saw the gun in her hand and the look on her face—one I recognized all too well.

I'd *invented* that look.

"Ali, you can't—"

"I can't fight because I'm human?" Ali said, cutting me off. "Or because you don't trust me not to get myself killed?"

There was no answering that question. I didn't even try.

"I may not be strong, I may not be fast, and God knows that I don't have even the tiniest sliver of psychic ability, but I am a part of this pack. I am a part of you, Bryn, and when I say that you are not going up against this coven without me, I mean it."

The message was clear in her stance and the set of her chin: alpha or not, I was *her* daughter. My fights were her fights, case closed.

"Can you shoot?" It was probably a stupid question, but I'd never actually seen Ali armed.

"Better than you can," Ali replied. "I've always been a decent shot."

She fell in beside me, and Chase took a step toward the two of us. I looked at him. He looked at me. We waited. And no matter how much I wanted to, I couldn't tell him that his willingness to trade the pack's safety for mine didn't matter to me. I couldn't tell him that everything would be okay, that we would be okay, and he knew it.

"Be careful," he said softly.

I pictured myself raising my right hand, waiting for him to do the same. I saw myself melting into him, but I didn't move a muscle.

"I will be," I said.

He nodded.

"Chase?" His name caught in my throat as he turned back to face me once more. "You be careful, too."

He nodded, and then I felt it—a prickling at the back of my neck, a shifting in the air around me as the Weres began to scent our prey. The psychics were close, getting closer.

This was it.

Pack. Pack. Pack.

The pull of the pack at the edges of my mind was unbearable, overwhelming. I hadn't asked for this battle. The human part of me didn't want it, but in those last moments before the enemy came into view, I could feel my humanity falling away, like sand through my fingertips, like the memory of a dream I'd never be able to reclaim.

Alpha. Alpha. Alpha.

Prey. Prey. Prey.

We were Pack. The coven had come here to hunt us. One way or another, this was bound to end in blood.

CHAPTER TWENTY-SIX

To my left, Ali readied her gun. On my right, Chase Shifted, flooding my mind with heightened perceptions from his wolf form: the sound of footsteps, the smell of gunpowder and lead.

"Lake." I was surprised that my voice could sound so human when the rest of me felt so *not*. "Now."

On short notice, we hadn't been able to round up more than three or four pairs of earplugs, but given the number of teens and tweens in our pack, we had iPods to spare. On my order, the girls turned up their music, drowning out all other sounds. If the coven wanted to get past our first line of defense, they'd have to do it the old-fashioned way—without the help of Bridget's knack.

As if on cue, a single note wafted its way through the forest on the wind, announcing the psychics' presence long before they appeared on the horizon, walking toward us like they hadn't a care in the world.

I knew what to expect, but the sound—sweet and simple and so full of longing that I ached to hear more—nailed my feet to the ground and brought my hands to my sides. I'd chosen to go without earplugs, because the one advantage I'd have in this fight was my own knack—and it only came out to play when I felt threatened, in mortal danger, trapped.

That was where Bridget came in. The sound—oh, God, the sound—rushed me, enveloping my body, my mind, drowning out everything and everyone else, until there was nothing.

Until I was trapped.

If it had been just me, it would have taken longer for my Resilience to flare up, but even as I lost all ability to care about the outside world, the rest of the pack gnawed at the gates of my mind, and their panic at my sudden stillness spurred a single spark of my own.

Trapped—Escape—Trapped.

For an instant, I saw the music as a physical thing, multi-limbed and snakelike. It held me in place. When I struggled, it tightened, but the overwhelming need for freedom burst out of me, and I saw the world in shades of red. Black dots played around the edges of my vision, but this time, instead of giving in to the haze, I rode it like a wave.

Fight. Fight. Fight.

Survive.

The psychics spread out—eight of them, Caroline and Archer nowhere in sight.

Fight. Fight. Fight.

I slipped sideways through the forest, far enough away from the rest of the group that—assuming the coven really was gunning for me—a portion of our attackers would have to follow. The first shot rang out, and the only reason I knew it wasn't Caroline was because the shooter missed.

The world was coming at me faster now. My heart raced, the amount of adrenaline coursing through my bloodstream an inhuman thing. I felt Chase throwing off Bridget's hold, and like dominoes, the others followed.

Now, I told them, and like horses bucking their riders, the girls gave up cover and rushed our assailants, crossing the space between them in a fraction of the time it took me to draw prey of my own.

Teeth snapped. Metal flew. A high-pitched whine cut me to the core, fueling my need to fight, to protect.

To survive.

"Hello, mutt-lover."

Archer's voice assaulted my mind, taking me back to my dreams. I saw the forest, the wolf, the fire—saw it as if it were real and the rest of the world had just faded away. Archer's hold on my mind wasn't a sharp, stabbing pain this time; it was burning, liquid flame: invincible, hungry.

Fire exploded around my body, and knowing it wasn't real didn't stop me from feeling the heat.

Trapped. Escape. Survive.

Power surged, crackling through my body and rendering Archer's interference useless. One second I was in my head, burning, and the next I was back in the real world, stalking toward Archer. He took a step backward and threw something at me—some kind of firecracker, maybe, or a mild explosive—and this time, I caught fire for real.

Fight. Kill. Survive.

My hair was burning, but I couldn't smell it. My eyes watered, and like a rubber band, the hold I had on my Resilience snapped.

At some point, I must have stopped, dropped, and rolled, must have extinguished the flame and disarmed Archer, but the only motion I was aware of was my fist plunging into his face, my body pinning his to the ground.

Fight.

I pressed my left forearm to his throat, cutting off his air supply. My skin was already beginning to blister from his assault, and the only thing that kept me from snapping his neck was a single sentence, issued from somewhere behind me.

"Let the boy go, Bryn." I heard Jed's voice, and it pulled me back, away from that lovely red haze in which I could fight, fight, fight without thinking, without hurting, without feeling anything at all.

Ignoring Jed, I dug my arm farther into Archer's throat, feeling his trachea give, and the older Resilient responded by wedging a shotgun against the back of my head. "I said to let the boy go."

Jed didn't shoot me.

Mistake.

In a single motion I caught the barrel of the gun with my leg and knocked it back into the older man's chin. He stumbled, and I whipped the gun around, caught it in my right hand, and rammed the butt into Archer's face, hard enough to knock him unconscious.

Jed shook his head, smiled through the blood. The sense of panic—and the fight-or-flight mode that went with it—left me the moment I let my eyes meet his. There was no threat there.

None.

"That boy isn't your enemy," Jed said. "Not really. Easy thing to lose sight of when you flash out."

"That boy," I said tersely, "set me on fire."

"You flashed out too early," Jed grunted, ignoring my complaint entirely. "Fight isn't over yet. You're going to have to go again, and sooner or later, the back-and-forth will start to wear on you."

I didn't have time for Resilience 101—not with my pack out there fighting for their lives. The smell of blood was thick in the air. The sound of teeth, of claws, of screams and howls was deafening.

"Caroline has to be in position by now," I said. Before Jed could reply, my words proved prophetic, and I felt—rather than saw—Chase take a bullet in the side.

My Chase.

White-hot pain. Silver in the blood. Hurts.

"She doesn't know what she's doing," Jed told me. Another shot sounded, another howl of pain. I felt it as if it were my own, wished it was.

Don't be dead, I thought, desperately trying to make the words an order. *Don't be dead. Don't be dead.*

"Explosives," I said out loud, my voice hoarse. "Very close to where I'm betting Caroline set up her little sniper's nest. If you can take her out of commission without hurting her, do it, because otherwise, we will."

For the first time, I had the experience of watching another human flash out. The look that came over the old man's face was completely animal: more than fury, more than need, more than the basest instinct I'd ever seen in a Were.

Whether he'd get to Caroline before the explosives detonated, I didn't know. With the smell of blood in the air and the feel of someone else's pain shooting through my body, I didn't care.

I had to get to them—to Chase, to the others. They were my pack. They were mine, and they were hurting.

Bleeding.

Dying.

"You really shouldn't wrinkle your forehead like that, Bryn. It's horribly unattractive."

I turned at the unsolicited advice, and there Valerie was, five feet away from me, completely unperturbed that I was the one holding a gun.

"Your little friends are certainly keeping us busy, aren't they?" Valerie said, casting her glance down at the battlefield below. A nagging sense of fear turned my stomach to stone, and I felt a sliver of ice sliding down the nape of my neck. I knew not to take my eyes off the woman in front of me, but I couldn't keep dread from forcing my gaze to the right, where what was left of my pack was facing off against the rest of the coven.

Wolf teeth met silver-plated knives held midair by a woman who blended in to the background like her entire body was painted in camouflage. Maddy, Lucas, and Sage were caught mid-Shift, bones frozen in the process of breaking, muzzles protruding from otherwise human faces. Lake was bleeding from her eyes and nose, Mitch was on his knees, and between them, the girls I'd seen at the breakfast table were moving their lips, saying something I couldn't hear, causing the others to writhe in pain.

"I promised not to kill the girls," Valerie said thoughtfully, "but I think my partner in crime will understand if we lose just one."

Maddy lunged, snapping her half-human muzzle at the old woman with the knack for influencing animals. She didn't see the snakes rushing down from the forest, didn't see the one close enough to strike.

I saw it, though—saw it and felt everything Valerie wanted me to feel as fangs struck at Maddy's body, only to be intercepted at the last minute in a blur of darkness and fur.

Chase. Bleeding. Hurting. He stumbled, turned, cut the snake down the middle with his jaws even as its head clung to his hind leg.

I stopped breathing.

Hurts. Hurts, Bryn. Maddy? Okay?

Chase's thoughts were a mess, as uncensored and jumbled as Lily's. I wanted to go to him, but I couldn't move, and all I could see was Chase beside me, Chase standing guard, Chase shielding Maddy's body with his own.

Maddy? Okay? Bryn?

Chase's voice was weaker in my mind now, and that was enough to tell me just how badly he was hurt. I could feel the burn of silver, the venom in his bloodstream.

Bryn . . . Protect . . . Mine . . .

I let down my walls, let him in. He filled me up, the way he and Devon and Lake had before, but this time, it was just the two of us. Chase and Bryn. Bryn and Chase.

Bryn. Protect Maddy.

For you.

I hadn't realized how far into my head Valerie had managed to get until Chase was there, too. His presence pushed against hers, and my body finally recognized the invasion for what it was.

She was attacking me from the inside out. She was violating me. She was hurting the people I loved.

Red, red, red...

Everywhere, there was red.

On some level, I knew that my own body was injured, knew that once I flashed out, there would be nothing to keep me from pushing too hard, too far.

It didn't matter. I could feel Chase lying on his side, bleeding, as his voice got softer and softer in my mind.

Red, red, everywhere, there was red.

Chase had saved Maddy. For me. He was going to survive this. He had to. *We* had to. With everything I had, I shoved Valerie out of my head. She blinked like I'd thrown something at her and stumbled backward.

"No bother," Valerie said, her hair falling into her face as she recovered. "You're a curious little thing, but I don't need to be in your head to win this fight—or any other. I've already got so many little soldiers. Can you feel how much they hate you? How much they want to see your people bleed? It's a delicate mixture—fear and loathing, the kind of curiosity they're ashamed of, sorrow and fury—rising, rising, until they can't stand it anymore."

"Hello, Mother." I didn't know whether to take Caroline's appearance at our side as a good sign or a bad one. At least if she was here, she couldn't be targeting the rest of the pack.

At least if she was here, everyone else was safe—from her.

"Hello, Caroline." Valerie sounded mildly pleased at her daughter's arrival—no more, no less.

I looked at Caroline's cherubic face, took in her doll-like features and the color of her eyes.

Watched them go from blue to black.

"Shoot her." Valerie spoke the words, and I dove to the ground, just as the world exploded around me. I knew a shot had been fired, but couldn't tell who had been shot. I was already in pain—so much pain—and I could feel all of the others', feel it everywhere.

Someone was shot.

Was it me?

No.

I clung to consciousness, clung to Chase as he began to fade away, and the last thing I saw before everything went black was Caroline's eyes changing back to blue—and Ali standing over Valerie's lifeless body, holding a smoking gun.

CHAPTER
TWENTY-SEVEN

I WAS LYING ON MY BACK, MY HEAD TURNED TO THE side, my eyes closed. I knew before I opened them that Chase would be there, lying on his back, his head turned toward mine. The night sky stretched out above us, stars burning so bright it hurt to look at them.

His hand wove its way through mine.

Neither one of us spoke, but I felt his heartbeat as if it were my own, and for reasons I couldn't pinpoint, tears began trickling down my face, slowly at first, but then faster.

This isn't real. I tried not to think the words, but couldn't hold them back.

I wanted it to be real. I wanted him to be okay, and barring that, I wanted the two of us to stay this way, my hand wrapped in his, his face close enough to mine that I could taste him.

Cedar and cinnamon. *Chase.*

He wasn't bleeding.

I wasn't burned.

And the ground beneath us was ... not ground, I realized. It was concrete, and though the sky stretched out in all directions above us, here on earth, we were surrounded by walls.

Bars. Titanium and reinforced steel.

It took me a moment to realize where we were: Callum's basement, the place where we'd first met, when Chase was newly turned and half wild with moonlust, and I was stupid and impulsive and unable to stay away.

This time, I was in the cage with him, and he was human.

"Caroline shot you," I said softly, wishing I could say something else. "You got bitten by a snake."

Chase blinked, his eyes brimming with acceptance—and something else. "Yeah."

I reached for his cheek. He nuzzled my hand.

"That snake was going for Maddy," I said, wondering if this was the last time I would ever touch him, feel the warmth of his skin. "You took its bite for her."

Chase reached out, touched my cheek, and I leaned into his hand. "I told you that if it came down to the pack or you, it would always be you. But if it comes down to me and them..."

I closed my eyes, rubbed my cheek against his hand.

"I'd pick them," he said softly. "For you."

Callum had said that being alpha was lonely—but all I could think, lying there next to Chase, sharing this dream, was that I wasn't alone.

"You're going to be okay," I told him, my lips a fraction of an inch away from his. "You're going to be fine."

"Bryn," he said, his breath warm on my face, his voice wild and irrepressible and sure. "Love you."

We'd shared dreams before, back when we were hunting the Rabid—enough for me to know that anything Chase said here was as real as words he said when we were awake.

There was no coming back from this moment, not now, not ever.

Somewhere his body was bleeding, poisoned with venom and silver.

Somewhere my body was burned.

But here, in this dream, as we lay side by side in a cage with all of heaven spread out above us, we were okay.

And I wasn't alone.

"Love you, Bryn," Chase said again, his voice hoarse. "Always you."

My mouth went cotton dry, and for a moment, I was scared—terrified—that I wouldn't be able to say it back. But somehow, I found the words, convinced my mouth to string them into a sentence—one that felt true.

"Love you, too."

The moment I said the words, his body gave in to the poison, and he began seizing. His limbs twitched, but he didn't Shift. He didn't blink. He didn't take his eyes off mine. He just faded away, bit by bit by bit, until I was lying there alone, the ghost of his touch lingering on my fingertips, my lips warm and swollen with the kiss we hadn't shared.

Bryn. Bryn. Bryn.

I sat up in the cage and willed myself to wake up so that I could go to him, save him, but instead, the world around me morphed, until the sky was nothing but stars, nothing but brightness, and I wasn't alone.

"You." The word ripped its way out of my throat, but I couldn't coax my body into moving, couldn't rip the intruder's jugular out, the way I should have the first time we'd met.

"Me," Archer said. The word sounded like some kind of confession. "It's just me this time, Bryn."

No nicknames, no gloating. This was a side to my psychic stalker that I hadn't seen before. I glanced at his eyes and noted the ring of lighter color around the pupil, and then I realized what he was trying to tell me.

"Just you," I repeated. That meant that Valerie was . . .

"Dead," Archer said, answering the question I hadn't asked. He flicked his wrist with halfhearted showmanship, and images flashed into my mind, courtesy of his psychic interference. This time, there were no flames—just a series of still shots of the coven's members, bleeding from the nose. "When Valerie died, her influence went with her. It was sudden. It hurt. But it was enough for the rest of us to realize that the monsters we were fighting weren't."

"Weren't fighting?"

"Weren't monsters." Archer looked at me with an expression somewhere between pity and pain. "You're just kids."

He couldn't have been more than five or six years my senior, but for a split second, I could almost see myself the way he did: sixteen, battered, old eyes, thin.

"I'd like to say that we didn't know what we were doing," Archer said, trying to sound like the words didn't matter to him nearly as much as they did. "But we weren't completely brainwashed. We knew. Valerie just made us feel like it didn't matter, made us hate you enough that we didn't want to question what that hatred was making us do. We let it happen. I let it happen."

I shut Archer down before he could say the word *sorry*, because I didn't want to hear it. "I need to wake up," I told him. "Now."

I didn't have time for apologies. I didn't need to be along for the ride as he worked his way through the question of whether he and the rest of the coven were villains or victims.

I needed to get out of here. I needed to wake up. I needed to protect what was left of my pack.

"Let me go."

"I'm not the one keeping you here," Archer said. "The fight's over. It's been over. You and some of the others—on both sides—were pretty beat up. You've been out for three days."

That wasn't possible. He had to be messing with me, playing with my mind, keeping me here when there was still something I could do to protect what was mine. I couldn't afford to take his words at face value, couldn't trust anything I'd seen through his mind—no matter how true it felt.

I had to make sure that the other psychics had stopped fighting when Valerie took a bullet to the head. For all I knew, while I was stuck in a dream with Archer, Caroline was out there in the real world retaliating for her mother's death. She could be taking aim at—

Ali.

The memory of my last conscious moment came rushing back. I'd been facing off against Valerie, against Caroline, pushing my body past every limit and clinging to consciousness by a thread. Caroline had pointed her gun at me. Valerie had given the order—and Ali, *my* Ali, had shot the coven leader dead.

If Archer was lying, if Caroline was still out there...

I moved to grab Archer by the lapels, but my hands sank through his body, like one of us was a ghost. "Wake. Me. Up."

Archer opened his mouth, then closed it. He took a step backward, his body solidifying once more. He held up one hand in invitation.

I didn't have the luxury of debating whether or not to take it. This was *Ali* we were talking about here.

The moment my hand touched Archer's, images flooded my brain in rapid fire: things he seemed to feel he owed it to me to share.

Not lies.

Like a slide show, the images flashed through my mind, bits and pieces of things that Archer had seen in other people's dreams, in reality.

I saw Devon Shifting from human form and Caroline's knuckles going white around the handle of a gun.

Flash.

I saw a little blonde girl, covered in blood. I saw her scramble backward as a large wolf—Devon? No, not Devon, not quite—approached.

Flash.

I saw Ali lifting a gun and taking aim at a woman exactly her height. I saw her pull the trigger, saw Valerie go down.

I heard Caroline say four simple words: "You shot my mother."

Flash.

I saw Ali releasing the clip on her gun. She lowered her hands to her sides. She met Caroline's eyes and waited for the girl to shoot.

"For what it's worth," Ali said, her voice catching in her throat as she looked back at Valerie's body, "she was my mother, too."

I woke up stiff, with morning breath and a body that felt like it had been put through a blender. It was dark outside my window, night just beginning to give way to the last moment before the dawn. Before I even opened my eyes, my pack-sense went haywire, flooding my body with thoughts and emotions, locations, tastes and smells.

Instantly, I knew where each member of my pack was. I knew who was awake and who was sleeping, who was injured, who was dead.

"You're awake." The voice was quiet, female, flat. I reached for the knife I kept on my nightstand, but it wasn't there.

"Devon didn't kill my father." Caroline said those words the way someone else might have said *hello*. "I didn't kill that Were."

That Were.

I knew who she was talking about. I could see his very human corpse in my mind—lanky and in desperate need of a haircut.

"His name was Eric," I said.

He'd been a freshman in college. The oldest of the Changed Weres. Excited to go to dorm parties. The first to speak up when things went awry.

"He was ours."

Words like *peripheral* meant nothing in death. Eric's absence was noticeable—a phantom limb, a gaping hole in my psyche. In human terms, we hadn't known each other very long or very well, but right now, I didn't feel human. I felt like I'd let Eric down. Like I should have protected him. Like I'd failed.

I didn't shed a tear, didn't even think about it. I wanted to go out to the woods, where the others had buried Eric, and howl.

"I could have killed him," Caroline said, her own voice catching. "I was so angry, so scared, it was *so much*—and I could have put a bullet right through his heart. I had the shot, and I didn't take it. I never miss, Bryn, but she couldn't make me aim to kill."

That was the first time Caroline had mentioned her mother, but I couldn't read any emotion in her words, other than something empty, something fierce.

"I shot that Were—Eric—but I wasn't the one who killed him. I didn't kill anyone."

I struggled to sit up, make myself taller, taking stock of my injuries as I did. In the time I'd been unconscious, I'd already started healing, but my left forearm was as good as useless, burned and wrapped in gauze. I thought of Jed and the layers and layers of scars decorating his aging flesh.

Werewolves healed quickly. Short of silver poisoning or being literally torn to pieces, they bounced back with minimal scars, but I wasn't a werewolf, and unless I turned, someday, I'd be as old and scarred and battle-worn as Jed, strong enough to survive, with the things I'd lived through etched into the surface of my skin.

"After I took that last shot, there was an explosion. Jed pulled me out, dragged me away. He tried to take my gun."

This time, I did see a flicker of emotion. Little Miss Huntress didn't like being disarmed.

"We fought. I let him think he'd won, and the second he came out of fight mode, I knocked him out and dragged him far enough away from the explosions that I knew he'd be okay. Then I went after you." Caroline shrugged, like nothing she'd said so far was important, like none of it mattered, to her or to me. "You know the rest."

She stayed in the shadows, her back against the wall, the distance between us the only thing that kept me from reaching out with my one good arm and grabbing her by the throat.

As much as I didn't want to, I believed her when she said that she hadn't killed Eric—but either way, she'd shot him, left him as easy prey for the coven and their bag of tricks. She'd put a bullet in Lake's dad and one in Chase, and the last time I'd seen her, she'd had a gun trained on the one person in this world who'd always been there, always been on my side, from day one.

"You didn't shoot Ali?" I meant the words as a statement, but they came out like a question.

Caroline didn't respond.

I could feel Ali, faintly, through the bond. Her mind was as much a mystery to me as always, and habit kept me from pushing past her walls. She was alive. She was safe. Everything beyond that—the sequence of events leading up to her putting Valerie down, the moment she'd recognized the coven leader as the woman who'd thrown her away, those final moments before Caroline had put down her gun—those things were hers alone.

"You're Ali's sister." I looked for a resemblance and found none. There was nothing of Ali in Caroline's baby-doll features, nothing that should have told me that the empath who'd abandoned Ali because she didn't have powers was the same one who'd taught Caroline to believe she was nothing without hers.

A memory—of Valerie reaching out and brushing my hair out of my face as she tried to stab her way through my mental defenses—flashed before my eyes, and I thought of the hundred thousand times Ali had done the exact same thing.

They were nothing alike.

"I'm not anyone's sister," Caroline said. "I'm not anyone. For what it's worth, I could have killed you, all of you, in that fight, but I didn't."

Caroline didn't sound like she thought that was worth all that much—and, fair or not, given the circumstances, I agreed with her appraisal. I knew better than most people what it was like to have the rug pulled out from underneath your very existence, to find out that everything you thought you knew was a lie, but I couldn't summon up any pity for her. I couldn't put myself in her shoes. I had no desire to understand.

"You're awake!" Dev glided into the room with the grace of a Broadway dancer. Clearly, he'd had time to heal completely, and just as clearly, he didn't hold it against the other occupant of this room that she'd been the one to shoot him. "Has Caroline been filling you in?"

He said her name so easily, like she was just any other girl.

"She shot you," I said, thoroughly disgruntled.

Dev shrugged. "Like Lake's never threatened to do the same. Ms. Mitchell's a menace with a shotgun. We love her anyway." Dev actually had the audacity to start humming an upbeat little ditty.

"'It's a Small World (After All)'?" I said. "Really?"

Bryn, she shot me because I look like Shay. Dev didn't elaborate on his silent statement, but the rest of the scenes Archer had shown me in my dream fell firmly into place. The werewolf who'd attacked Caroline when she was little, the one who'd killed her father, looked so much like Devon did now that unless you knew wolves—really knew them—you wouldn't have been able to tell one from the other. They shared the same massive size, the same markings.

The same parents.

Shay killed Caroline's dad.

That truth was like a splash of cold water in my face. Jed had told me that Valerie had taken to leading the coven a little too easily, a little too well. She'd never shown the hatred for werewolves that she'd instilled in the others. She was the type of person who could throw her own daughter away.

It wasn't a stretch to think that she could have orchestrated the death of her husband.

I'd wondered about the terms of the deal Valerie had made with Shay, and now they were inescapably clear. She hadn't attacked us to curry favor with Shay; she'd been paying off a debt—an old one.

Turning this over in my mind, I looked at Caroline—really looked at her—and wondered if she'd connected those dots.

Probably best not to ask, Bryn, Devon said quietly. *She doesn't talk about it, but she's dealing.*

She. As in *Caroline.* Ali's sister, the self-proclaimed hunter of werewolves.

"Eric's dead," I said, unable to forgive her that, even if she hadn't been fully in control of her own mind, even if she'd resisted the urge to shoot to kill. "She shot him, and now he's dead."

Devon fell into a standstill, the expression on his face 100 percent wolf.

I know, he said silently, the words echoing through the pack-bond between us like a cry of mourning, a song for the dead. *I know. I know. I know.*

"I was supposed to protect him," I said softly.

Dev nodded, accepting my words. "I wasn't even there."

I felt the weight of that. So did he. It would have been so much easier to put it all off on someone else—say, for instance, the person who'd put a bullet through Eric's leg.

Caroline didn't feel like a threat to me, not anymore, but I didn't want to see the tear tracks on *her* face.

I wanted her gone.

She's Ali's sister, Bryn. Her mother is dead. Devon's words inside my head were like a gentle nudge with a massive wet nose. *You do the math.*

I didn't want to do the math.

"I want to see Chase," I said, clinging to that instead. His presence on the other end of the pack-bond was muted, but it was there. He was weak, but he was healing.

He was alive. Impossibly, undeniably, wonderfully *alive*.

"We had to move him to the far side of the property." Dev held up a hand and wiggled his fingers, holding off my protest. "Nuh-uh-uh," he said. "You don't get to complain about this. The closer he was to you, the faster he healed, but neither one of you was waking up. You shouldn't have been out more than a couple of hours, but whatever it is you all can do, however that pesky little knack of yours works—yours was doing the work for him."

I thought of the dreamworld, where Chase and I had lain side by side. I thought of the walls between us melting away and the things I would have given—*everything*—to make him okay. Chase was Resilient. So was I. We'd shared dreams often enough that I didn't question the idea that we'd done it again, and it seemed right that after everything he'd given up for me, I'd somehow funneled some of my strength to him.

I didn't know how it worked or what it meant, but at that instant, I didn't care.

"Chase was getting better. You weren't." Coming from Devon, that was clearly a condemnation of Chase. "You usually have more sense than that."

Apparently, it was also a condemnation of me.

I gave Devon a look. "Did you actually just accuse me of normally having common sense?"

Dev finally cracked a smile. "Touché."

I didn't realize that Caroline had left the room until I looked for her and discovered her gone.

Good.

"I need to see Chase," I said, allowing myself one moment of selfishness before the alpha in me reared its head, forcing me to amend the statement. "I need to see everyone."

I needed them near me. I needed to touch them, to know that they were okay.

Injured or not, I needed to run.

CHAPTER
TWENTY-EIGHT

WAITING FOR NIGHTFALL WAS TORTURE—WORSE than the searing ache in my left arm, worse than the itching underneath the gauze. Somehow, against all odds, my pack had survived this confrontation. Shay's wolves were already pulling back from the border. The psychics—with the exception of Caroline and Jed, who had stayed for her sake—had dispersed. Aside from Chase, who was dealing with the aftereffects of being poisoned in more ways than one, and Mitch, who'd taken his share of hits—including a bullet—while defending Maddy and Lake, the pack was no worse for the wear, but like me, they felt the loss of one of our own keenly.

Even the babies, who didn't know what they were feeling or where that aching, fathomless loneliness had come from, were in a state, mourning a loss they wouldn't begin to understand for years. And then there was Lucas, his presence a jarring reminder of the outside world, one the pack wasn't in the mood to tolerate, let alone accept.

"Bryn?"

I was lying in Chase's bed, his body curled next to mine as he slept, when Maddy approached. Her gaze was aimed at the floor, her eyes round and her breathing shallow. I listened for her through the pack-bond, but for once, her mind wasn't on running, or the pack, or what we'd become together as soon as night fell.

There was only one word in her mind, only one emotion.

LucasLucasLucasLucas.

I didn't try to make sense of the intensity of it. I didn't weed through her mind to find the moment when she'd known, the way Chase had with me. Instead, I sent my words through the bond to her.

Look at me, Maddy.

She lifted her eyes, and I wondered how we'd come to this: her approaching me not as a friend, but as a member of my pack. I'd never asked for that kind of deference. I didn't want it. Now that the threat was gone—for now, at least—I just wanted things to go back to the way they were before.

Even with Chase beside me, Callum's words about being alpha—the weight, the responsibility, knowing beyond a shadow of a doubt that someday I'd die to keep my pack safe—were still there.

"We're running tonight," Maddy said, interjecting the words into my thoughts.

"Yeah, Mads. We are." I kept my voice soft, unwilling to spook her. "What happened, with Eric . . . We need to be together. We need to let go."

"Will you claim Lucas?" There was strength in the tilt of Maddy's head, just like there was a simple grace to her words. She'd fought long and hard to be this person, and now she was willing and ready to fight for him. "I know it seems wrong, with Eric and everything, but Lucas needs a pack, and I need it to be ours."

As I looked at her and listened to the pattern of her thoughts hovering just out of reach, it was easy to see the truth in Ali's cautionary tale, easy to believe that Maddy's wolf had made this decision for her, that love was an instinct for werewolves, not an emotion. Chase had told me once, a lifetime ago, that as a human, before the Change, he'd loved four things—and one of them was me. Forget that he hadn't ever seen me or talked to me or even known in any concrete way that I existed. Forget that when he'd spoken the words, we'd met exactly twice.

His wolf had known, and Chase had known, the same way Maddy—and Lucas—did now.

"I was always going to claim him, Maddy. I didn't win him from Shay just to send him away."

It didn't matter if Lucas was damaged, or that he'd come

here believing that doing so would put our pack in danger. He'd never really had a chance, and I could give him that. For better or for worse, he was Maddy's, and that made him ours.

"Tonight," I told her, and the strain melted off her body like she was shedding a second skin. She glowed, practically luminescent, and I felt a deep hum of approval, of contentment through the bond.

For the first time since we'd saved her from the Rabid—since she'd saved herself—she felt sure of herself.

She felt whole.

The moon wasn't full. The snow on the ground was fresh. Our numbers were diminished, and the forest still smelled like blood, but the energy running through and around us was no less palpable than it had been the last time the Cedar Ridge Pack had met.

The need to shed my own skin, to be one of them, was no less real.

Five feet from the spot where the others had buried Eric, Lucas stood, hunched and waiting. To a lone wolf, standing in the middle of another pack, knowing he didn't belong must have been torture.

I glanced sideways at Chase. As far as I was concerned, he shouldn't have even been out of bed. As far as he was concerned,

I shouldn't have granted Maddy's request to claim Lucas until I'd had at least a few more days to heal myself.

And there it was again. I was the alpha; Chase was putting my welfare above the pack's. Love was so much less complicated when I was halfway dead.

As if he knew exactly what I was thinking, Chase gave a wry little smile and brought his head to rest on top of mine. *I can't help it,* he said. *And neither can you.*

Alpha. Alpha. Alpha.

The call pushed Chase back from my body, and as he melted into the rest of the pack, I searched for the right words to say to the others. Our pack had never been much on ceremony. On the nights when we ran together, the power just burst out of us, like water breaking through a hole in a dam. At most, I nodded to usher it in, but this wasn't just another night at the clearing.

Too much had happened, and for better or worse, every single one of us was changed.

"Brothers and sisters." Those were words I'd learned from Callum—or at least, the *brothers* part was. "Tonight we mourn the loss of one of our own. He will be remembered." For a moment, I felt less like the alpha and more like myself. "I will remember him."

Unbidden, Lucas stepped forward, and Chase matched the lone wolf's movement with a subtle movement of his own, quiet and understated, even as he kept one eye on Lucas and one eye on me.

"We protect each other," I continued, the words coming faster now. "That's what packs do, and I like to think that even when we're hurting, none of us are the kind of people who could hear a request for protection and turn that person away."

I nodded to Lucas, who took another step toward me. The pack spread out around us, then crowded inward, until we were surrounded on all sides, alpha and lone wolf separated only by inches from the rest of the pack.

"We know what it's like to be kicked around, to be small and weak and feel like no matter what happens, there's never going to be a place where we really belong." My breath turned to frost in the night air, and unwillingly, I shivered. "We were wrong."

Normally, at this point, the alpha would call Lucas by his family ties, but I didn't know his mother's name, or his father's, and I wasn't about to mention his severed relationship with Shay.

"Lucas," I said slowly, "beloved of Maddy, step forward."

There wasn't much of anywhere for Lucas to go, but the words and the ceremony of the moment seemed to have taken on a life of their own.

Pack. Pack. Pack.

The feeling rose inside me—unbearable ecstasy, unbridled joy. I lifted my right hand. Lucas knelt. The lines on the back of his neck—a half circle embedded with a four-pointed star—were still faintly visible, and in a single motion, I slashed my nails through them.

A tiny bead of blood rose on Lucas's skin, mixing with sweat and adrenaline and the smell of things to come. I closed my eyes and reached for the connection, the invisible cord that tied me to Maddy and Chase and Lake, Lily, the twins, and all the others. I felt it.

I owned it.

And then I threw it at Lucas. Power surged through me. All around us, the others began to Shift. Lucas's back arched, and his pupils went wild and wide.

Pack. Pack. Pack.

"You're mine," I whispered, "and you're theirs, and all that we are is yours."

The low hum of the others' minds gave way to Lucas's as a familiar scent filled the air.

Pack. Pack. Pack.

Lucas rose on unsteady legs. Maddy was beside him in an instant, and they leaned into each other, as if his body had been made only for hers. My stomach lurched, and without thinking, I reached for Chase, and he was there, beside me.

There as the urge to run became overwhelming.

There as I tasted something sharp and bitter and electric on my tongue.

Maddy must have felt it, too, because her face went pale and she stopped breathing, her chest frozen and still.

"I was always the weakest," Lucas said, and though neither his tone nor his words surprised me, there was something about the set of his eyes that made my stomach roll. "I never hurt anyone, but that never stopped anyone from hurting me."

I wanted to tell him that it wouldn't be like that here, that he could trust us not to do to him what had been done again and again and again. I wanted to make him see that he could trust me, but now that I could feel his emotions, now that I was in his head, I could taste the tinny, sour flavor of blood in his memory and see for myself the number of times he'd been forced to swallow his own.

I looked in Lucas's eyes. I looked inside him. And no matter how hard or how far I looked, I saw nothing but hurt.

Anger and hurt and helplessness—and the desire to never be helpless again.

"I know what Shay must have been thinking when he sent me here. I know what he wants me to do, and the real kicker is that as much as I hate him, I hate myself more. I hate *weakness* more."

"Lucas—" Maddy choked out his name, and he silenced her, pressing his lips to her temple in a tender, bittersweet kiss.

"You understand, Maddy," he said, his voice a hoarse and heady whisper. "I know you do." His eyes flickered from hers to mine, and this time, there was no submission in his gaze. He met my stare with his own, and he spoke down to me.

"I told you once, for reasons that I can't really fathom, that by the time this was over, I'd be six feet under, or I'd be free."

The real meaning of Lucas's words—his definition of *free*—hit me a moment too late. I'd believed—we'd all believed—that Lucas just wanted to be free of Shay and the psychics, that he'd wanted to transfer to Cedar Ridge because he knew we'd keep him safe.

It had never occurred to me that to Lucas, giving himself over to another alpha—any alpha—might feel like a trap. I'd never thought, even for a second, that he might have something else in store for us—for me—once his transfer into our ranks was complete.

I should have seen it. We all should have, but for a werewolf, Lucas was small, weak—not a threat to anyone or anything.

Unless you were human.

Dead-eyed and sure, Lucas spoke. "As a member of the Cedar Ridge Pack, I question your right to lead us. I question your power over me."

I felt the pull of the pack-bond like a noose around my neck. The hair on my arms rose, and a growl worked its way up from my diaphragm. My lips curled in warning.

Don't do it, I told myself. *Don't say the words, Bryn.*

But as alpha, I had to say them, and the instinct that propelled me to do so became clearer and more insistent in my mind. "Are you issuing a challenge to your alpha?" I asked, Shay's warning that Lucas would bring me nothing but trouble echoing through my memory, taunting me with every sign I hadn't wanted to see.

"Yes," Lucas said in the same throaty whisper he'd used with Maddy. "I am."

Pack. Pack. Pack.

There was growling and howling and the snapping of teeth. The pack, already on edge before our run, felt the call of darkness and blood at the very sound of our newest member's words.

Challenge. Challenge. Challenge.

The word passed from one mind to another, and it didn't matter that none of us had ever seen a challenge. It didn't matter that our pack wasn't supposed to be like any other pack. The animal part of their psyche knew what this meant. I knew what this meant.

Saying no was never an option.

A direct challenge to the alpha always ended with a fight to the death.

CHAPTER
TWENTY-NINE

INSTINCTIVELY, THE PACK MOVED OUT, ENCIRCLING us, but leaving space enough to fight.

I had no weapons, a bum arm, and none of Lucas's speed or strength. I was human. He was a Were. It didn't matter if he was weaker than others of his kind. It didn't matter if he was smaller. It didn't even matter that I was Resilient.

I would have stood just as much of a chance against an atomic bomb.

The only reason I'd lasted this long as the Cedar Ridge alpha was that the others had chosen me to lead in the first place. Any one of them, at any time, could have done what Lucas was doing now. They could have challenged me, they could have killed me, and they could have claimed leadership of the pack themselves.

The laws that forbid one werewolf from killing another only applied *between* packs. Within our own ranks, Pack Law and survival of the fittest were one and the same—at least when it came to being alpha.

Think, I told myself, my breath coming quickly and my chest tightening. *Think, think, think!*

But I couldn't. There was nothing to *think*. There was no answer. There was only me—human and breakable.

Meat.

I remembered, suddenly, what it had been like growing up in Callum's pack, knowing that if he hadn't protected me, one of the Weres might have killed me. I remembered knowing how dangerous werewolves were, but life as the Cedar Ridge alpha—in their heads and out of them—had undone a lifetime of lessons.

You'll never be as strong as they are.

You'll never be as fast as they are.

If they lose control, you're dead.

I'd forgotten. I'd let myself forget, and now there was nothing to be done.

I couldn't run. I couldn't hide. I had to stay and fight and *die*, because I'd wanted to help. Because I loved Maddy. Because I couldn't let myself believe that some people were too far gone to save.

In an ideal world, I would have had time—to think, to prepare—but this wasn't an ideal world; it wasn't even a human one, and any challenge to the alpha had to be settled at a breakneck pace.

Sometimes literally.

I tried not to think about all the ways this could end, tried to concentrate on the here and now, but the more I concentrated, the direr the situation seemed.

Lucas was already on one side of the circle. He took off his shirt, and any remaining hope I'd had that he might fight me as human evaporated from my mind. He was going to Shift, and he was going to devour me whole.

I turned to walk to the opposite end of the circle, my head held high. Damn him for doing this to me. Damn him to hell and back, but I wasn't going to die crying. Given half a chance, I'd take out his eyes.

Devon caught me roughly by my good arm as I walked by, and I turned to glare at him. This was hard enough without thinking about all the people I was leaving behind, all the people I was letting down. This was hard enough without looking at Devon's face and realizing that he was going to have to watch me die.

"You'll challenge Lucas," I said softly, my voice full of knowing. "The second this is over."

That was the real tragedy here, the thing that made this whole exercise pointless. Absurd. The moment Lucas had issued this challenge, he'd signed his own death warrant as much as mine. It didn't matter if he was stronger than I was. There were plenty of people in my pack who were stronger than him, and they wouldn't allow him to lead. They wouldn't let him kill me and live another day.

Lucas was so far gone he couldn't see it, and somehow, I doubted that Shay had pointed out the inevitability when he'd planted this suggestion in Lucas's head.

Layers upon layers upon layers.

Shay had known that Lucas was going to do this. He'd broken him and sent him, broken, to me. He'd played me—the bet, the stakes, scratching on the eight ball when he must have always intended to lose. This was his fail-safe.

This was the endgame.

"You're not going to die." Devon spat the words right in my face. "You are not *allowed* to die."

"Fine," I said. "You win. I'll just—oh, wait. *I don't have a choice.*"

I didn't want to be doing this—not with Dev, not with any of them. I didn't want to say good-bye.

"There's always a choice." Dev tightened his grip and pulled me up onto the tips of my toes. "Do you think for one second that if all of this was going to end with you dead, Callum would have taken a hands-off policy and just let you die? Don't you think he saw at least a hint of this coming? And if so, do you think he would have let you accept Lucas into this pack if he'd thought there was even the remotest chance that you might die over something so preventable, so useless?"

I thought of Callum telling me on the phone that I might die, never indicating, even for a second, that the danger extended past the coven per se.

Something caught inside me, like a breath catching in my throat.

"He must have seen it, Dev. He must not have cared."

Devon let go of my arm, but he leaned down, bringing his face very close to mine. "You," he said, "are the most *impossible* person I have ever met. You're bulletproof and self-sacrificing and beautiful in ways that you will never understand. You are Bronwyn Alessia St. Vincent Clare. You turned the entire werewolf Senate upside down. You laugh in the face of danger. You are the alpha of this pack, and you *are not going to die.*"

As far as pep talks went, it was a good one, but Dev couldn't stay there next to me. He couldn't fight my battles for me. There was a mandate buried deep in the biology of his species that said he had to step back and watch.

So he did. He faded back into the circle, next to Maddy and Lake, next to Mitch, next to Chase, who was trying to get to me but couldn't quite get his body to move.

I could feel his anguish, sewn into the air all around me, and the hum of the pack's acknowledgment that a challenge to the alpha had to be met.

It didn't matter that I wasn't a Were; the mandate was there in my head, too. I felt it in the marks Callum had left in my skin. I felt it in the bond that made me who and what I was.

Fight. Fight. Fight.

It would have been so easy to give in to the instinct, to let the world go red and go out fighting without feeling a single instant of pain, but this time, flashing out seemed like giving up.

There had to be another answer.

There had to be.

The sound of Lucas Shifting tore me from my thoughts. How could I ever have thought he was scraggly or malnourished? He was *hungry*—there was a difference.

I felt the pain of his Shift as an echo in the bond that I'd thrown at him, and an image came to mind, of an old woman standing in front of three grown Weres, forcing them to halt mid-Shift.

I'm the alpha, I thought. *Until he kills me, I'm the alpha.*

Physically, I might have been the weaker party, but mentally, I was dominant. I always had been. There was a reason the Cedar Ridge Pack had chosen me as their leader, and it wasn't my physique.

I pictured the bond that tied Lucas to the rest of the pack. I pictured the portion of it that tied him to me. I'd done that. *Me.* I couldn't take it back, but there was a chance I could use it.

Lucas came toward me, and I stepped forward to meet him. I caught his eye, and I pushed. His lip curled and he leapt forward.

Stop! The command snapped out of me like it had been shot from a cannon and traveled through the pack-bond to Lucas, who jerked back suddenly to land a foot in front of me, just short of his goal. His teeth flashed and he let loose a sick and bone-crunching bark, but his body didn't move. I could see the nails on his feet digging into the frozen ground as he strained against my hold.

Somebody hadn't realized that to take down an alpha, you had to be able to fight them in more ways than one.

For a few seconds, I stood there, staring at him and *willing* him to lie down, belly up. He fought me. He pushed back, and as he lost himself to animal rage, to panic, it got harder and harder to hold him.

Keeping him from killing me wasn't enough.

I had to end this, but I didn't know how. Even as my own instincts surfaced, even as I threw everything I had—Resilience included—into the bond, I couldn't fathom the idea of *ordering* someone to die.

If I could keep him still enough, if I was sure I could hold him—

No.

It wasn't working. I was *fighting, fighting, fighting,* and it wasn't enough. I needed *more*. More power. A stronger will. *Something.*

An image began to form in my mind, a ridiculous image that I didn't have time for, one of me and Chase lying in Callum's cage, looking up at the stars. I heard Devon's voice telling me that when Chase had been on the brink of death, somehow I'd taken everything I might have used to heal myself and given it to him.

The stronger the pack, the stronger the alpha.

That was the way it worked. That was why Shay wanted greater numbers. That was why the rest of the alphas would have sold their souls for what was mine.

I was Bronwyn Alessia St. Vincent Clare. I was impossible. And I was not giving up. My body started to shake with the strain of holding Lucas off. He inched closer. I gritted my teeth. I pictured the pack-bond that connected me to Chase, to Lake, to Devon and all the rest.

I pictured *their* power, and I pulled.

The rush was like nothing I'd ever felt before, and with it came the rest of their instincts—the bloodlust and the adrenaline and the need to force this challenger *down*.

My body alive with that power, I turned my attention back to Lucas and said a single word: "Down."

Lucas fell to the ground. His mouth snapped shut. His eyes opened wide with fear. Even with the power of the pack—and their animal instincts—flowing through me, like charge through a wire, I wanted to let him live.

I wanted to give him another chance.

I wanted to, but I couldn't.

Over, I told him, my mind-voice echoing with power that wasn't mine. Lucas rolled onto his side. I knelt next to him, fear nothing more than a memory, a distant memory, like maybe every time I'd ever felt it was nothing more than a dream.

Challenge. Challenge. Challenge.

Kill. Kill. Kill.

I held Lucas there in wolf form. I looked into his eyes. I ran one hand gently over the fur on his neck, and then, with the power of an entire pack behind me, their Resilience bleeding into mine, I told him to go to sleep.

Forever.

CHAPTER THIRTY

EVERY MORNING, I WOKE UP AND I SAW THE PERSON who'd killed Lucas staring back at me in the mirror. Every night, I went to bed wondering if there was ever a point where I could have stopped him from drawing that line in the sand. Like clockwork, I stared up at my ceiling, analyzing all the moments, big and small, that had led to his challenge. I searched for an answer that wouldn't have led to my looking into his eyes and watching him die.

I knew Lucas wouldn't have survived long without the protection of a pack. If I hadn't been so trusting, if I'd turned him away, the outcome would have been the same—at least for him.

I blamed myself for not being able to get through to him. I blamed Shay for setting me up. But mostly, I blamed the fact that when Lucas had challenged me, he'd had reason to believe that he would win.

If I'd been stronger, if I'd been faster, if I'd been the type of opponent that other people feared, Lucas would still be alive.

He'd challenged me because I was human. I'd won because I wasn't—not really, not anymore.

Chase slid into bed beside me, the way he had every night since the fight. We didn't talk about it. He didn't yell at me, the way Devon had beforehand, or say that he'd recognized the darkness in Lucas, the desperation, even though he had. He didn't ask questions. He didn't push. He just held me, and I breathed in his scent.

Every night, he was there.

And even though I was lonely, I wasn't alone.

A week before Christmas, Maddy came to me. It had been eleven days since Lucas's challenge.

"I'm leaving." She said the words calmly, but I knew what they had cost her. The Wayfarer was Maddy's home. We were her family.

She was already gone.

"I don't blame you," Maddy said. I stared at her, and she amended her statement. "I don't want to, but every time I see you, I see him. Every time I hear you, I hear *him*, and I know it was his fault. I know that he's the one who did this to you and to me, and I want to hate him for it, but I don't. I can't, and I can't be here. I can't stay here."

"Maddy, it's okay." I'd known she was going to leave—probably before she did.

"No," Maddy replied. "It's not. I'm not. But someday, I will be."

I recognized that as both a promise and a statement of fact. Whatever it took, whatever she had to do, Maddy was going to survive this. I just wished she didn't have to do it alone.

I wished that I hadn't been the one to kill the boy she loved.

"There's a stretch of land along the Colorado border," I said. "Sage's family lives there. They know. You'd be safe there, and you wouldn't have to see me—"

"You're there, Bryn. You're everywhere, every day, all the time." Maddy met my eyes, but it wasn't a challenge. It was a request, one that told me she was beyond dominance, beyond submission, beyond everything other than the need to get away. "You have to let me go."

It took me a moment to realize what she was asking.

"You want me to let you go," I repeated. "As in *go* go?"

"You're a part of me, and if I'm going to get through this, I need you not to be."

I saw in her eyes that she'd thought this through, that while I'd been lying in my bed, looking up at my ceiling, she'd been doing the same in hers.

"If you're not Cedar Ridge, we can't protect you. Any alpha who sees you could take you by force and make you theirs."

Lone werewolves were dangerous. A lone female was more or less unheard of. The other alphas would hunt her to the ends of the earth if they knew.

"No one is going to see me," Maddy said with that same quiet dignity she'd always had. "I'll stick to No-Man's-Land. I'll lie low."

I couldn't let her do this.

"If you force me to stay, I'll hate you. Maybe not right away, but sooner or later, I won't be able to help it anymore, and I'm not going to do that to either of us, Bryn. I'm going to go away, and I am going to get better, because if I don't, the next time someone challenges you, it's going to be me." She paused, her chest heaving with the effort of saying the words. "I don't want to be that person. *Please*."

She didn't give me the chance to respond.

"Being Resilient means having the ability to shake off pack-bonds. I did it with the Rabid. If you force me to, I'll do it with you. But I'd rather you just..."

She closed her eyes, lowered her head, and finished the statement in a whisper, from her mind to mine. *Let me go.*

I nodded then, because I couldn't speak. I closed my eyes. I reached out and touched her face gently.

I dragged my nails over the flesh of her neck, lightly leaving my mark.

And then I let her go.

The world realigned in an instant, and I did my best to tune out my senses, the ones that recognized what Maddy was now—and what she wasn't anymore.

"Anytime you want to come back, you can. No conditions,

no questions asked." I sounded calmer than I felt, and that somehow tricked my brain into thinking I could handle this. "If you get into trouble and can't or don't want to come here, go to Colorado."

I might not have been sure of much when it came to Callum, but I was sure that he wouldn't use Maddy the way the other alphas might. She'd be a person and not just a power play to him.

"Bye, Bryn."

Just like that, Maddy was gone.

For the first time since Lucas's challenge, I let myself cry.

I woke up on December 24, looked in the mirror, and made a decision. I didn't tell anyone, because I knew they would argue with me. I brushed my lips against Chase's, and his curved upward in response.

I willed him to keep sleeping.

I walked toward the door and paused at the dresser, just long enough to look at myself in the mirror one last time and pick a small wooden carving up off the base. I tucked it into the pocket of my jeans, helped myself to the keys to Ali's car, and drove.

It took hours to reach my destination. I threw the car into park and slipped out of the driver's seat. Then I walked right up to the edge of the sign—WELCOME TO COLORADO— and I waited.

I didn't have to wait long. Callum seemed smaller than I remembered, and he looked younger, right up until we were standing less than two feet apart, and then my eyes adjusted and saw him as they always had.

For a few seconds, we just looked at each other, poker faces firmly in place, Callum on his side of the border and me on mine.

"I don't suppose Ali knows you took off with her car," he said finally. I would have taken his speaking first as a sign of victory, but I recognized a hint of mischief around the corners of his eyes.

"Actually," I said, "I'm pretty sure she does, because I'm betting you called and told her."

Callum ran a hand over the five o'clock shadow on his face, but the motion couldn't quite hide his sheepish smile. "Old habits die hard, Bryn."

I felt a few "old habits" of my own flaring up. Reaching into my pocket, I pulled out the carving he'd sent me on Thanksgiving Day, and I slammed it down into his palm.

"A Trojan horse?" I said. "Seriously, Callum? You saw what was going to happen, you *knew*, and all you could give me was a cryptic carving whose meaning wouldn't register until *after* Shay had sent a ticking time bomb into my ranks?"

The poker face fell back into place. "I wanted to be there.

I wanted to help you, but this was something you needed to do on your own."

This tune was already old. "I'm Sorry for It, but I'd Do It Again" was quickly becoming Callum's theme song.

"There are things you don't know, Bryn, things I can't tell you about the person you're meant to become."

I swallowed the urge to tell him that the next time he could take his cryptic warnings and put them where the sun don't shine. Instead, I asked him the question I'd come here to ask, the one he'd almost certainly known he would be answering when he drove here to meet me.

"Will you do it?" I didn't specify what *it* was. I didn't have to.

A flicker of sadness passed over Callum's face, and something tender flashed through his eyes, but a moment later, all of that was gone. Callum reached across the border and ran one hand over my head and down the length of my hair, the way he had a million times when I was growing up.

"Yes," he said softly. "I will."

"Now?" I asked, and he let out a bark of laughter that made me wonder exactly what memory from my youth my request had provoked. I'd never exactly been what one would call patient.

"No," Callum replied sternly. "Not now. You have some time yet, Bryn-girl. Human time. I'd not have you giving that up."

I didn't like his answer, but there was no one else I could ask to do the unthinkable. Chase and Devon would have refused,

Lake would have found a way to beat the tar out of me just for asking, and I didn't trust anyone else to do it right. If the werewolf who attacked me pulled his punches, all I'd have to show for it would be a boatload of scars, and if he went too far, I'd be *dead*.

This wasn't a science. There were no guarantees. But this was Callum, and if there was one person I trusted to know exactly how much he could hurt me for the greater good, it was him.

"You won't tell Ali?" I asked. I'd thought this through, but given that I valued my life, I didn't think cluing my foster mother in would be a good idea.

"She'd never forgive me for even considering it," Callum replied.

I snorted. "She's never going to forgive you anyway."

"Brat."

I accepted the word as a term of endearment but didn't take that one extra step to cross from my territory into his, and as much as he might have wanted to, he didn't cross over in my direction, either.

I had my pack, and he had his. I had my reasons for asking. Knowing Callum, he had his reasons for saying yes.

Maybe this moment had been inevitable from the day Callum had saved me and taken me in. Maybe he'd always known it would come down to this. Maybe he'd hoped that it wouldn't.

In any case, if there was one thing the past month had taught me, it was that the stronger a pack was, the stronger their alpha—and the stronger the alpha, the stronger the pack.

I wanted my pack to be safe.

I wanted to be able to protect them.

I didn't want a giant target forever drawn on my very human head. What had happened with Lucas wasn't going to happen again.

Ever.

"Merry Christmas, Callum," I said.

He smiled and handed me back the carving of the Trojan horse. "Merry Christmas, Bryn."

I closed my fingers around the token. I walked back to Ali's car, buried this entire conversation so deep in my mind that no one else would ever know it had taken place, and drove home.

Alpha. Alpha. Alpha.

Pack. Pack. Pack.

Soon.

In any case, if there was one thing, the past month had
taught me, it was that the strongest steel was, like copper,
then iron—and the nuances that... those caught he put
instead of my body to be safe.

I wanted to be able to protect them.

Little even a glance at Lucas forever drawn on my very brain in
head. What had happened with Lucas was a long road to open
again.

Fine.

"Merry Christmas, Charlotte," I said.

He reached and handed me back the drawing of the major
a noise. Merry Christmas, Birdy.

I closed my fingers around the token. I walked back to the
car bench seat, and, legs crossing, as deep in my mind that
made the place with our money. I had to replace, and drove
home.

Alpha Alpha theme.

R Birdy task two.

home.

ACKNOWLEDGMENTS

I owe a huge debt of gratitude to everyone who's helped this book come to life. Thanks first and foremost to my editor, Regina Griffin, whose keen insights whipped this puppy (no pun intended) into shape and who continually floors me with her enthusiasm and love for Bryn and her world. Thanks also to Elizabeth Harding, agent extraordinaire, who keeps me sane—I sleep better at night knowing I have you on my side. To everyone at Egmont USA, who are all among the kindest, funniest, smartest bunch of folks I know, I cannot tell you how lucky I feel to be a part of your pack! And a big thank-you to the team at Quercus, especially Roisin Heycock and Parul Bavishi, for bringing the Raised by Wolves series to the UK and taking such good care of me last fall.

I would be absolutely lost without my writing friends, who lend an ear on everything from plotting to procrastination. Thanks to Sarah Cross and Melissa Marr for reading early drafts of this book, and to Ally Carter, for being on the other side of the phone line every single day. And a shout-out to the Smart Chicks, my RWA roomies, and Bob!

As always, I couldn't do even half of what I do without the love and support of my family. Mom, Dad, Justin, and Allison—you all are the best.

Bryn's adventures continue in

Taken *by* Storm

Jennifer Lynn Barnes

A Raised by Wolves Novel

Available from Egmont USA in Summer 2012.
Turn the page for a sneak peek.

CHAPTER ONE

I RAN AS THOUGH MY LIFE DEPENDED ON IT. Branches tore at my ankles and legs. My bare feet—caked with blood and mud and who knew what else—slammed into the forest floor, again and again and again. It hurt. Everything hurt.

It didn't hurt enough.

I pushed harder, faster, choking on air, my lungs on fire and my chest tightening like a vise around my heart.

I couldn't run like this indefinitely. I couldn't keep going, but I couldn't stop. Muscles screaming, heart pounding—any second, my body would give in. Any second, it would be over.

No.

I fought. I fought to breathe, fought to hold on, to keep going, to—

Survive.

There it was: a whisper from somewhere deep inside of me, a familiar feeling creeping up my spine. I tasted copper on the tip of my tongue, and my vision—already blurred—shifted.

Red, red. Everywhere, there was red.

And just like that, I couldn't feel the pain, not in any way that mattered. I ran faster, the burst of energy coming out of nowhere, the need to escape overwhelming, all consuming....

And then gone.

As suddenly as I'd shifted into the altered state, I fell out of it.

No, I thought. *No, no, no.*

I'd been so close. For a moment, I'd almost had it. I'd felt it. I'd *controlled* it, but now I was just me again: sweating and exhausted and human, as incapable of summoning up my Resilience as I would have been at fighting back the tide.

Spent, I collapsed on the ground, my back up against the trunk of an old tree, my lungs and legs and common sense rebelling against the ordeal I'd just put myself through: the physical pain, the strain on my endurance, the panic I'd worked myself into on purpose.

At least I'd managed to get there this time. At least it had worked. If I could flip into fight or flight mode at will on Cedar Ridge land, in the safety of a forest that felt like home, there was hope that I'd be able to do it elsewhere, that I might be able to control this power I only halfway understood.

There was still a part of me that resisted the idea that some people were born with unnatural aptitudes: psychic knacks that pushed the bounds of possibility. Until I'd run into a coven of psychics bent on my destruction, I'd never identified that way myself. I was just a girl with a habit of surviving things that would have killed a normal person—things like being attacked by a werewolf or set on fire by a coven of psychics.

Just, you know, for instance.

Avoiding a trip down memory lane, I waited for my jagged breathing to even out and ignored the burning ache in my chest. It took a full five minutes for my heart rate to go back to normal, and even then I knew that I'd be feeling the effects of this little experiment tomorrow. This was the third time I'd attempted to jump-start my knack—which typically flared up only when I was in danger—and the first time I'd actually managed to tap into the power, for a few seconds at least.

"Damn fool thing you just did, Bryn," someone opined from behind me.

I didn't bother turning around. At seventeen, I liked being called foolish about as much as I liked people treating me like I was some fragile little butterfly, best kept under glass.

"I'll live," I replied. I'd spent my entire life surrounded by werewolves, whose animal instincts didn't always line up with human ideas about "violence" and what was and was not an acceptable form of "conflict resolution." Running on my bare feet wasn't going to kill me.

"I don't know," my companion drawled, coming into view and rubbing the back of his hand roughly over his chin. "That mother of yours might kill you if you come in from the rain looking like that."

"It's not raining," I replied, deliberately sidestepping the older man's point about Ali that was probably true. My foster mother was not enamored with the fact that, as the alpha of a pack of werewolves—the only human alpha in history—my life was pretty much the textbook definition of *dangerous*. Ali certainly wouldn't take too kindly to the idea that after seven and a half months of relative calm, I was willingly putting myself through the wringer.

For practice.

Beside me, Jed said nothing, letting me mull over his words. Of all the people currently living at the Wayfarer, the old man was probably the only one who could have taken one look at me and known what I was up to—and why. Like me, Jed was Resilient. And human, which put him in the minority around here.

Reflexively, my mind went to a series of numbers ingrained in my very being. *Eight females. Ten males. Two humans.* The rest of the Cedar Ridge Pack were always there in my mind, their names a constant whisper in my subconscious. As alpha, I could feel each and every one of them—four-year-old Lily was waiting impatiently for Katie and Alex to wake up from their naps; Lake was spinning a pool cue around her fingers like it was a baton; Devon was in the shower, singing into a bottle of shaving cream at the top of his lungs; and Chase . . .

Chase was gone. Not for good. Not even for the night. He was checking in on the peripherals, the members of the pack who'd chosen to live at the edges of our territory instead of at the center. As much as Chase hated leaving me—leaving what we had together—I knew there was a part of him that felt the distance as a relief. He wasn't wired for pack living the way I was.

He was used to being on his own.

"Penny for your thoughts." Jed's voice was as gruff as always, but there was something about the set of his features—old and worn and wrinkled—that made me think that he was being generous with his offer, that he didn't need to pay a fictional penny for my thoughts when he understood why I'd been running fast and hard enough that I'd come close to throwing up.

"Things have been quiet," I said finally, answering Jed's question carefully. "They won't always be quiet."

And there it was. The reason I couldn't just sit back on my haunches. There was a threat out there, and every day was like waiting for the guillotine to fall. I had to be ready. I had to do something. The rest of the pack trusted me to be prepared. They trusted me to make the right decisions, even when there wasn't a right decision to be had.

They trusted me to lead, but I didn't trust myself.

Sure, I'd make the decisions, I'd do whatever I could to make them safe, but at the end of the day, I was human. I was slower, weaker, more fragile—and if the previous year's events had taught me anything, it was that to protect my pack, I might need to be something else.

Since I hadn't heard one word from the werewolf who'd promised to Change me into one myself, that left only one option. I had a psychic knack. I had power. I just didn't know how to use it.

Yet.

"Seems to me, a girl like you could think of better uses for quiet time than running around and getting her feet all cut up."

I opened my mouth to reply, but Jed preempted the words.

"Seems to me, you could have asked someone."

"For help," I clarified, since Jed was a man of few words. "Asked someone for help."

There were days when I relied on the rest of the pack as much as they relied on me, and days when the concept of help seemed as foreign as the idea that most girls my age were just starting to look at colleges. Being an alpha was impossible and lonely and bigger than anything my human half might have wanted.

"I don't need help," I said softly, willing that to be true.

Jed rolled his eyes heavenward. "I'm not suggesting you go belly-up and ask your Weres for pointers," he said. "I'd wager the ability works differently once there's another set of animal instincts at play."

Like Jed and me, a large number of the wolves in my pack was Resilient. At one point in time, they'd been human.

Just like I was.

Just like I wouldn't be anymore, once Callum made good on his promise to Change me.

In the distance, I heard a rumble of thunder. Looking up, I noticed the blue sky turning a dark and ominous gray.

"How'd you know it was going to rain?" I asked Jed.

He snorted. "I've broken just about every bone in my body

at one point or another, Bryn. I can feel a storm coming from a mile away."

Jed's body was covered in scars. I'd gotten so used to seeing them that I barely even noticed anymore, but his words reminded me that he'd had a lifetime of experience coming out on top of fights he had no business winning.

If anyone understood that a few scratches were a small price to pay for what I was seeking, it was Jed.

"You'll help me?"

Jed nodded, gazing out at the horizon, looking oddly at peace as it started to rain. "I'll help you," he said. "But we'll do it my way."

I was going to go out on a limb and guess that his way did not involve putting myself through hell in hopes of convincing my body I was under attack.

"Fine by me."

Jed gave me a look that said he thought I was constitutionally incapable of doing things any way but my own. Once upon a time, that might have been true, but now I'd do whatever it took to keep my pack safe. To be the kind of alpha they deserved and make sure that what had happened last December never, ever happened again.

With nothing more than a nod in my direction, Jed started walking back the way he'd come, but I just sat there, letting the rain beat against my body and thinking about a broken boy with hungry eyes.

A boy I'd invited into my pack.

A boy who'd tried to kill me.

A boy I'd killed.

Bone-tired and sopping wet, I went home.

CHAPTER TWO

THE CLOSER I GOT TO THE WAYFARER, THE MORE aware I was of the rest of the pack, and the more aware they were of me. Being alpha meant that the others didn't have an all-access pass to my mind, the way I did to theirs, but even without the benefits of the pack-bond, my friends knew me well enough to know that a quiet Bryn meant trouble with a capital T.

I wasn't altogether surprised to find someone waiting for me at the clearing.

"Halt! Who goes there?"

If ever a werewolf had mastered the art of yelling from the diaphragm, it was Dev. Like a knight guarding a princess's tower, he put his hands on his hips and threw his head back haughtily.

I could so feel a Monty Python impression coming on.

" 'Tis I," I yelled back, playing along. "Queen Bryn."

With any luck, I could distract my best friend—and second-in-command—enough that he wouldn't pay much attention to the fact that I looked like I'd been mud wrestling—and lost.

"Queen?" Devon repeated, looking down his nose at me. Since he was six foot five, he had a long way to look. "Thou dost not look like a queen."

I rolled my eyes, but amended my previous statement. " 'Tis I. Peasant Bryn."

Dev's lips twitched, but he didn't crack a smile, which was not a good sign. That Peasant Bryn line was comedy gold.

"You okay?" he asked, dropping the accent and searching my face for the answer.

"I'm fine," I told him. "I just went for a run."

To a werewolf's nose, those words would have smelled true. I *was* fine—as fine as I could be, given everything that had happened in the past two years.

"You want to tell me why you're not wearing any shoes?" Devon asked, quirking one eyebrow to ridiculous heights.

"Not really," I replied. "Peasant Bryn is a girl of few words."

Maybe I should have given him a real answer, but this was Devon. He couldn't stand to see me in pain. I doubted he'd understand why I'd sought it out.

Behind us, a twig snapped—fair warning that we were about to have company. If I'd been in a more charitable mood, I might have acknowledged the fact that "company" had probably stepped on that twig on purpose. I knew better than anyone that if Caroline didn't want to be heard, she wasn't heard. She came out of nowhere and disappeared the same way. She was a natural hunter, a psychic with supernaturally good aim.

We weren't really what one would call best buds.

"Heya, Caro," Devon called, perfectly amiable. I didn't understand how he could call her by a nickname. She'd been a part of the coven that had waged war against our pack. She'd made our people bleed—Devon included.

"Did Jed find you?" Caroline met my eyes and ignored Devon. Dev wasn't usually the type to be ignored, but for some reason, he let Caroline get away with it.

If you asked me, Caroline got away with a lot.

"Jed found me," I told her. I didn't elaborate, and she didn't seem to expect me to.

"In that case," she said, turning back the way she came, "I guess there's not really anything else for me to say."

As she turned, I caught a glimmer of something in her eyes, and I couldn't help but think of the way Ali looked, gritting her teeth and breathing through the worst life had to offer, the memories that cut her to the bone.

"Wait."

Caroline paused. She waited. I didn't know what else to say to her, didn't want to be talking to her at all, but the resemblance to my foster mother, however fleeting, had reminded me that no matter what this girl had done, she was family. Ali's family.

Her biological family.

"You should come by to see Ali more," I said finally.

That was as close to an olive branch as I could come.

Caroline lived with Jed: on our land, but not in the house I shared with Ali; she was privy to what the rest of us really were, but not a part of the pack. If I'd had my way, the girl who'd shot Devon and—whether she'd meant to or not, whether she'd had a choice in the matter or not—helped kill one of our own would have been living in another hemisphere. But Ali cared about her. She wanted a relationship with her, and I couldn't be the one to screw that up.

Family mattered to Ali the way Pack did to me.

Family. Pack. That combination of words made me think of another person who should have been standing here, but wasn't. A person whose absence I couldn't blame on Caroline in any way, shape, or form.

Maddy.

Maddy, who'd been one of us. Maddy, who'd loved an angry, broken boy.

Maddy, who'd left, because I'd killed the boy she loved.

For a moment, Caroline actually met my eyes, and I wondered if she played Eric's death over and over again in her head, the way I obsessed over Lucas's. I wondered if she felt even an ounce of my guilt, if she sat up nights, staring at the ceiling.

Caroline broke eye contact first. She turned on her heels and left, without snapping a single twig.

What happened last winter wasn't her fault, Bryn, Devon told me silently, for maybe the thousandth time. *Caroline never stood a chance against her mother's mind-control mojo. You know that.*

Maybe that was true and maybe it wasn't, but my pack should have had twenty-two people, and it didn't. Eric should have been starting his sophomore year in college, and he wasn't.

Your mother never had a choice when Callum ordered her to beat the crap out of me, I retorted. *But I don't see you rushing out to mend bridges with her.*

That was a low blow, and I knew it. Growing up, Devon and I had both been a part of the same pack—Callum's. Devon's mother was the second-in-command, and the moment Sora had laid hands on me, she'd changed everything—for me, for Ali, for her son.

Suffice it to say, Devon was much less willing to forgive and forget when the person who ended up hurt was me.

For a second after I snapped at him, I thought Devon might turn around and leave me standing there by myself, but he didn't. He put an arm around my shoulder and pulled me close.

"Come on, brown-eyed girl," he said. "Let's get you some food."

I'd never done a thing in my life to deserve Devon. I probably never would.

We passed the restaurant on the way back to my cabin, and Lake—who'd heard us coming—shot out the front door like a jackrabbit. Or a werewolf under the influence of too many Pixy Stix—take your pick.

"Got room for one more?" she asked. Dev inclined his head in a gentlemanly fashion, and Lake was on my other side in an instant, her arm flung around my shoulder, just like Devon's.

Pack. Pack. Pack.

Physical contact sent my pack-sense into overdrive, and my body was flooded with the feeling that this was how it was meant to be. We were together. We were safe. I could feel their wolves, feel the emotion rising up inside of them, the same way it did in me.

And then I felt something else.

Foreign. Wolf.

Devon and Lake went absolutely still, and I knew they'd felt it, too. Each of the twelve packs in North America had its own territory. The last time a foreign wolf had crossed into ours without permission, things had gone badly.

Very badly.

Foreign. Wolf.

Dev stepped in front of me, his jaw granite hard. Lake's upper lip curled, and I could physically see the growl working its way up her throat.

And that was when I felt it—a tremor in my pack-sense, horror and recognition that whoever had come here without seeking my permission first wasn't just a wolf from another pack.

Wasn't just a threat.

Our visitor—whoever he was—was an alpha.

ABOUT THE AUTHOR

JENNIFER LYNN BARNES has been writing for as long as she can remember, completing her first young adult novel, *Golden*, at the age of nineteen. She is also the author of *Platinum*, The Squad series, *Tattoo*, and *Fate*. Currently pursuing her PhD in developmental psychology at Yale University, she splits her time between New Haven, Connecticut, and her home in Tulsa, Oklahoma. You can visit her online at www.jenniferlynnbarnes.com.